"A stunning, funny, frank, and beautiful look at loneliness, friendship, and the risks taken to love and be loved. In a career of standout books, *You Are Here* takes its place at the top. David Nicholls is my favorite writer."

—Chris Whitaker, author of *We Begin at the End*

"David Nicholls is one of the best writers at chronicling the way annoyance and resentment are often irretrievably mixed with love and empathy. This is a love story but never predictable—Nicholls stays one step ahead of the reader in the sharpest, funniest way. If you're looking for a great comic novel, *You Are Here*."

—Katherine Heiny, author of *Games and Rituals*

"*You Are Here* is everything I hope for from a David Nicholls novel: beautifully observed, very funny, a little heartbreaking, and at its core, full of hope about people and love."

—Monica Heisey, author of *Really Good, Actually*

"*You Are Here* is David Nicholls's funniest, warmest, and most addictive novel yet. Perfect."

—Clare Chambers, author of *Small Pleasures*

"Nicholls's best book ever, which, given he wrote *Starter for Ten*, *Us*, and *One Day*, is saying something."

—Caitlin Moran, author of *What About Men?*

"A beautiful book. Nicholls perfectly judges the balance between humor and pathos. I was often on the verge of tears even when I was laughing."

—Tracy Chevalier, author of *A Single Thread*

"Brilliant: just perfect and exquisitely written. Every page is a delight."

—Jill Mansell, author of *Promise Me*

"Nicholls wears his formidable intelligence so generously and so lightly that you scarcely notice the skill it takes to write a book like this: a story at once passionately funny and richly human. *You Are Here* is gorgeously witty and joyful, kind and sad: a book you do not want to be away from."

—Katherine Rundell, author of *Super-Infinite*

Praise for
You Are Here

"The genius who gave us *One Day* has written another classic and funny love story, set on a ten-day hike. You breeze along and get caught up in it like a leaf in the wind. Witty and joyous."

—Matt Haig, author of *The Midnight Library*

"What a rare find this is! Beautiful writing and authentic characters supported by a dry and honest wit. I loved it."

—Bonnie Garmus, author of *Lessons in Chemistry*

"A romantic, funny, hopeful story of what it is to lose and keep faith in love. The characters became my friends in an instant, and I enjoyed every moment spent with them."

—Dolly Alderton, author of *Good Material*

"Any love story by David Nicholls is a treat, but this one is especially tender, wise, and joyful. I inhaled it."

—Jojo Moyes, author of *Me Before You*

"Oh this book! What's better than rooting for two shy, once-burned characters to recognize that love is within reach? I stopped often to reread and savor its sparkling, wry sentences. *You Are Here* is both up-to-the-minute and old-fashioned in the best way: sharp, yet so very kind, funny, and bittersweet."

—Elinor Lipman, author of *Ms. Demeanor*

"A witty, touching love story. The writing is magnificent: taut and vivid. I was so happy while I was reading it and now I'm bereft. Gorgeous."

—Marian Keyes, author of *Rachel's Holiday*

"Pure and utter delight! *You Are Here* is a fun, poignant post-pandemic romantic comedy that takes us across the hills and moors of Northern England, grapples with loss—of people, of direction—and reminds us vividly and viscerally what it feels like to fall in love."

—Lily King, author of *Writers & Lovers*

"I loved this book. A story about loneliness and the beginnings of love, with the backdrop of England's lakes and fells and relentlessly changeable weather. As a read it is warm, unsentimental, hilarious, and *so* acutely observed. Nicholls has given us a master class in writing. I want to buy it for all my friends."

—Annie Macmanus, author of *The Mess We're In*

"David Nicholls is at the peak of his considerable powers—*You Are Here* is not only packed with the delicious observations, profound truths, and moving encounters we expect of him; it's the funniest thing he has written. Even if it was twice the length, it would have finished too soon."

—Sathnam Sanghera, author of *Empireland*

"*You Are Here* is a gorgeous, grown-up love story. I fell for Marnie and Michael hard and fast—this book is honest, raw, yet profoundly hopeful. This is the work of a writer at the peak of his enormous powers—it's one of the saddest stories I've ever read, and one of the funniest. A future classic."

—Daisy Buchanan, author of *Insatiable*

"David is the laureate of the modern love novel, and this is his best yet."

—John Niven, author of *O Brother*

"*You Are Here* encompasses all of David Nicholls's characteristic warmth, humor, and observational insight. But it also asks fundamental questions of life, love, and loneliness in such a beautifully delicate way that you don't even realize it's happening or that the fundamental truth of human happiness has been staring you in the face all along. I don't know how he does it, but he does, and he's the only person who can."

—Elizabeth Day, author of *Friendaholic*

"I devoured this book. . . . It's a lovely, uplifting, at times laugh-out-loud novel about love and finding a proper connection in the most unexpected places. Put it on your 'To Read in 2024' list."

—Sophie Raworth, journalist, newsreader,
and broadcaster for the BBC

"David Nicholls is a wonderfully gifted writer. His trademark wit and sensitivity bring light and life to his characters, allowing him to explore difficult subject matter with an admirable lightness of touch."

—Okechukwu Nzelu, author of *Here Again Now*

"For anyone who has pounded a pavement or even climbed a mountain, wrangling with the stuff of life, love, loss, loneliness, betrayal, and failure, or simply destiny's strange peculiarities that can upend life, this book is both journey and destination. It will make your heart soar with the climb. It's so tender and wise that I found myself walking every step of the way with Marnie and Michael, through the rain and shine, hoping, praying that they would find each other, and at last see the view. It has pain and bliss in its pages and does what David Nicholls does best: cracks open your heart to show love in all its infinite beautiful chaos, imperfect, funny, yet always true. Loved it."

—Abi Morgan, author of *This Is Not a Pity Memoir*

"A lovely book."

—Nigella Lawson, author of *Cook, Eat, Repeat*

"Marnie and Michael are two characters who I will carry in my heart for a long time. This is a love story for all ages, an epic journey, a moving tale of second chances. I don't know how David does it, but his characters are real to me, and I know I will want to go back to them, to reread *You Are Here*, the way I have his other novels."

—Georgina Moore, author of *The Garnett Girls*

"I finished this novel in two breathless sittings, as invested in its outcome as I would be in the happiness of a friend. This is the magic of *You Are Here*: warm, generous, and funny, it invites readers into the world of Marnie and Michael with the promise that everyone is welcome, and that choosing happiness and being courageous in any small way we can is always possible. I loved this book."

—Kaliane Bradley, author of *The Ministry of Time*

"What a beautiful, beautiful novel, sensitive, witty, and brilliantly insightful and kind about us messy, stupid humans. I loved every single step of it. I will miss it now that I'm finished and I know that it will be one of those rare novels that will dwell in my memory and my heart."

—Donal Ryan, author of *The Queen of Dirt Island*

You Are Here

You Are Here

A NOVEL ·

David Nicholls

HARPER

An Imprint of HarperCollins*Publishers*

HarperCollins books may be purchased for educational, business, or sales promotional use. For information, please email the Special Markets Department at SPsales@harpercollins.com.

First published in Great Britain in 2024 by Sceptre, an imprint of Hodder & Stoughton.

Maps designed by Barking Dog Art

FIRST U.S. EDITION

Library of Congress Cataloging-in-Publication Data has been applied for.

ISBN 978-0-06-339405-6

24 25 26 27 28 LBC 5 4 3 2 1

To Hannah, Max and Romy,
for all the walks

*She was sure of his having asked his partner whether
Miss Elliot never danced? The answer was 'Oh, no,
never; she has quite given up dancing. She had rather
play. She is never tired of playing.'*

Jane Austen, *Persuasion*

THE COAST TO COAST WALK

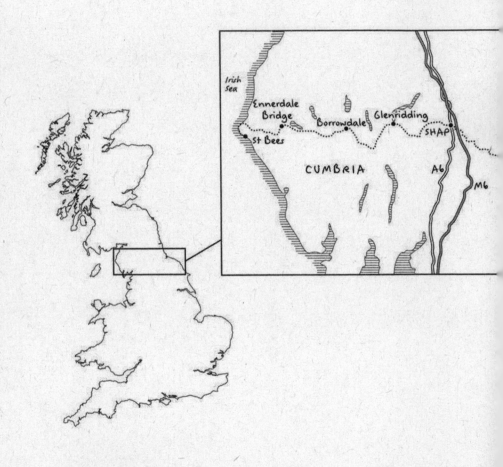

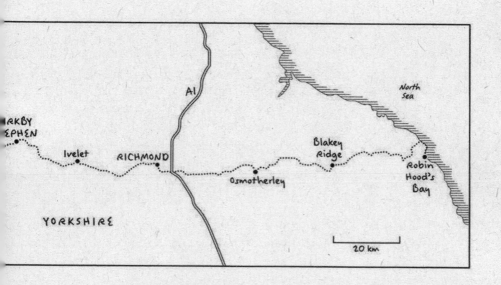

RKBY
EPHEN

Ivelet

RICHMOND

A1

Osmotherley

Blakey
Ridge

North
Sea

Robin
Hood's
Bay

YORKSHIRE

20 km

Part One

HOME

–

To what purpose, April, do you return again?
Beauty is not enough.
You can no longer quiet me with the redness
Of little leaves opening stickily.
I know what I know . . .

Edna St Vincent Millay, 'Spring'

Imaginary Photographs

In all her youthful visions of the future, of the job she might have, the city and home she might live in, the friends and family around her, Marnie had never thought that she'd be lonely.

In her adolescence, she'd pictured the future as a series of imaginary photographs, densely populated, her friends' arms draped around each other, eyes red from the flash of the camera in the taverna or lit by the flames of a driftwood fire on the beach and there, right in the centre, her own smiling face. The later photos were harder to pin down, the faces less defined, but perhaps there'd be a partner, even children among the friends she would surely know and love all her life.

But she hadn't taken a photograph of another person for six years. The last time she'd had her picture taken was at Passport Control, where she'd been instructed not to smile. Where had everyone gone? Now thirty-eight, she had grown up in the golden age of friendship, when having a supportive, loving community around you was a far greater priority than the vexed business of family, the strained performance of romance or the sulky obligations of work. The late-night phone-calls, the texts, the outings and board games, it had all been so much more exciting and fulfilling than her erratic love life, and hadn't she once been good at it? A nice addition to the group if not the core, well liked if never adored or idolised. She was not one of those girls who hired a nightclub for her birthday but she'd easily filled a room above a pub for her twenty-first, a long table in an Italian restaurant for her thirtieth. For her fortieth she thought she might go for a walk in the park with a friend or two, a once popular band obliged to play ever smaller venues.

Year by year, friends were lost to marriage and parenthood with partners she didn't care for or who didn't care for her, retreating to new, spacious, ordered lives in Hastings or Stevenage, Cardiff or York while she fought on in London. Others were lost to apathy or carelessness, friendship like a thank-you letter she kept meaning to write until too much time had passed and it became an embarrassment. And perhaps it was natural, this falling away. Real life was rarely a driftwood fire or a drunken game of Twister, and it was part of growing up to let go of those fantasies of perpetual skinny-dipping and deep talks.

But nobody took the lost friends' places, and now she had revised her vision of the future to one of self-containment and independence, tea from a nice cup, word puzzles on her phone, control of the TV, her books, her bed. To eat, drink, read and ignore the clock, to live without the intrusion or judgement of another soul; the fantasy of being the last woman on earth. She couldn't say whether a falling tree in a forest made a noise, but no vibration that she made would strike another eardrum and so she'd taken to speaking to objects. Not *you* again, she joked with the damp patch in the bathroom. Nice and fresh, she complimented the eggs. *There* you are, she bantered with the corkscrew, waving its arms in the air. In a film on TV, Marnie watched a solitary character give a long pep-talk to her reflection. Nobody does that, she told the TV.

But solitary conversation was like playing yourself at Scrabble, it was hard to be surprised or challenged. Sometimes she didn't even bother with words, instead developing a vocabulary of small noises, fwa and petah, flu-ah and cha-ha, their meaning ever shifting. The radio helped, her days marked by the schedules, though the news was increasingly an hourly jolt of pure anxiety or rage that left her scrambling for the switch. She played music, listening to playlists called things like Coffeeshop Essentials or Rainy Day Piano, but no one had yet compiled a playlist for those sluggish Sunday afternoons in her one-bedroom flat, listlessly foraging on social media, incontinently liking posts, present but as anonymous as someone clapping in a stadium crowd. Time is a sensation that alters depending on where you are, and the cursed hours between three and five on a February afternoon lasted forever, as did the same hours in the morning, times when she had nothing to contemplate but the same circling anxieties and regrets, times when she was forced to acknowledge the truth.

I, Marnie Walsh, aged thirty-eight, of Herne Hill, London, am lonely.

This was not seclusion or solitude or aloneness, this was the real thing, and the realisation came with shame, because if popularity was the reward for being smart, cool, attractive, successful, then what did loneliness signify? She had never been cool, but she wasn't clueless either. People had told her she was funny, and while she recognised that this could be a trap, she was never intentionally sarcastic or spiteful and far more likely to mock herself than others. Perhaps that was the problem – her ex-husband had certainly put it high on the list – but she was kind too, thoughtful, always generous within her means. She wasn't shy. If anything she tried too hard, a people-pleaser, though no one ever seemed that pleased.

There is who we want to be, she thought, and there is who we are. As we get older the former gives way to the latter, and maybe this is who I am now, someone better off by themselves. Not happier, but better off. Not an introvert, just an extrovert who had lost the knack.

But it was not romantic loneliness, or only occasionally. She had married and divorced in her late twenties, in that alone a prodigy, and this great central calamity of her life had gone some way to cauterising those emotions, even if the scar still itched now and then. Since the divorce there'd been no one, not really, though she thought about it sometimes, that it would be nice to feel the warmth of another body in bed or to get a text that was not an authentication code or scam. It would be nice to be desired but let's not get carried away. The risks involved in romantic love, the potential for hurt and betrayal and indignity, far outweighed the consolations. For the most part, she just missed other people, specifically and generally, and if the prospect of social contact sometimes felt daunting, exhausting, intimidating, then it was still preferable to this small and shrinking life inside her fifty-four square metres on the top floor.

Sometimes, she thought, it's easier to remain lonely than present the lonely person to the world, but she knew that this, too, was a trap, that unless she did something, the state might become permanent, like a stain soaking into wood.

It was no good. She would have to go outside.

Mighty forces beneath your feet

'The trick is to change the way you think about time. It's no use thinking in minutes or hours or days, or even generations. You've got to adjust the scale, think in terms of *millennia*. Then everything you see here is temporary, the lakes, rivers, mountains, all in motion, the changes taking place over millions of years. This valley wasn't always here: it was *created*, gouged out by a great glacier, because ice is a moving thing, just a couple of feet a day but scouring and chewing away with these great teeth made of stone, snapping off boulders, gnawing into rock in a process we call . . . a process we call?

'Anyone? That's right, glacial erosion, consisting of . . . ? Wake up, you lot, you know this. Yes, abrasion and plucking! Why's that funny, Noah? Any reason why the word "plucking" is funny? Tell the class. No, I thought not.

'So ice is unimaginably violent, much more violent than fire. It destroys but it creates too, like those hollows called . . . That's right, corries or cwms here in Wales, those mountain pools where people like me and Mrs Fraser go swimming, unlike you cowards. Phones away, please, unless you're taking photos for your project. No selfies. Have you been eroded by a glacier, Chrissy? Then no selfies.

'Go back even further, about 480 million years, and this mountain, highest in Wales, wasn't even here. It was formed in what's called the Ordovician period. No, that won't be in the exam but that doesn't mean you shouldn't know it. O-r-d-o-v-i-c-i-a-n. Long before dinosaurs . . . No, long before. But, yes, at some point there were dinosaurs here . . . No, not any more, don't be daft. Dinosaurs *are* cool, Ryan, but this is cooler, these forces, these immense forces . . .

'Listen to me, please, if you want to get back! When continents collide, these plates of rock buckle and rise above the water and you get volcanoes, here, volcanoes, can you believe it? Close your eyes and look. You know what I mean. Close your eyes and *imagine* . . . Yes, imagine dinosaurs if you want, it's not accurate but pop 'em in. The point is to remember this process doesn't stop just because humans are here. It's happening now and it'll happen when the last human is long gone. Mighty forces beneath your feet. Nothing permanent, everything changing. Sarah Sanders, don't yawn right in my face, please. Let's keep walking. Yes, open your eyes first, see if that helps.'

They began their descent. Like rivers, all jokes had to begin somewhere and he sometimes wondered who had started the notion that geography teachers were dull. Was it a book, a disgruntled kid, an embittered physics teacher? He would never dream of criticising a colleague's discipline, but were the historians really so interesting, bouncing back and forth between the Tudors and the Weimar Republic? No one in the English department was jumping on the desks, and the mathematicians could preach all they wanted about the beauty of numbers: it was all so much Sudoku. And yet somehow, somewhere, the geography joke had come to be and now it was up to Mr Bradshaw, Michael, to defy those expectations and inspire. He led the way, Mrs Fraser – Cleo – herding the stragglers, and down in the valley he spoke of alluvial fans.

'Just eighteen thousand years ago, which is nothing, the day before yesterday in deep-time terms, the glaciers receded and left this great gift behind.' He stomped on the ground and they looked dutifully down and saw the gift of mud. 'This soil, this beautiful dark soil, came from beneath the glacier, like grain ground into flour, washing out over the valley floor in a rich, fertile . . . Alluvial. Fan. Alluvial, what a great word. And these minerals spread out and made their way into the trees and plants and crops, into the apples you ate, should have eaten, in your packed lunch. Isn't that amazing? Debris from an ancient glacier inside you now, calcium in your bones, iron in your blood . . .' Here Michael paused and wondered if he should take things further, segue into the origins of these elements, of the universe itself, tell them they were all made of stars. The teenage mind was so easily blown but that was chemistry and physics and, besides, the apples were from South Africa.

'So – any questions?' he asked, looking out at thirty oily, unfinished faces, some glaring sullenly inside their hoods, others whispering or giggling at private jokes. He was a passionate and committed teacher who tried his best to punch through adolescent indifference, but the questions that preoccupied these kids were not his to answer. Who can identify stratocumulus when your mind is on the hipflask and the vape and whether she likes you? How can a mountain compete with the boil on your chin? Tonight at the youth hostel there would be another game of cat-and-mouse, torch-lit patrols at three a.m., *I'll pretend I didn't see that. Put it out. Back to your room. Big day tomorrow*, and at the end of the residency he would return home, stooped and pale with exhaustion. Still, he would rather not go home.

He was a teacher but not a parent. They'd tried but there had been complications and obstacles, and he struggled to imagine the circumstances now. There was no comparison

9

between the roles and only the most superficial overlap: a parent might teach a child but it's a mistake for a teacher to parent a pupil. Still, it sometimes seemed as if all the turmoil and angst of adolescence were crammed into the five days of the field trip, not just the mischief and squalor but the emotional stuff too. The popular, self-assured kids could be left to their plots and schemes. Instead, Mr Bradshaw chose to focus his attention on the nervy, awkward kids left to dangle from the end of abseil ropes. Looking at their fizzing, anxious faces it seemed unlikely they were made of stars but, still, he felt a certain professional tenderness.

'Landscape is life,' he told them, 'and when you take in a view like this rather than your phone, Sarah Sanders – I've told you before, I will throw it into the next ribbon lake – then you can see its beauty and read it too. Why are farms here? Why's the soil this colour? Why are clouds over the mountain but not the valley? Why does the rock glint in the sun like that? Look, how magnificent it is! Look!'

He noted the boys at the back, hoods pulled into snorkels, shoulders vibrating with suppressed laughter. He was well liked as a teacher, more than he knew, though he could no longer pull off the larky irreverence required to be adored. He was sincere in his passion for the subject but sincerity invites ridicule and the more passionate he sounded, the more they'd laugh, just as they'd laughed when Mrs Bradshaw moved out and some boys had seen him crying in his car. Really, there was nothing some kids wouldn't laugh at, nothing at all.

Accept All Changes

Work was not the answer. Self-employed, solitary, Marnie was a copy-editor and proofreader, working from home where the only water-cooler was her own fridge. The pay was low, the idea of a holiday fanciful, the fear of illness all too real, but she enjoyed the work, was good at it, fast and accurate, and much in demand. Publishers were loyal and authors requested her in the same way that they might ask for a particular hairdresser or surgeon. In return, she was aware of her regulars' foibles and fetishes; the author who made everything 'hazy', the author addicted to 'sophomore' and 'eponymous', to triple single-syllable adjectives or 'either/or' constructions or three 'buts' in a sentence. Were these mistakes or style? Marnie knew the difference, and while it was not in her power to turn a bad book into something good, she could smooth over the potholes that might jolt the reader on their journey. For the most part authors were grateful and many simply 'accepted all changes' without a second look. She was flattered by this trust, a wise counsellor, unobtrusive but essential, touching the author's elbow and letting them know they had spinach on their teeth.

A certain amount of pedantry came with the job – in some ways pedantry *was* the job – though she tried to be open-minded and collaborative. The young ones, she'd noticed, were abandoning quotation marks and she'd seen lower-case come in and out of fashion several times and all of that was fine, though she felt that there were too many semi-colons these days, so that reading was like climbing over a series of fences, and she was particularly conscious of the distinction between British and US English. She'd once had a heated email exchange with a belligerent right-wing author, male, of an espionage thriller, who was determined to put things atop one another, cheese atop the burger, the villain atop the hero. No British person had ever used the word, least of all the head of MI5, whose gun was atop the mantelpiece. A dentist can't lie awake and worry if her patient is flossing, and she rarely checked to see if her advice had been followed, but months later she'd seen the published novel on display in a bookshop and there they were, 'atop' atop 'atop'. *Ah, well*, she thought, *he's the one with spinach on his teeth*. She put another book atop his and moved on.

Still, it would be a knife through her heart should a 'whose' pass for a 'who's'. She was respected and in demand, always gratified when editors came to her, pleading, an assassin being pressed to accept one last job. Consequently, she'd not taken a holiday for three years. On her last solo trip to Greece, she'd worked in her hotel room, returning paler than when she'd left.

Like many self-employed people, she found it hard to leave the work behind. Once, in a bar, her husband had ordered a vodka tonic. 'Vodka *and* tonic,' she'd said before she could stop herself. He'd closed his eyes and exhaled slowly. 'Marnie,' he'd said, 'please do not fucking *dare* to edit me,' and she'd been glad then that he was leaving.

The Deal

'I think,' said Mrs Fraser, Cleo, his old friend, 'you spend too much time alone.'

They were talking on the long coach journey back to York. Teachers' privilege had given them the front seats, the kids hyped up on service-station snacks or sleeping off all-night card games, the stagnant air barely breathable for the smell of wet trainers and inadequate deodorants. 'I would love to be alone,' said Michael, over the tinny rattle of thirty mobile phones. 'Aren't you *desperate* to be alone?'

'That's not the same thing. Come to us for Sunday lunch.'

'I'm sorry, I'm out.'

'All weekend?'

'I'm walking.'

She narrowed her eyes. 'With people?'

He shrugged. 'I like being by myself.'

Work aside, he was always by himself. Natasha had moved back to her parents' place near Durham nine months before, seizing her opportunity between lockdowns as if rolling under a descending metal shutter. In her absence, he found it hard to be at home for any length of time. A neat and pleasant two-bedroom terrace house with a new side return, she had left enough of her possessions to keep it comfortable but he could never quite escape a feeling that something had gone missing, as if he'd been visited by neat and courteous burglars.

Of course, something had gone missing, and though he lived alone, it was always in her presence. Weekends and holidays were particularly hard so he had taken to setting out at dawn to remote spots to walk himself into exhaustion. To Cleo and his colleagues, there was something masochistic about these expeditions, medieval almost, the head-down trudge through wind and rain and fog. 'I think it's weird,' said Cleo. 'Where are you actually going?'

'In a circle usually. I park the car. I walk away from the car. When I'm far enough away, I walk back to the car.' Cleo sang Chic's 'Good Times' and Michael laughed. 'I like it. Clears the head.'

'A clear head. I want a clear head too,' said Cleo. 'I should come with you.'

'Maybe,' he said warily.

'I could bring Sam and Anthony.' Anthony was their son, thirteen now. Michael had watched him grow up. 'We could make a trip of it!'

'Perhaps,' he said, and hoped that this would be enough, because it wouldn't work with other people there. The solitude was the point and nowhere he had walked was ever unpopulated enough. Perhaps Cleo would forget the idea. Already, she had turned and was shouting the length of the coach. 'Please don't stand on the back seats. Please just leave the lorry drivers alone!'

And that, he hoped, was that. Somehow, he got through a brutal winter break, returning to his parents' home at their insistence, to be cheered-up with an exact recreation of Christmas from 1997, the same dry food in super-heated rooms, the same decorations and films on TV, a bottle of advocaat that was literally the same. The unspoken policy on his wife's absence was not to speak of it so that this was Christmas in a parallel world where he'd never married. There was no antipathy: his parents had loved Natasha very much, had seen her bring their son to life, but they didn't have the words to talk about it. *Probably just as well*, Michael thought, lying in the same teenage bed. Truly, this was a Festival of Melancholy, and he'd left like a teenager too, fleeing at the earliest opportunity to go and walk in the rain instead. 'Shall I come with you?' his dad had offered. 'I've got my boots.' Michael preferred to go alone.

On the first day of the new term he was called to Cleo's office. Though she'd joined the school after him, she'd always been the ambitious one and now addressed him from behind the deputy head's desk.

'How was Christmas? Shit get wild?'

'Midnight mass, sherry, Queen's Speech—'

'Caning it again. No wonder you look shattered.'

'Thank you. So do you.'

'Unfortunately, you can't say that to me,' she said, rapping the desk between them. 'It's a rank thing. We'd hoped to see you on New Year's Eve.'

'Yes, I was going to come, but the TV's always so good—'

'Michael—'

'I'm sorry, it's not a big festival for me.'

'What *are* the big celebrations in your life, Michael?'

He knew this tone too well, the voice she deployed when talking to a promising kid who was not fulfilling their potential. But he was forty-two years old. Cleo was his friend, they'd been on holidays together, first the four and then five of them when Anthony was born, and while it was touching to be looked after, it was humiliating too. He let his eyes drift to the window, yelps and screams from the playing fields below. 'I'm fine. I had a nice break, very quiet, very peaceful.' He'd had a panic attack on Boxing Day, had gone to hide in his dad's shed to steady his breathing.

'Did you speak to Natasha?'

'I did, briefly, Christmas Day. We had a nice chat.'

'She said it was like talking to someone on a prison visit. Through one of those screens.'

'Well, that's my brand of chat.'

'Okay. Because I just wanted to know that you're all right.'

He was not all right but that need not concern anyone. 'I'm absolutely fine. I'm just not ready for company yet. That's allowed, isn't it?'

Cleo sighed. 'Come for dinner on Saturday.'

'Can't, sorry—'

'Friday—'

'I can't Friday. Early start.'

'Lonely walk?'

'I'm going away for a few days, yes.'

'Okay, we'll come with you!'

He laughed. 'No.'

'I won't wear these shoes. We won't eat your horrible sand-wiches—'

'I like being on my own.'

'Fine, we'll follow behind. Shout conversation at your back. We'll invite people!'

'I'm not quite ready.'

'I think you are.'

'Can you just . . . overrule someone on how they're feeling?'

'It's pastoral care.'

He looked back to the window. 'I'm grateful but not this time.'

She leant forward, sensing an opening. 'Ah, but *another* time!'

'Maybe.'

'After Easter, second week of holidays, nice big walk.'

'Possibly.'

'Okay. It's a deal.'

'Is it a deal if I don't want to do it?'

'Yes. We're all going away together in a big fun group.'

'You're only *deputy* head.'

'A matter of time. There, it's decided.'

This was the crux of it. For Cleo, the solution to a problem lay in the presence of other people, while Michael depended on their absence, and while the kindness of a friend was a precious and touching thing, it could also feel like an imposition. 'All right,' he sighed, 'when the days get longer.' Earth's tilt and its orbit around the sun made this inevitable but he'd have time to think up an excuse before then.

The Slideshow

She had become addicted to the buzz of the cancelled plan. It was a small and fleeting high and no one would ever look back fondly at all the times they'd managed to get out of something, but for the moment no words were sweeter to Marnie than 'I'm sorry, I can't make it.' It was like being let off an exam that she expected to fail.

Ideally, the other person would cancel first, but she was quite prepared to take the initiative. Like an actor in an emotional scene, it helped if she could draw on some personal truth, so that when she woke on the morning of New Year's Eve – most terrible day – with a tingle at the back of her throat, her first thought was 'I can *use* this.' Her friend Cleo, the deputy head of a secondary school in York, had invited her to a party but it would be irresponsible to travel – she'd be no fun, it was a long way, she was going to stay in, sweat it out. She lay on the sofa to give a bed-bound quality to the voice, the sticky croak of a child possessed by demons, and made the call.

'I *knew* this would happen,' said Cleo. 'I *knew* it.'

'You knew I'd get ill?'

'We can all do the voice, Marnie.'

'I have a temperature!'

'A normal temperature.'

'I'm shivering, I'm . . . Why would you want me if I'm not going to be fun?'

'We don't invite you because you're *fun*.'

'Oh.'

'We invite you because we love you and it's important to see people. You spend too much time alone.'

'It's not my fault if—'

'Sat there like . . . Eleanor fucking Rigby.'

'Cleo!'

'Sorry, but I really wanted to see you. Anthony too.' Anthony was Marnie's godson, someone else she'd neglected.

'I want to see him too, and you. I just want to be at my best.'

'You don't have to be at your best. No one's interested in you being at your best. We want you exactly as you are.'

'That's nice.'

'Isn't it? I might throw up.'

'Me too,' said Marnie. 'And that's why I can't come.'

'All right. Happy New Year, I suppose.' She was gone, and now the room seemed very quiet. She loved Cleo, a good and constant friend, fiercely loyal but also fierce, and while it was humiliating to be told off, she knew this feeling would pass, replaced by immense relief. She ran a bath and opened wine. She drafted several humorous posts about her wild-night-in for social media, but she'd found in the past that the jokes she made online led to messages asking if she was okay. Instead, she lurked and read her feed and felt as if she was looking up at a party from beneath a lamppost.

So deep was her commitment to the fake illness that it soon turned into the real thing, a feeling that the back of her throat was somehow chipped, a sweetly metallic taste, a whole-body ache. The pleasure of cancelled plans depended on the belief that she was having a better time than the fools who'd made

19

an effort, and that was no longer the case. She toasted herself with a pint of water, swallowed two Paracetamol and a sleeping pill and, at ten fifteen p.m., squeezed beneath the weighted blanket that turned her bed into a giant flower-press.

At midnight, all the fireworks of London came punching through her sleep and the first hours of the new year were spent in a fevered haze, imagining where she might be if she'd chosen yes over another no. In a branching timeline, she imagined herself in the corner of Cleo's kitchen, being animated and funny with a nice-looking man, his dark eyes crinkling, his teeth less than perfect and all the better for it. *Shall we step outside?* he'd say. *It's too bright*, and maybe they'd scrounge a cigarette, share it in some corny way. *What time's your train tomorrow?* he'd ask. *I don't have to rush back*, she'd say (although it was an advance ticket, not a flexible one, and even in the fantasy, she worried about the cost). *So*, she'd ask, *how do you become a tree surgeon?* and here he'd lean in to kiss her.

The trouble with alternative timelines was that they really were full of the most mortifying nonsense. Back in the universe she'd chosen for herself, the alarm clock read two fifteen and she chiselled her feverish body into the cool side of the bed. In a documentary on the emergency services, she'd heard the story of an old man who had died with the electric blanket on, simmering gently over the course of several days. What might her weighted blanket do over time? Press her flat, splayed like an Archaeopteryx? Would a fireman roll her up, like her yoga mat, carry her out beneath his arm?

On New Year's Day, shivering on the sofa, she turned on the TV to find that her streaming device had compiled a sarcastic slideshow of her photographs, entitled *What A Year!*: her oven light-bulb, a recipe for hearty lentil soup, a close-up of an ingrowing hair, her National Insurance number, the flapping sole of a faulty shoe, the mole on her shoulder, a gas-meter reading, a dry-cleaning receipt, the shard of green glass she'd found in a salad, then back to the oven light-bulb, all accompanied Carole King's 'You've Got a Friend'.

A resolution. This year the photographs would be different. There'd be no more self-willed illness, no more cosiness, no candles sucking the oxygen from the room, no more relentless self-care. Instead she'd care for others, revive her friendships and make new ones, engage in the messy, confusing business of other people.

Resolutions fade with time but this one lingered, and when Cleo phoned with a new invitation Marnie hesitated, suspended between the desire for change and the need for everything to stay the same. Three days of walking with strangers. It was the kind of potentially awful experience she needed and, in her mind, she decided to give it some thought. In the real world, out slipped 'Yes.'

Napoleon

Something terrible happened to Michael when presented with a map. Cleo had tasked him with plotting the route, challenging but not punishing, picturesque but not touristy. In return, she'd find accommodation (a strict no-tent policy) and get a nice group of people together, no one to be scared of. Long, bright days on the high fells, then the pub in the evening. A pleasant, easy mini-break: that was the brief.

Well, he'd see about *that*. The map transformed him into a general, leaning on his fists, contemptuous of these amateurs with the price tags still on their boots. A conqueror, he examined the terrain and elevation but everything seemed too puny, too easy, too short, marsh and bog a few dashes, the miles mere inches.

Three days would not be enough and he wondered, what if he simply left the others behind and kept on walking? How far could he cover before he was obliged to go home? If he started at the west coast, he thought he could make it to the east, a high belt cinched under Scotland's arm, crossing the Lakes, over the Pennines, along the Dales and across the Moors, then descending down the Yorkshire coastline to dip his toes into the North Sea. It was the famous route devised by Alfred Wainwright, 190 miles usually covered in twelve or thirteen days, though he felt sure he could do it in ten if he didn't stop or rest.

Once formed, the idea proved unshakeable, the kind of obsessive project that overtakes men in the middle of life, like marathon running or carpentry. Recognising it as such did not make it any less compelling and he felt sure that if he were to complete the journey he would feel . . . what? As a pilgrimage it lacked a spiritual purpose but he hoped at the very least for a sense of achievement, well-being, closure. A deep immersion in the natural world – surely that would bring calm, not happiness but peace of mind. There'd be great beauty along the way, some discomfort, too, and other people, of course, but only for a few days, after which they'd drift away and he would be able to fall silent and think over the last few years. At the very least he'd sleep, the fells and moors a kind of natural sedative, and even if it rained every step of the way, surely it would be better than ten days in this haunted house. At home he was merely lonely. Stepping outside transformed loneliness to solitude, a far more dignified state because it was his choice. He imagined arriving on the slipway at Robin Hood's Bay, trim and weather-beaten, dirty but cleansed, purged and transformed in ways he couldn't quite define.

Looking at the map he noted, too, that the route would take him close to Natasha's new home, though he found this scene harder to imagine.

Waterproof

She went shopping for what she thought of as 'gear'. Her London wardrobe, the clothes she wore in company, the opaque tights, the long black coat, the midi-dresses and knitwear in grey and black and blue-black, were a kind of adult school uniform and would not do for the high fells. Instead she would need nylon and fleece and 'technical garments', whatever was needed to feel comfortable, warm and dry, to feel, in short, that she was still indoors.

In the shop, the clothes rails glowed with reds and yellows, purples and oranges. Marnie preferred camouflage and bought a green cagoule composed entirely of pockets and zips, a pair of waterproof trousers that rolled into a ball the size of an apple. She bought socks of an unimaginable complexity, based on a design by NASA, and a red woolly beanie because wasn't 95 per cent of body heat lost through the head? She bought thermals in case of snow, sunblock in case of sun, she bought maps and a clear waterproof pouch for the maps, and a rucksack with a pocket for the map pouch plus the capacity to carry forty litres of clothing, though she struggled to imagine what forty litres of clothing would look like. Hydration was key and so she bought a rubbery bladder with a tube attached, grisly and sinister, like something you'd find hanging by a hospital bed.

She'd need a compass, because what if she wandered off in

the fog or was ostracised by the group? As a kid, she'd always assumed that a compass somehow pointed where you needed to go but life was more complicated than that. A high-tech slice of plastic, marked with impenetrable scales and signs, it seemed inconceivable that this device could help her find her way, but imagine the embarrassment of being rescued without one. Carrying a compass on a walk was a way of saying, 'Look, I'm trying, all right? I'm doing my best.'

She bought new boots. Ideally a shop like this would be staffed by weathered, bear-like rangers in checked shirts, but the boy in charge of boots was a pale, intense zealot who insisted that it was all about the boots, the wrong boots would break you, never skimp on boots, so that selecting the correct boots seemed as momentous as buying a horse. Too small would mean blisters but too big would mean blisters, plus impacted toenails, corns and keloids, and with this in mind, he led her to a small fake bridge paved with varnished cobblestones to replicate the experience of country walking. The pretend bridge was patently ridiculous.

'You seriously want me to walk over this?'

'If you could.'

'Is there a shop troll? You know, fol-de-rol?' The assistant stared at her with such ferocity that she had no choice but to trot back and forth, clip-clopping across the puny bridge in a variety of boots, frowning in concentration, head cocked as if talking to her feet telepathically, until she wanted to throw herself off it. She settled on a ruinously expensive pair in glossy brown leather, something to spray them with and wax to rub them down. 'You must wear them *now*,' ordered the assistant, 'wear them in', so she packed her flats into the rucksack and hiked back down Charing Cross Road. The money she'd spent had left her with a sick feeling and she struggled to justify the expense to critics who didn't exist.

Back at home, she put everything on and looked in the mirror, the labels dangling like baubles, the room seeming to shrink as she bulked up. The green cagoule with the red beanie made her look like a stuffed olive, and the noise alone would send her mad, the roar of nylon against Gore-Tex. Was she imagining it, or were the boots too tight? In profile, if she held on to the straps of the rucksack, the low-slung bulk made her look like a tyrannosaurus. From the front, she was self-conscious about the way the straps framed her breasts, pushing them forwards in a single solid unit, like the nose of a submarine. Should she pack something elegant for the evenings, devote one or two of her forty litres to a nice dress? Would there be parties? Should she get her legs waxed? She felt sweat trickle down her back.

Four single people, a married couple, a teenager. It was like a murder-mystery, though she hoped it wouldn't come to that.

Part Two

THE LAKES

—

I will clamber through the Clouds and exist. I will get such an accumulation of stupendous recollections that as I walk through the suburbs of London, I may not see them.

Keats, in a letter to Robert Haydon, April 1818

Day One:

ST BEES TO ENNERDALE WATER

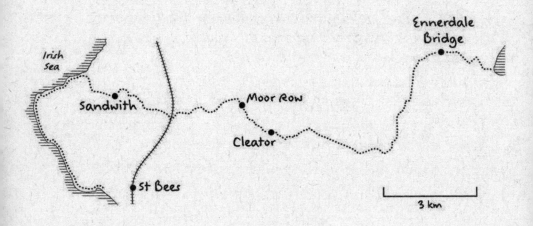

The Wigan Orgy

It was a shame not to depart from a more romantic station, the graceful curve of Waterloo, the great glass vaults of King's Cross and Paddington, the black-and-white matinée of Marylebone. But travel to the north-west meant the doomy black box of Euston, a building whose exterior is somehow disguised – no lifelong Londoner can draw a picture of it – as is its function, the trains departing furtively from a back room. Even on a bright, crisp April morning, it felt gloomy and dystopian, her fancy-dress costume now absurd, the sports bra a tourniquet, the thermals deployed far too soon, forty litres of clothing tugging at her back so that she thought she might pass out in the queue for coffee, roll backwards on to her pack, arms and legs waving uselessly, a beetle in a shoebox.

She felt better on the train, the first of the day, claiming her forward-facing window-seat with table: the dream. Now she was an executive, laying out her laptop, pen and notepad, charging her devices unnecessarily, because this was the key to surviving in the wild, charging devices and using a toilet whenever the chance arose. She laid out her ancient copy of *Wuthering Heights*, which she'd brought to get in the mood, and now the train crawled out into the light, emerging behind the terraces of Mornington Crescent, an address that still retained an atmosphere of old kitchen-sink films, sad, shabby love stories, the kind she'd aspired to when she'd first moved to the city. She saw closed shutters and grimy curtains, imagined new lovers slumbering in rented rooms. Then, above the terraces, came a knife of brilliant blue and she felt sorry for anyone who was still in bed.

City faded into suburb. She saw gasometers, horses in a stable-yard, dog-walkers on a frosty recreation ground, articulated lorries on the ring roads, everyone going about their business, as in a Richard Scarry book. She'd become so used to the view from her kitchen table, the short lens of London life. Now England was a model village blown up to life-size. Look, canal boats! A recycling plant! A wind-farm! Infrastructure, was that the word? The suburbs faded and stagey swirls of mist lingered in the dips and hollows. Wild cows! She was observing the hell out of things, remembering the power of a train journey to turn life into montage, a sequence conveying change. Why hadn't she done this before? What had she been so scared of? Would she care for anything on the trolley? She would care for everything.

She'd agreed to come along for three nights, the first leg of the Coast to Coast, which was apparently some big deal. It seemed feeble just to be doing the one coast but even if she hated it, if they didn't get on or ran out of things to say, surely she could survive for three nights. She'd see the Atlantic and some of those famous Lakes, then sprint back from Penrith on Tuesday, and in the afternoons, she would find a quiet spot and work, because all of this adventure would need to be paid for.

She opened up the new assignment. *Twisted Night* was the sequel to the highly successful erotic thriller *Dark Night*, which took the lid off the glamorous, shocking world of Hollywood's private sex clubs. 'Very spicy,' said the editor, 'but possibly written a little *too* quickly.' Even the title seemed to demand a margin note, because a night might be hard or hot or endless but in what sense could it be twisted?

She soon found out. The opening orgy alone took her through the Cotswolds to the West Midlands and Marnie had never felt more grateful for the empty seat beside her. So disorienting was the action that she had to make notes on her napkin to establish everyone's whereabouts, a complex web of arrows and initials, like a diagram of the Battle of Austerlitz. Was S on top of B now or behind and, if so, where did that put L and what was in her hand? A vibrator hopped from left to right to left, like a nightclub singer's microphone, and the author alternated 'PVC' and 'latex' as if they were synonyms. Marnie was pretty sure they were not, though when she searched on the train's Wi-Fi she was told that *latex PVC* was a forbidden term.

She deleted her search history and would fact-check later. In the meantime there was plenty to be getting on with, not least the wild punctuation, the commas scattered like rose petals, the yelp of exclamation marks, paragraph-length sentences that gave the text a kind of hallucinatory, high-modernist intensity. Marnie had not attended an orgy, though she had copy-edited many, and while this was not the same thing, she couldn't deny the author's skill in conveying a sense of disorientation and sex-panic, so that you really couldn't tell who was doing what to who, or 'to whom', or 'to who what was being done by whom'. An orgy was like trying to pat your head and rub your stomach at the same time, except the head and stomach belonged to other people and it wasn't their head and stomach. Was it S's hot tongue on L's salty skin or B's sharp nipple in L's soft mouth, and was 'sharp' really the right word?

As a civilian reader she might, she supposed, be turned on by all this, sleazy and facile though it was, but a certain professional distance was required and so she worked on methodically, wondering if anyone's sex really did taste of the ocean and, if so, was this a good thing? Maybe it was a question of which ocean. No one wanted to taste of the English Channel.

Marnie sipped her tea. She had not shared a bed with anyone for – oh, God, terrible arithmetic – six years now. She knew that this was not unusual and that celibacy was a perfectly acceptable choice, but when she'd tested the statistic on Cleo, she'd simply said, 'Yikes.' Her friend had always carried an aura of sexual confidence, a kind of heavy-lidded, tousled air, never boasting exactly but hinting at her satisfaction in 'that department'. Marnie had tried not to resent this but that 'Yikes' had stung. It's like driving on a motorway, she'd told Marnie. You can't avoid it for too long or it becomes frightening, and Marnie had felt another little twist of resentment because she'd always liked driving on the motorway, had been complimented on her driving, would like to drive on the motorway again. Even marriage had not cured her of that.

But it seemed unlikely on this holiday. Whether it was the fresh air or the paraphernalia of wipe-clean trousers and cling-filmed cheese rolls, there was something powerfully anti-aphrodisiac about the English countryside. The smell of wet wool and an unwashed Thermos flask, the taste of boiled sweets . . . no, sex belonged in cities. In Los Angeles, for instance, they'd been at it for three hundred miles now and she longed for someone, anyone, to orgasm so that she could look out of the window. But on it went, page after page, through Warrington, Wigan and Preston. She had a headache. Would someone please just fake it? By Lancaster, the words were beginning to lose their meaning. At Oxenholme, she typed the note 'close repetition of "cock"', saved the file, then looked up.

It seemed they'd crossed the border into another country, all purple and sage green, and off to the left she could see – this was not the right word – lumps, less than a mountain, more than a hill, each rising abruptly, like a child's drawing of a volcano. Somewhere beyond those hills was the Irish Sea, which meant she'd have to traverse this landscape to catch her train back. She reached for her books, *A Pictorial Guide to the Western Fells* and *The Central Fells* by Alfred Wainwright, facsimiles of the old editions, the text hand-written, the prose fine and sturdy as a dry-stone wall, the illustrations densely cross-hatched, lovely but as gloomy as a walking map of Mordor. She laughed at the notion that these might ever help her find her way. Opening a page at random she began to read but the Hollywood orgy lingered.

She gave up on Alfred Wainwright. Silly to lug them around, a rural prop of no more practical use to her than the briar pipe the author chewed in his photo. She looked back to the window, hoping to spot a lake through the trees in the same way you might spot a giraffe on safari, suppressing a sacrilegious thought that, while the view was lovely, she'd got the idea. Penrith shortly, then Carlisle, where she was due to change trains then curl back south along the Cumbrian coast. The dawn start was catching up with her. She closed her eyes and dreamt of clear forest streams, lofty parapets of granite, red squirrels in their high heels with their hot, soft mouths.

A Connection

It was easy to spot the Londoners, their clothes too new, too bright, worn in too many layers, boots fresh from the box, neither properly seasoned nor broken in. Waiting on the local platform at Carlisle, they had a wide-eyed look, pioneers venturing bravely north. The train opened its doors to let them on, two carriages only, and Michael waited patiently behind a woman with a rucksack the same size as her torso, the straps too long so that the weight tugged her backwards. He thought for a moment about advising her.

But he must not teach. He would be travelling with adults who had no need or desire to learn about drumlins and moraines. The train ticked and hummed, then began to crawl, rattling past sooty Victorian buildings, warehouses, the new light industry at the edge of town, the sky widening like a cinema screen, opening on to farm and woodland. Seated diagonally across the aisle, the woman with the poorly fitted rucksack was typing noisily but without a table, so that the laptop kept slipping down her new trousers towards her new boots. What was so important that it should take precedence over the view? She was certainly making a big show of it, tutting and blowing up at her fringe. It was a nice face, amused and amusing, attractive and expressive, with a city haircut (was it a 'bob'? He wanted to call it a 'bob') and more make-up than you'd expect on a walker, sometimes rolling her eyes or clapping her hand to her flushed cheek at the words on the screen. He noticed that she was perspiring slightly. Noticed, too, that he'd stopped looking at the view.

But he must not stare at strangers on trains and he must not play the Lakeland poet either, though there was a kind of poetry to the towns they were passing through now: Wigton, Aspatria, Maryport, Flimby. Look, look up, he wanted to tell her, though in truth the landscape was not yet beautiful, at least not to a tourist, a belt of old industry between mountain and coast, small towns exhausted by winter, exposed terraced houses that seemed to regret their sea view. As they curved around towards Workington the Solway Firth appeared, a great slab of polished pewter with Scotland beyond, and still she shook her head at the screen, her hand a visor, one eye clenched shut as if she couldn't bear to look. If it was causing her so much pain, why was she still reading?

Now the train was hugging the black cliffs, the sea some distance below. They entered a tunnel, long and sinister, then back into the light at Corkickle, where they both began to gather their belongings. Wary of the dawn start, the others had driven on ahead and were all staying overnight at a hotel in St Bees. They would meet on the beach at the start of the walk, seven of them. Cleo and her husband Sam were bringing their son Anthony who, they insisted, could handle it. Sam was bringing an old friend from London, Cleo two old friends. 'Female but don't worry,' she had told him, as if this were a phobia. He did not have a phobia, it was just . . .

He'd read somewhere that people found it easier to talk frankly when walking, something about the forward gaze and the rhythm. He'd have to watch out for that. Not too open, not too reserved, not the teacher or the poet or the northerner or the grizzled old man of the mountains; not too judgemental, because all boots were new boots at some time or another. As to which role he should assume, well, he wasn't sure. Cleo had told him *just be yourself* by which she meant *be your former self* and that was no longer possible. So much of his social life had been led by Nat and he'd yet to work out how to perform as a solo act. He would do his best to appear cheerful, and if he could keep that up for two days, he would be on his own again, unobserved and therefore invisible, racing to the North Sea. At nearly two hundred miles it was the furthest he'd ever walked and his pack, as he heaved it on to his back, felt impossibly heavy. He'd get used to it, he had no choice, and in nine days he'd be the other side of England, aching, browned by spring sunshine, everything thought through and resolved. 'Walking it off', that was the phrase, and though it was more usually applied to indigestion or rage, it was worth a try.

The train pulled into St Bees station, red brick and wood, like something from a model railway. He let the woman descend, so that she might go ahead.

But on the platform she was looking at the town map quite unnecessarily, blocking his way. *The sea's right there. Just point yourself at the sea.*

'Excuse me,' he said.

'Oh, I'm so sorry.'

'It's this way.'

'Yes, I know,' she said, a little prickly. 'Thank you.'

It would be embarrassing to fall into step with a stranger and he accelerated past her. 'Good luck,' he said, but without looking back and, in turn, she didn't reply.

Names for Stones

She had misplaced the Irish Sea, but only for a moment. Back on track, she hurried down the lane and across the car park, past the playground and the municipal toilets – should she? Stop worrying about toilets! Look at the cliffs! Look at the sea! Did seagulls count as wild birds? Here they were, swaggering, large enough to be men in costumes, menacing the tourists for chips. Marnie hurried on and began to feel the first pang of social anxiety, as if she was about to give a presentation, which in a way she was. Cleo was her oldest and best friend but also her most successful, and the qualities that had brought this success, her confidence and directness, sometimes left Marnie feeling daunted, as if their friendship was a job for which she must continually reapply.

She hurried along the promenade. And then there would be new people to contend with – my God, new people. *Hi! I'm Marnie! Pleased to meet you!* Was that how it went? Should she shake hands? Touch cheeks? Curtsy? When had it started, this wild self-consciousness? The pandemic had certainly played a part. The first lockdown had been tough but she was single and self-employed, had been able to work, had not lost anyone, fully expected to emerge when the time was right. But something had happened to her confidence in those months, and even when restrictions eased, her own life barely altered.

It was as if she'd returned from a foreign country and not let anyone know. The threshold of her flat seemed like a high diving board, too big a leap, too many people watching, and even when she made it out, what did she have to say? Conversation required a warm-up now, time set aside to workshop smiles and responses, and she no longer trusted her face to do the right thing, operating it manually, pulling levers, turning dials, for fear that she might laugh at someone's tragedy or grimace at their joke. In Japan and California, they were developing robots with a more natural and spontaneous set of responses than she currently possessed.

But too late to cancel now. There they were on the slipway, Cleo whooping and laughing, waving her arms madly as if flagging down a passing ship. She waved back and hurried down, Cleo enveloping her then holding her at arms' length as if she were an outfit to try on. 'Look at you! You've got all the kit!'

'Well, it's the wilderness, Cleo!'

'All that olive green!'

'Is it too matchy-matchy?'

'Not at all. I've never seen you looking so . . . waterproof! Oh, it's good to see your face! You didn't cancel!'

'I don't always cancel.'

'Sam had you down as fifty/fifty.'

'Where is Sam?'

'He cancelled! I know, can you believe it? He had too much work on. Also, he doesn't "agree" with the countryside.' Sam was an architect, as successful in his field as Cleo but with a tendency to patronise his wife's humble friend, and Marnie felt a small, shameful relief that he wasn't there. 'Anyway, the main thing is – look who *is* here!'

Anthony, her godson, stepped out from behind his mother's

back and once again affection was tangled with guilt. God-parents are appointed for a reason and she'd initially imagined that her role was to be a kind of children's entertainer, perpetually finding things behind his ear. She'd failed in that, but as he'd got older, she'd hoped she might become a confidante, his parents' laconic sidekick. This hadn't worked out either. Anthony was earnest, reserved, a maths prodigy by his parents' account, but the words 'godmother' and 'grandmother' are a little too close and the last time she'd seen him, eighteen months ago now, that was how she'd been, gasping stagily at his academic achievements, palming cash into his hand and making corny jokes. *Don't spend it all on sweets!* Since then, adolescence had set in and she noted the raised dots across his forehead, the glitter of braces as he tried a smile. She knew not to point these out and it would be inane to observe that he'd grown taller, but this was the material she had to work with so . . .

'Look how tall you've grown! I swear, I look away for one minute!'

'Bit more than one minute,' said Cleo.

'Come here!' said Marnie, opening her arms for a hug but noting the flash of fear in the boy's eyes. Instead, she placed both hands on his shoulders and waggled them vigorously, like a locked steering wheel. 'So handsome!' she said, and thought, *Well, that's creepy, right there.*

And then, as if on the subject of handsome, another man stepped forward, perhaps the most handsome man she'd ever seen, so handsome that she gave a little laugh, and he smiled at her laugh, as if to say, *I know, it's ridiculous, isn't it?* 'This is our friend Conrad,' said Cleo.

Looking back later, she didn't *think* she'd pushed her godson to one side, though she might have curtsied.

'Pleased to meet you, Marnie,' he said, his voice incongruously pitched, as if the helium was just wearing off. 'I've been hearing all about you!'

Don't say, *Nothing bad, I hope*, she thought but it seemed she'd already said it.

'Oh, *only* bad things!'

'Ohhhhh, like what?' she said but what if he *had* heard only bad things? He said nothing and for a moment they all stood, listening to the sea.

'And there's one more of us!' said Cleo, brightly, indicating the man standing at the water's edge, tapping at the advancing tide with the toe of his boot as if nudging the sea back into place. He turned and smiled briefly and Marnie recognised him as the man who'd stolen looks at her, then later told her to get out of his way. 'This is Michael, one of my junior colleagues from school.'

'Pleased to meet you,' he said. A low voice, slight accent, a blue fisherman's jumper, beard and scruffy hair that might all have been home-knitted.

'Hello, Michael!' and she walked down the slipway, hand extended. His palms were full of wet pebbles, which he looked at in confusion then tossed on to the beach. 'Don't just throw them on to the ground!' she said, and he laughed, shook her hand then went back to his search, looking down with the touching concentration of a child hunting in a rock pool. 'Lost your keys?'

'Hm? No, I'm looking for a pebble.'

'Well, you've come to the right place!' she said brightly. Then, 'What do you want a pebble for?'

He bit his lip and winced. 'I'm embarrassed to say. Just a daft tradition.'

'What is it?'

'If you're walking right across the country you're meant to dip your toes in the water, pick up a pebble on one side and carry it all the way to the other.'

'Michael's walking to the North Sea,' said Cleo. 'Like a lunatic.'

'Oh. Wow – really?'

'Two hundred miles!' said Cleo.

'Hundred and ninety,' said Michael, 'give or take.'

'You know they've got trains for that, mate,' said Conrad. 'You can get taxis, you can get buses . . .'

He shrugged. 'I like to walk,' he said simply, and Marnie noted his face, which had something old-fashioned about it, a kind of crumpled nobility, like someone leading a doomed expedition. Was this it? Was this the doomed expedition?

'You do realise you could drive it in, what, four hours?' said Conrad, but the other man, whose name she had forgotten, had gone back to scanning the beach.

'Well, I'm getting one too,' said Marnie, and she jumped off the slipway and began turning the stones with her foot.

The man frowned. 'You only have to do it if you're going all the way across.'

'What if I get lost? Anyway, I want one as a souvenir.' She picked up a small stone, rubbed at it with her thumb. 'What are we looking for? What makes a good stone? Surely they're all as good as each other.'

'Nice colour. Not too big.'

'They're always disappointing when you get them home, don't you think?' she said, then, bizarrely, 'Like men.'

'It's because they dry out,' said the man. 'Lose their shine.'

'Like men?' they said together, and smiled.

'This one won't,' he said, and held out the pebble between finger and thumb, sleek and grey but banded with an elegant white line. 'Nothing flash. Understated, classic. It's called a rounded dolerite.'

'Rocks have different names? Christ, it was bad enough when

they did that with birds. Rounded dolerite. Nice. Okay, what have I got here?' It was a pale red stone, the size, shape and colour of a supermarket raspberry.

'Red sandstone. It's very typical. Did you notice it in the buildings here, all the red buildings?' She shrugged, as if to say, *Don't be ridiculous.* 'It's softer, easier to work. That's sedimentary, this is igneous.'

'Which means?'

'Yours was laid down slowly in layers, mine came out of a volcano.'

'See, now I want what you've got. Look at you!' she said to her pebble, turned towards her like a ventriloquist's dummy. 'Why didn't *you* come out of a volcano?' She stopped herself abruptly. 'Sorry. Literally talking to a stone. Sorry.'

He gave what she thought of as a not-today-thank-you smile. 'It's a good choice,' he said, drying his hands on his hair. 'I think you should follow your instinct. Stick with it.'

'I will,' she said, and slipped the pebble into one of her many pockets. 'I'm going to dip my toes in the water too. Just in case,' and she walked down to the water's edge and tapped at the surf, careful not to get her new boots wet before they'd even started.

Lighthouse

They settled their bags on their backs and began the ascent, zigzagging towards the cliff-top on worn wooden steps. Fifteen miles to go, but once they'd left the cliffs behind it was just farmland, a few small towns, plantations rather than natural woodland, only one serious ascent, and with this in mind he walked ahead, partly to set the pace, partly to admonish himself.

Talk to them, talk to them, talk to them. Absurd for it to be this hard. Given a class of thirty adolescents, he was usually capable of being confident and eloquent, often engaging, sometimes even funny, and surely this was an easier crowd. But here he was, banging on about igneous and sedimentary, a geography teacher straight out of the gate and things had scarcely gone any better with Conrad, who, judging by his new trainers and skinny jeans, really wasn't taking this seriously at all. He heard his dad's voice – *bit flash* – and told himself to keep an open mind, but encounters with other men always seemed pre-loaded with rivalry and suspicion, the handshake tight, the smiles too, and he wondered if, after a certain age, men could ever really like each other. The window for friendship was always small, and narrowed with age, and a new male friend after forty? What a strange, uneasy relationship that would be.

Did the same apply to female friendship? He was unlikely to find out. Glancing behind him, he could see Conrad and the woman who'd talked to her stone already creating scenes for their montage, the man telling some story, the woman laughing and slapping at his arm with the back of her hand. In the corridors and common rooms, this behaviour was a daily rite but, like the school musical, it was more fun to take part in than to watch, and he thanked God that the other woman had failed to turn up. 'Look at the view!' shouted Cleo, further back, and they all turned to take in the town and its beach, the gauzy sea and beyond it, in their own grey haze, the chimneys and cooling towers of Sellafield.

'I particularly like the nuclear power station!' shouted Conrad. 'Very picturesque!'

Michael estimated the gradient here as approximately one-in-ten. With a good push, he would probably roll all the way to the car park.

They carried on, the slow rollercoaster of a cliff walk, the others shifting and forming into pairs or threes as they descended to Fleswick Bay, a vivid example of coastal erosion but best keep that to himself. Soon the lighthouse, white and bright in the midday sun. Surely everyone liked a lighthouse, kids especially.

'Hey! Wait!' Here was Cleo, trotting to catch up.

'See the lighthouse?'

'The large white building?' she gasped, clutching her knees as if holding them in place. 'I missed that. Very nice.'

'Does Anthony want to get a closer look?'

'He's all good. He's past the lighthouse stage now.'

'That's a shame. I love a lighthouse.'

She stood, head back. 'Maybe it's something you come back to later in life.'

'I'm just making it entertaining for him.'

'He's thirteen, Michael.'

'I'd have been interested at thirteen.'

'Oh, I absolutely believe *that*. Hey, you are going to talk to people, aren't you, not just walk ahead?'

'I will. I just have to, you know, get into the zone.'

'It's two new people.'

'I know. I will!'

After a while, she said, 'I'm sorry Tessa couldn't come. She still really wants to meet you.'

'Some other time.'

'I mean, it's never come up but I bet she's a lighthouse *freak*. I'll fix a dinner.'

He sighed. 'I thought I told you—'

'Remind me.'

'—no matchmaking.'

'Oh, come on, what am I meant to do? Days are long. I need something to distract me from all this . . .' she gestured to the landscape '. . . all this *geography*.'

'You can watch them.' He nodded towards the woman from the train and Conrad, who was at that moment kicking at a molehill.

'Hm. The jury's still out on Conrad. He's a nice guy but that's very much Sam's suggestion. I'm sceptical. I think he might be here for a good time not a long time, if you know what I mean.'

'I don't.'

'Whereas you're here for a long time not a good time.'

'Just toying with people's emotions.'

'A puppet-master. "As flies to wanton boys . . ."' Cleo was an English teacher and it slipped out sometimes. 'Such a shame about Tessa. When I think what might have been . . .'

'We're going this way now.' The path began to turn inland. 'Say goodbye to the sea.'

'So are we nearly there yet?'

'You see that hill?' He pointed towards a wooded peak, sentry to the mountains beyond but still impossibly far away. 'Just the other side of that.'

'God, really? Are you trying to kill us?'

'That's what ten miles looks like. Over that, we're in the Lakes.'

'Are we nearly there yet?' shouted Anthony, slouching behind.

'Almost, sweetheart,' shouted Cleo, 'not far now.' Then, to Michael, 'He's a little sulky. He wanted to see his friends.'

'This'll be better,' said Michael.

'Oh, you think so?' said Cleo, laughing as they turned their backs on the sea.

Hobbies and Interests

Conrad was telling her how awful the hotel had been.

'I had to send the towels back because, well, you don't want to know. And the sheets were nylon, polyester, whatever, so if you moved too much, you got a shock. A substantial shock, like a cattle prod, three or four times in the night. If I'd had sex with someone, we'd have been electrocuted.'

Was this flirting? It seemed like flirting, so she said, 'Oop,' calling on her vocabulary of not-quite-words: oop, wah, fum, bah, owa, phla.

'It's not what I'm used to. I like a nice hotel, something a bit more . . .'

'Boutique?'

'Boutique. Don't think I'm going to get that here.'

'But it *is* beautiful.'

'Yeah!' he said, looking a little startled, as if he'd only just noticed. 'It is!'

'Look at the view!' shouted Cleo, from ahead. They looked back to the town.

'I particularly like the nuclear power station!' Conrad shouted back. 'Very picturesque!'

'Phla,' mumbled Marnie. She felt moisture forming below her hairline from the effort of the climb or conversation. Why did her voice sound so strange? Perhaps it was the outdoor acoustics. She had not spoken at length to someone in the open air for, what, three, four years? Was that true? He was asking a question. Concentrate.

'So you came up on the early train?'

'From London. I did. It was very nice. I had to do some work, but—'

'And where do you live in London?'

'I'm in Herne Hill.'

He frowned. 'Is that even *in* London?'

'Hey, you!' she said, putting a laugh into her voice and hating it. 'It's Zone Two borders!'

'South London, though.'

'Yes.' Wasn't he meant to ask about her work? 'Why? Where are you?'

'Kensington,' he said.

'By the museums, the Palace . . . ?'

'More west. Barons Court,' he said and they both made their private judgements, as Londoners will do, while also working out the route they'd take, should the situation ever arise. A tricky one, overground to Victoria then the District line or was it Piccadilly? Best not worry about that. Best say something.

'Have you noticed, Barons Court has no apostrophe, but Earl's Court always does? Why *is* that?' It seemed that living there gave him no insight, and so, 'What do you do, Conrad?' she said, and thought, *My God, why not ask him his National Insurance number?* This was the form-filling part of the conversation, name, address, place of birth, education and employment. Once completed, they could move on to the emotional heft of Hobbies and Interests. *Reading, going to the cinema, meeting people.* Well, maybe not meeting people.

'I'm a pharmacist,' he said. 'I run a little pharmacy in West Brompton,' and she had a happy little fantasy of him smiling, handing her a white paper bag, stapled at the top, an ointment perhaps or some delicious sleeping pills.

'So, uh, you can get your hands on all kinds of good shit,' she said, with narrowed eyes and a croaky voice. 'The reeeeal gooood shiiit.'

'There are systems in place.'

'Yeah, yeah, yeah, you *say* that, but I bet a few pills "fall on the floor".'

'No, really,' he said, stern now, 'we're very strict about security.'

'Oh, Okay. Okay. I wasn't suggesting—'

'And, anyway, what am I going to do with some old guy's blood thinners? No, we take stock-keeping very seriously.'

'Well, *good*,' she said emphatically, 'good for *you*,' and she tried to remember where she'd had this experience before, of panicked improvisation, of being scrutinised, assessed and lightly scolded, and recognised that it was from dating, that she was on a date, and that instead of some small plates restaurant in Clapham, she'd been dropped off out of doors with a wardrobe on her back. Her own fault. She'd asked Cleo not to match-make but with the conviction of a toddler demanding not to be tickled and now she was paying the price. She told herself brusquely, Enjoy yourself. Enjoy this real-world interaction. He was, after all, an absurdly attractive man, with his bright eyes and lovely mouth, and pharmacist was a noble and responsible profession, someone who might witness a passport application. He was neat and trim, and easy access to moisturisers had given him extraordinary skin, a smoothness untouched by time and life, as if he were his own action figure. If he'd grabbed his chin, pulled sharply upwards and removed his face, she wouldn't have been at all surprised.

'You, okay?' he said, and she realised she'd been staring.

'Look, a lighthouse!' she said. 'We're literally going *To the Lighthouse*!' and when that didn't land, 'I'd be a good lighthouse keeper. When I was a kid, that was my perfect job, hanging out in my little round rooms, with my round tables and round carpets—'

'You've really thought about it, Marnie.' Using her name, that sounded nice.

'Little hermit lady, flat cap and a jersey, pipe on the go, checking the weather, keeping the light burning, loads of time to read. I'm sure there's more to it than that, changing bulbs and reading, but . . .'

'You read a lot, do you?'

'That's practically all I do.'

She was about to add 'these days' but it had always been the case. 'When I was a kid, my parents actually told me to read less. They thought I wasn't going out enough. You know, the shops, sleepovers, social stuff.'

'Didn't you like those things?'

'I did. But I liked reading more.'

She did not elaborate and they fell into silence once again, but perhaps there had been something a little obsessive about it, the way she'd consumed the shelves of the local library, Blyton to Jansson, C. S. Lewis to P. G. Wodehouse, Christie then du Maurier then the Brontës, reading indiscriminately but always passionately, so that even her dislikes were passionate. Dickens, she thought, was preachy and silly, like a teacher putting on funny voices, but never mind, here were Jane Austen and Sue Townsend, Ursula K. Le Guin and Jean M. Auel, and each Saturday morning she'd return her stack of library books, the maximum permitted, placing them on the counter, like a gambler cashing in chips. Books saw her through the pupal stage of thirteen to sixteen, frowning at Kafka and Woolf, then tearing through John Irving and Maeve Binchy, widely read in the proper sense, making no distinction between Jilly Cooper and Edith Wharton. There were stories on film and TV and, a little later, in the rolling melodrama of the internet, but those were team activities, noisy and social. Private, intimate, a book was something she could pull around and over herself, like a quilt.

Perhaps her parents would have worried less if all that reading had been reflected in her schoolwork, but she was only an average student. English was her best subject, and on an autumn evening that she still recalled, they'd talked about the possibility of university. Yes, she read a lot, but reading was a hobby, not a job, and while there were literature degrees, why spend three years studying something she was already doing for free? In the novels she read, parents might be wild and glamorous, bohemian and complicated, villainous or absent. Her own were steady, cautious, conservative people, nervous of debt, modest in their own aspirations and their aspirations for their child. With only some private tearfulness on her part, it was agreed. For now, best get a job.

She sometimes wondered what might have happened if she'd persisted, stated her case, put her disappointment on display rather than secretly crying in her room. 'We met at university' was such a familiar phrase and perhaps that version of her life might have been fuller, more populated. Somewhere in a parallel timeline that story was unspooling but there was no point in dwelling on it. Resenting her parents for not supporting her education felt too much like 'Why didn't you buy me a present?', a small and sour grudge to carry.

After all, it was not an unhappy childhood, not exactly, just steady, suburban, as constant as the thermostat in the hall that she was forbidden to touch, and if she sometimes wished that she was an orphan, it was only for the narrative possibilities. At no point did her parents move house, gamble, use an overdraft, change jobs, have affairs, go abroad, shout in public, park illegally, eat on the street or get drunk, and while they must have had sex at some point, this was covered up as carefully as a past murder. Marnie was the only evidence, and while she always felt sure that her parents loved each other and presumably her too, there was no need to say this out loud. She loved them even as she rolled her eyes at them, and in turn they worried about her and protected her from anything too complicated: illness, sex, unhappiness, the larger human emotions.

A classic only child. Neil, her ex-husband, had used the phrase, though she couldn't recall the circumstances. Perhaps she'd been too quiet, left a party early, gone to bed to read. Perhaps with a sibling or two there might have been more noise in the house, more friction or affection, though she'd never resented the absence, had quite liked having the back seat of the car to herself, all the presents at Christmas. The three of them fitted on the sofa perfectly well and when she'd had enough, she could slip upstairs with a book.

'Did you read much as a kid?' she asked Conrad now.

'Not really. I was into sport mainly. Football, cricket.'

She didn't want to talk about that. 'What about now? Do you read now?'

'Sure. Business, economics, sports psychology.'

'Not novels?'

'I don't like wasting time on things that are made-up.'

There was a lot she might have said to this, but instead: 'You know, I've not read any sports psychology. How to win, that sort of thing?'

'Building confidence, stamina, setting goals. Going for it!'

'It must be hard to get a whole book out of going for it.

Anyone ever written anything good on, you know, just doing what you can manage on the day? "Bronze Is Fine!"' Here she stumbled on one of the piles of earth that dotted the otherwise perfect green . . . *sward*. Was that the word? 'Molehills! I've only ever seen them in cartoons.'

'God, you really are a city girl.'

'Well, Zone Two borders. I always thought, with molehills, that if you knocked the top off quickly enough you'd see a little mole inside. Like taking the top off a boiled egg, except . . .' and here she gave a little impression, nose to the sky, teeth bared, squinting, fingers waggling at her chin. Go for it!

'Let's find out, shall we?' he said, ran up and gave the nearest molehill a footballer's kick, sending earth flying. Now that he'd made the effort, it seemed rude not to look. 'Nope. Just mud,' he said, brushing the dirt from the trainer's toe.

'Another childhood dream shattered,' she said, and walked on, feeling that it had been a mistake to impersonate a mole.

Human Geography

Inland now, they walked down lanes and across farmyards, Michael leading the group and raising his hand to the farm workers, as if to say, Yes, tourists, bear with us. They passed through small towns, old mining communities that had never quite found a replacement, the terraced streets silent and melancholy in the afternoon sun.

'Where is everyone?' said the woman from the train.

'Maybe it's siesta time, like in Barcelona,' said Conrad, and Michael felt his teacherly instinct twitch. Towns don't appear from nowhere: they need a natural spring or harbour or a seam of tin, and when that loses its importance, the absence will be felt. He thought of his own hometown, his father a lifelong employee of the printing works, not books but brochures, catalogues, directories and calendars. Dad had started there as an apprentice, educated on the factory floor and promoted into the lower levels of management. Everyone's dad had worked there, some of the mums too, and the fortunes of the factory had mirrored the trajectory of Michael's childhood, the certainty and prosperity of his early years giving way to the insecurity and angst of adolescence as the business faltered. Phone directories and catalogues – they might as well have been making wagon wheels, and when the last scraps of production moved abroad, the whole town lost its purpose. Like a car without an engine, it had begun to fall apart, shops and pubs closing, the town centre taking on an aggressive air so that people were more than ever inclined to stay indoors. Dad, who'd long carried the stress of keeping the business open, now felt the guilt of watching it close. All that time at home, it was unbearable and he'd often disappear all day into the Peaks. His mum, a piano teacher, once as glamorous and bright as Dad was blunt and self-contained, stayed home and strove to hold on to a few students, but she, too, seemed to shrink and fade. His younger brother, less academic than Michael, had always expected to find a role in his hometown and now seemed dazed, furious with Michael who, with rude timing, was making his escape.

Aspiration had been his parents' great project: a nice house in a cul-de-sac, holidays in Spain and even Florida, dinner-dances with the lord mayor, a presence in the church and the town hall and now the first Bradshaw in higher education. Yet even as he packed his suitcase, Michael had felt as if he was elbowing his way on to a lifeboat. At parties or flirting in the student bar, he'd suddenly remember his parents and reassure himself: maybe they can just retire.

But his father was forty-two when he'd lost his job, the same age as Michael now. Neither young nor old, too late to start again, too early to stop, the future simultaneously a great swathe of time but also not enough. *Maybe they can just retire.* He shuddered now to think of how blithely he'd dismissed his parents' anxieties, though he knew that this was at least part of the reason he'd chosen his own profession. 'People'll always need teachers,' said Dad, who had not always been needed. At the time he'd thought his father had been proud but at least part of it was relief.

They walked on. He would phone him later, tell him his route and progress – no matter where he walked, Dad had always been there before him, walked further in worse weather. They no longer asked if he'd spoken to Natasha but, still, best stick to what they were having for their tea. He would ask Dad, How's Mum's arthritis? He would ask Mum, How are Dad's feet? and in this way, they would avoid anything substantial.

They were back in woodland now, industrial conifers, all identical, a battery farm for trees really, but at the end of the tunnel, framed and illuminated, a great, golden hill, like something from a church painting. He turned to address the group with his best tour-guide smile. 'So. How are we all doing?'

'Are we climbing again?'

'How much longer?'

'Because I can't climb again.'

'Who's got water? I'm out of water.'

He heard Dad's voice: *Bloody hell, this lot.* 'Okay, team,' he said, 'a quick march to the top, and then down to the Lakes. Two hours.'

'There's something on my boot. It's yellow. Wow. Wow, that stinks.'

He found Anthony and put his hand on his shoulder. 'How you feeling, kid? All right?' The boy covered his forehead and nodded sadly. 'You're doing brilliantly,' and they headed up through the shade of the forest to the golden hill beyond.

Five fire extinguishers strapped to his head

Note to self: remember the great gulf between how physical exercise looks and how it actually feels. On billboards, in commercials for sportswear, in movie montages, nothing seems more exciting, ecstatic even, than the stretch and the burn, the pumping heart and the surging blood, the air-punch, then afterwards that moment of standing hands-on-knees, sweat dripping on to the athletics track. No accident that it resembled sex. Who wouldn't want to do *that*?

The reality was discomfort, edging into pain. Breathing, usually an unconscious act, now felt impossibly hard, as if her sports bra was being wound tighter with a windlass. Halfway up the hill she felt she was inhaling through a pillow, her lungs rattling with great gouts of phlegm, her heart rebelling and trying to punch its way out through her sternum. Was this what a heart attack felt like? She had once vomited into a hand towel during a spin class, and here it was again, that same feeling of distress and discomfort and embarrassment. Her nose was blocked and yet some kind of liquid, some unnameable salt-sweet combination of snot and sweat coursed down her philtrum into her open mouth. She might put a finger to her nostril and blow, like a footballer, but was there a way to do this coquettishly, to hawk and spit with élan, to kittenishly throw up? She wouldn't be pulling this face in a Clapham small plates restaurant, her Stallone-arm-wrestling face, teeth bared, squinting through the perspiration that had combined with eye make-up and moisturiser to create a concoction of salt, acid and oil, a vinaigrette basically, that burnt her eyes. She dug at the sockets with her knuckles, saw the smudges, thought *Great, two black holes.*

They were still on Hobbies and Interests, and for some time Conrad had been talking with knowledge and passion about Formula One racing, how it was a mistake to think it's all about the car, how those guys are actually athletes. 'People think it's just driving in circles, but at a hundred and seventy miles per hour that's 5G, enough to snap your neck.'

Would her own neck snap? She felt it might, and perhaps that would be a good thing. The weight of her pack felt like a great hand pulling her backwards, a big capital W of sweat had appeared beneath her breasts and now some other object, the heel of her evening shoes or the corner of Wainwright's *The Central Fells*, jabbed her liver every step and meanwhile—

'A driver's heart rate's a hundred and eighty-five beats per minute, that's bam-bam-bam, three times a second. Can you imagine?'

'I can actually.' Why wasn't he out of breath? 'Tell me more.'

She had no strong feelings about Formula One, placing it in a category of things that appeal to men, like wetsuits and samurai swords and big watches. Conrad's own watch was the size of a pub ashtray. Her ex-husband Neil had something similar, though his was a ten-dollar fake, bought on Canal Street in New York on their honeymoon. Like the marriage, it had stopped working almost immediately, but though the purchase had been a joke, she knew he'd longed for the real thing. She'd laughed at him once, affectionately, she'd thought, that had been the intention, for buying a men's health magazine and following a regime that promised the arrival of killer abs in thirty days. Each morning she'd counted down the days to their appearance, twenty-three, twenty-two, twenty-one, until he'd snapped, 'Could you please stop jeering at me for one fucking minute, please?', startled once again by the venom Neil could impart to the word 'please'. She had apologised, of course, though the apology might have been more muted if she'd known that he was getting in shape for the benefit of his girlfriend at work. She would never know if the abs arrived because he'd left on day fifteen. He certainly looked better the next time she saw him, healthier and happier, so something good had come out of it.

'With the weight of the helmet, the force on a driver's neck at that speed, it's like having five fire extinguishers strapped to their head.'

'I'm sorry, wait. Why do they have fire extinguishers strapped to their head?'

'They don't, they don't – that's just what the force feels like.'

'Sorry, I lost the thread . . . Can we just . . . ?'

She stopped for a moment and doubled over. There were various questions she might ask about Formula One – is it a sport or an engineering competition? What about women? – but they all seemed hostile, and it was important not to mock things that others enjoy. But she'd been awake now for twelve hours, home was impossibly far away, and she wanted more than anything to lie in a dark room. She squinted at the summit through burning eyes.

'You okay?'

'Yes, yes! Call my sports psychologist! Let's keep moving. I don't want to die here,' she said, and thought of a joke. She would put her hands on her hips indignantly, exhale and say, 'Well, *this* is not a hill that I'm prepared to die on!' If she did it now, she'd fumble the timing. She'd save it for the summit. For now, she asked, 'So in a Formula One car, is the gear box manual or automatic?'

'Semi-automatic. With eight gears!'

'Eight! Wow. And is there a reverse?'

'Surprisingly, there is.'

'For the big shop in Sainsbury's?'

'Ha. Right.'

'You're a real petrol-head, Conrad.'

'A little, maybe. Do you like cars, Marnie?'

'No, I'm a public-transport-head. Ask me about buses. Near me, you've got the three, the one nine six. Along South Lambeth Road, the eighty-eight can reach speeds of nearly twelve miles an hour.' But it sounded like she was jeering again and now the breathlessness was back. 'Tell me, what's the best race you've seen?' she said, just to get them to the top of the hill.

At the summit they gathered by a pile of stones; she threw off her rucksack and wiped the vinaigrette from her eyes. This, she supposed, was the air-punch moment and she could certainly have punched something – the man who'd sold her the boots or Jenson Button. She drank water, caught her breath and looked dutifully at the panorama. To the west, a patched green plain unfurled towards the sea, which reflected the low sun back at them, but she refused to be awed. Big things in the distance look smaller. Fine, get over it.

'Very nice,' said Conrad.

Marnie saw her chance and put her hands on her hips. 'You know, *this* is not a hill that I'm pre—'

'That's Scotland over there, the other side of the Solway Firth.' The knitwear model had stepped on her joke. 'There's the Isle of Man. Over there, that's where we've come from. And now look over there . . .'

Resentfully, she turned and there they were, the Lumps, erupting abruptly from the plain, too steep and suddenly near as if they'd somehow snuck up. 'That's where we're going,' he said, 'over that range tomorrow, those mountains the day after, then the biggest climb on Tuesday.'

'Well, rather you than me, mate,' said Conrad.

'When are you leaving, Conrad?' said Marnie, as casually as she could.

'Monday morning.'

'Fnuh,' she said.

'Back to work Tuesday.'

Marnie felt a little panicked. 'When are you leaving, Cleo?'

'Eh, Monday morning too.'

'Oh. Oh. I thought you were staying on longer.'

'Anthony's got something, haven't you?' Anthony nodded. 'What about you?'

'Tuesday night,' she said, and wondered if perhaps she saw the other man flinch. 'But the ticket's flexible so . . .'

The ticket was not flexible. She'd thought they'd have longer. All those expensive plasters, the rubber water bladder. She'd brought twelve pairs of pants.

'Or you can drive back with us, get the train from York?'

'Okay. Okay. That's okay. Let's see. Let's see.'

The other man was scanning the ground for another stone, a freak for rocks and minerals. 'We should get going if we want to be there before evening,' said Gravel Boy, selecting and placing a pebble reverently on the top of the cairn as if it were the star on a Christmas tree. They picked up their bags, fell into step and Marnie asked Conrad if there was a Formula Two and Conrad said, funnily enough there was and told her all about it.

The Valley

It's not always easier to walk downhill, and as they descended, he smiled at the yelps and groans behind him as the hand that had held them back on the ascent now shoved them forward. Finally the ground levelled, and they crossed a beck swollen with the recent rains and followed its bank into a valley, sickle-shaped, steep-sided, exquisite in its pale greens and russet browns, like a perfect apple. The path was well-worn but it felt as if they'd stumbled on some hidden kingdom, reed buntings flitting alongside them, like perfectly skimmed stones. The adults were together now, and rather than join them, he fell into step beside Anthony.

'How's the walk? Not too much?'

'A bit too much. We're nearly there, yeah?'

'About an hour.'

'And tomorrow?'

'Don't tell anyone,' said Michael, 'but tomorrow is hard.' Anthony clapped both hands to his face and dragged them downwards. 'Kids love nature walks with middle-aged people. Is that not right?' He felt more comfortable, talking to Ant. In the school corridors, the boy occupied that strange role of the pupil whose parent is also a teacher, both privileged and vulnerable, like a young prince in a treacherous court. Michael watched over him, had known him since he was born, had been on holidays with him, applauded his grade-1 guitar pieces, had taught him card games and football (his father was not the type to kick a ball). He and Natasha had looked after Anthony for long weekends at a time when they'd been trying hard for a child of their own, and on his departure, they would be left silent and dazed, struck dumb by a kind of surrogate love for the boy.

Since then, Anthony had watched him go through break-up and breakdown, had even visited him in hospital, and Michael wondered how that changed things, to see an adult in the aftermath of a catastrophe, stripped of the illusion of authority and control. He wondered what Cleo had told him. *Our friends Michael and Natasha are spending time apart.* Was the boy curious or was this all just grown-up stuff, as irrelevant as mortgages and pensions? Whatever he knew, Michael was keen to reassure him all was well, but again the question, how to be? The older the kid, the harder to impress, and while Michael had no ambition to be a role model, he should try not to be weird.

'You see that bird, there, in the trees? With the black stripe on its cheek? That's called a reed bunting.'

'Yeah,' said Anthony, not looking up. He might as well have told him that it was called Steve. Best let the bunting go, though he found himself wondering, as he often did, how he would have fared as a father. They'd both wanted it – had they even needed to ask? – had tried for years. When nothing happened, he had taken the tests and, while scrupulously avoiding the language of blame, there seemed to be an issue with sperm count and motility. The problem was, he was assured, not insurmountable: the sperm were there, but were variously shy, lazy, sluggish, so he took on the advice about bicycle saddles and boxer shorts, spinach and hot baths, and they made the stoical jokes that couples are expected to make in such circumstances.

But nothing diminished his mounting . . . 'broodiness'? No other word existed and yet it seemed a frivolous, imprecise term for a feeling that had once, after Anthony's departure, left him in private tears at the end of the garden. They did what they could to improve their chances and it was at this point that he'd had the incident, the fight, and had ended up in hospital and nothing, not a single thing, since then had gone right. Natasha had been gone for eighteen months now. He was forty-two, with idiopathic oligospermia, and what was he to do with the broodiness now?

Concentrate. Buck up. 'How's the manga?' he asked, a tourist who has taken the trouble to learn a few words of a foreign language. 'Or is it anime? I get confused.' He knew the difference, but Anthony was telling him anyway, regaining the touching effusiveness of pre-adolescence. Michael asked questions with no need to know the answer, enjoying instead the sound of the boy's fluent speech in the final days of his high register, the miles passing easily until they were back on tarmac, a shaded lane that rolled down towards the village where they'd spend their first night.

Gateway to the Lakes

Like a Regency novel, the etiquette of walking required that she spend time in conversation with each of the guests, and now that it was nearly over, it seemed a good time to mark the card of the man who'd spoilt her joke.

'Ah, Ennerdale Bridge!' she said, reading the village sign. 'Gateway to the Lakes!' and he smiled lightly, still looking ahead. 'I think we were on the same train.'

'You were working hard. I was going to tell you to look at the view, but I didn't think you'd thank me.'

She typed in the air. 'Busy city girl, lot of pressure, deadlines to meet.'

'What d'you do, if you don't mind me . . . ?'

'I'm a copy-editor. Fiction mainly, checking over books before publication.'

'Like marking homework.'

'Sort of. You're a teacher?'

'Yes.'

'Let me guess. Geography.'

'Is it the beard or just a general . . . ?'

'The knitwear, the pebble fetish.'

'Not a *fetish*. It's called geology.'

'I don't know, you do pick up a *lot* of stones. We passed that pile of rocks, you picked one up, gave it a little rub, sniffed it—'

'Clearly, I didn't *sniff* it.'

'—put it carefully on top.'

'That's a cairn, an ancient marker. You're meant to do that, so it lasts.'

'Oh. Now I feel bad. I was never very good at geography. Sorry.'

'We are not a vengeful people.' They reached the old bridge and stood for a moment looking down into the whorls of black water. 'This is the River Ehen,' he said, as if introducing them at a party.

'Geography field trips, is that still a thing? Are they still wild?'

'Not on my watch. And not for the teachers.'

'I should hope not. My God, we went on one to the Isle of Wight and I swear, it was like the last days of Rome. Is that what drew you to the subject?'

'The packed lunches? The hostels?'

'Kids throwing up on the coach?'

'Not *just* that. What drew me to . . . ?' He thought for a moment, as if considering the question for the first time. 'I liked knowing why things are where they are. Used to walk with my mum and dad, liked being outdoors, interested in the environment, the politics of it. Was crap at everything else. What did you study at uni?' he said.

'Oh, I didn't go to university.'

'I thought that was where you met Cleo?'

'People meet in other places.' She was punishing him a little. 'I'm sorry, it's just when people find out I work with books but don't have a degree, they're all *Really?* As if it's a scam, like I'm a self-taught heart surgeon or something.'

He seemed to think for a moment. 'I don't *think* I did that.'

'No. You're right. You didn't,' she said, and this was true. They walked on.

'So how *do* you know Cleo?'

'We met in the office where I was working. Commercial advertising.'

'You worked in advertising?'

'Doesn't that sound glam? Used to. Small-time stuff, just selling space, admin, answering the phone, writing the odd bit of copy. Cleo came in as a temp in the holidays, slumming it while she was studying, and we talked about books, so I've known her, what?, eighteen years. She was sort of my mentor, trying to get me back into education. Except I never took her advice. Long before she was this superstar head-teacher.'

'Deputy.'

'*Deputy* head-teacher. Did you meet at school?'

'Yeah, me and my wife used to—'

'Oh. Oh, you're married?'

'Separated. Cleo likes to keep an eye on me.'

'I know that feeling,' said Marnie. People who said they were separated, not divorced, were like people who insisted that a tomato was a fruit, not a vegetable: technically correct, but on shaky ground. No one ate tomato ice-cream. 'I'm divorced,' she said emphatically, professional to amateur. 'Also Anthony's godmother.'

'You're Anthony's godmother. We've met you!'

'Your wife's name was . . .'

'Natasha, Nat.'

'Natasha! Pretty, well-dressed. You're a nice couple. Or you were.'

'Oh, well, thank you,' he said. 'I thought so.'

This was definitely a bump in the road, but if she kept going. 'Sorry. Sorry, I'm . . . I've forgotten your name.'

'Michael, Michael Bradshaw.'

'So we met at the christening.'

'We must have.'

'Clearly I made quite the impression.'

'I'm sorry.'

'Don't worry about it. I have one of those memory-foam mattresses at home and every night absolutely *no* idea who I am. You might remember my ex-husband, though, he was there. Do you remember talking to a little shit?'

'Nope.'

'Anyone patronise you, start an argument, talk over you?'

'Everyone seemed very nice.'

'You missed him, then. Lucky you.'

'Was it a *very* happy marriage?'

'Flah,' she mumbled, then took him by his arm. 'Let me look at you again.' They stopped in the road, and she squinted at his face while he glanced around awkwardly. It was a good, strong face, though a little scuffed, nothing fine or delicate. The creases around his eyes might have been laughter lines, though surely no one laughed that much. Yet when he smiled, as he did now, there was something reassuring about it, dependable, a sense of being in good hands. 'I didn't have the beard then,' he said, turning in profile. 'Or this,' with his finger he traced a pale line, a scar running parallel to his jaw, 'though I'm sure there are other reasons not to remember me. Anyway,' he said, turning away as if stuffing something back into its box.

She recalled the summer afternoon, a secular christening, a kind of ceremonial barbecue: well-dressed families, kids running around, prosperity, community. A gazebo, a bouncy castle as imposing as the real thing. Natasha she remembered as likeable and only slightly competitive, but she did not remember the husband. In the what-have-I-done days of her own marriage, the main emotions she recalled from that afternoon were love for her friend and an equally profound envy.

A common mistake in manuscripts was confusion over the words 'envy' and 'jealousy', the first meaning to want what someone else has, the second including the fear that someone might take what's yours. She was not jealous. Neil did not get on with Cleo, did not like meeting strangers, being with other people or being left alone, and had strident opinions about barbecuing. She remembered venturing on to the bouncy castle with Cleo, the slow shake of his head, her shoes dangling from his index finger.

They were walking again. 'So, in theory, if anything happens to Cleo and Sam, God forbid, then I get to keep Anthony.'

'Um, well, I suppose so. I imagine there'd be some discussion with the executors of the will. And there'd be the godfather.'

'I don't know him. Some friend of Sam. Would I have to fight him?'

'I don't think godparents physically fight over orphans, no.'

'Well, good because I'd cave straight away. Do you think I could have him?'

'In a fight? I don't know him but, yes, if you were determined enough, I'm sure you could beat up Anthony's godfather.'

'Ah, that's nice. Thank you!'

The man seemed serious again. 'Let's just hope it doesn't come to that.'

'I bet he's a much better godparent than I am, too. I always thought I'd be boxes of oil pastels and tickets to the RSC but I'm ten quid in an envelope every second year. In fact, I'm not even sure, hand on heart, that I could renounce Satan.'

'What about all his works?'

'I'd renounce *some* of his works,' she said. 'The early stuff.' He laughed so nicely that she almost forgave him for spoiling her hill-joke. 'By the way, is it "Michael" or "Mike"?'

'Michael. Strangely, hardly anyone calls me Mike.'

'No, I get that. I think it's that k – it's like x, it's quite racy. Mike's a DJ but Michael's a saint.'

'Well, I'm no saint.'

'That's what they're saying in the staffroom,' she said, and thought, *That's enough for now. Leave them wanting more.* Was Conrad tantalised by her absence? She fell back, turned to see him with Cleo, their heads close – was he talking about her? *She's so compelling, the way she clears her throat.* He caught her eye – and was that a wink, or was he squinting into the low sun? No definitely a wink, and she turned and walked on, attempting to add a certain Monroe-quality to the pendulum swing of her rucksack. She took in nature in a generalised way and soon enough they were on a single-file path, through an ancient wood, damp and mulchy with a vegetal smell, bad in a fridge but fine here, circle of life and all that. Then, through the trees, a lake.

'We're there, everyone!'

An amber sunset illuminated the Trout Inn and they picked up their pace. She wrenched off her backpack before they were through the door. The saloon bar smelt of beer and coal, and room keys were handed out by a harassed landlord, his face a scribble pad of broken veins, spectacles hanging from a chain around his neck, like the weight of the world. An ancient by-law requires all country pubs to have themed rooms and here it was freshwater fish. Marnie was Gudgeon. 'What are you, Cleo?'

'Eh, Tench?'

'Conrad?'

'Stickleback.'

'Wish I was in Stickleback,' said Marnie.

'Play your cards right,' murmured Cleo, and Marnie blushed and thought, *Oh, it's on, it's definitely on.*

'How about you, Michael?'

He was filling in the registration form. 'What?' He looked at the fob. 'Oh. I'm Chub.' They laughed and he smiled tightly. The Wi-Fi code was 'wainwright2017', all lower case.

'There's another room here,' said the landlord.

'Yes, that's my friend Tessa. She couldn't make it. We did cancel.'

The landlord sighed, preparing for the fight, and Marnie grabbed her bag and hurried up the narrow stairs to her room to use the toilet and charge all her devices.

Kintsugi

At last, alone. There was a sharp, artificial tang of lemon cleaner and the lighting was a little stark, but he shrugged off his ruck-sack, fell back on to the bed and recklessly gorged on complimentary shortbread, listening to the crumbs rattling into his ears, wondering about Tessa.

He'd already been briefed. In the weeks leading up to the trip, Cleo had contrived mentions of how attractive she was, how fit (triathlons apparently), how successful, a dentist with her own practice. Best of all, said Cleo, she was 'outdoorsy', though he was less sure what this meant: that she didn't wear make-up? He knew, from history lessons and Nat's costume dramas, that olden-time court artists would often be commissioned to paint flattering portraits for approval in advance of marriage, and that these portraits were not always representative. When he tried to picture Cleo's Tessa, he imagined her on a moor, minty-breathed, shrugging off her white coat to run, then cycle, then swim. Was this what Cleo thought he wanted? He did not want anyone.

And even if he did, he could not imagine them at dinner in the Trout Inn, flirting over pie and chips, looks and smiles and self-revealing anecdotes. He had not been on a date since the Italian restaurant with Natasha fifteen years ago, and wasn't that one of the great joys of a long relationship, to be free of that kind of performance? Trying to picture himself on a date now was like trying to imagine himself bungee-jumping, theoretically possible but under what circumstances? No, it was just as well she hadn't come. On the wall opposite him, a TV leant dangerously on its bracket, and he reached for the remote and scrolled through the channels. When did TVs in hotel rooms start to seem so archaic and quaint? On their trips away, it was almost the first thing they did, turn on the . . .

There she was again. As if she'd walked into the room, he sat up, shook the crumbs out of his ears and got undressed, catching sight of himself in the mirror. The naked body of a middle-aged man. It could have been worse. He'd always looked after himself, running, hiking, five-a-side, not out of vanity but for the same reason he brushed his teeth and put the lids back on pens, but there was no doubt things had slipped a little since Nat's departure. He was getting through a lot of chilli sauce, these days, and, he had to admit, did not always eat off a plate. He'd put on weight in some places, lost too much in others, and while his injuries had largely healed, he still felt cracked and vulnerable, like a cup with a glued-on handle. Apparently, there was meant to be beauty in cracks, cracks were how the light gets in but, more importantly, they were how the liquid gets out. No one really wants a leaky cup.

The shower was like a kettle poured on to the back of his neck and he stepped out quickly and wiped steam from the mirror, pouting, moving his mouth from one side to the other. His face. He'd been quite the catch at teacher-training, though that was some time ago. At Christmas, Mum had a habit of picking up wrapping paper and smoothing it out to use again, and his skin had taken on that quality, especially around his eyes, of tissue paper used more than once. He'd stopped shaving so that he wouldn't have to explain the scar on his jaw, and he'd once hoped that there might be some kind of Renaissance-painting handsomeness to it, not the subject but a disciple maybe, lurking at the back. That was the theory, but what were these new filaments high on his cheek, like bristles on a broom? Tessa or no Tessa, he should have trimmed the thing. He blinked and tightened his jaw. At least he had his hair and he scrubbed at it now with his fingertips, arranging it to look like it hadn't been arranged. The outdoorsy look.

The trick to walking two hundred miles was to travel light. He would have to wash and dry his underwear each night, and as he filled the basin, squirting in hand soap and squeezing his socks and pants in a milking motion, it occurred to him that there was a very real possibility that this might be considered depressing. He smiled and wondered if this was part of the portrait Cleo had painted for Tessa. He's outdoorsy. Not bad-looking, always prompt. He still has his hair. Would she describe him as shy? Not shy, he just wanted to be left alone.

From Stickleback came the sound of Conrad's music, the generic tsk-boom of an aerobics class and he thought, *What kind of fop brings a Bluetooth speaker on a long-distance walk? What kind of amateur wears jeans? Don't be judgemental.* He heard the music build and Conrad shout, 'Let's goooo!', grooming complete. Testing the radiator, Michael draped his underwear and socks along the top as if laying bacon in a frying pan. His one 'night-life' shirt lay on the glossy eiderdown, porridge-coloured, frayed at the cuffs. Arms out to the sides, the shirt seemed to say, Look, it is what it is. It is what it is.

Crime Scene

The single word that best described her room was 'gudgeon'. A monolithic wardrobe, a clot-coloured eiderdown, duvet and pillow filled with something fibrous, asbestos perhaps, it was the kind of place you might stay the night before a relative's funeral. She boiled the miniature kettle and looked out at the lake in the last of the light. This at least was beautiful, the miles of black water, the rocky shore and the misted valley beyond, tomorrow's adventure. She felt a shudder of anticipation then corrected herself. Pack it in, Frodo.

Tonight she intended to bring the silvery tinkle of cocktail-bar laughter to this humble country inn. She knew that Conrad owned an electric Audi but was not yet sure if he had a sense of humour, so tonight she would be witty, effervescent, a guest on a seventies chat show, walking into the saloon bar as if she was walking on to a yacht. Such natural vivacity would require effort, a state of intense but tension-free concentration, the kind of focus a swimmer finds on the starting block. Timing was key, verbal and mental dexterity, clear diction, a little alcohol but not too much. In company, her best jokes often went unnoticed or were spoken over, white doves released into the air while everyone was looking the other way, but not tonight. *Isn't she great?* he'd whisper. *Almost* too *vivacious. Where has she been hiding?*

Taking care not to slide down the bedspread, she hauled herself to the bathroom and peeled off her damp clothes. A mirror confirmed her fears: black smudges around her eyes, a German Expressionist painting. Cleo had lured her with the promise of rural luxury, roll-top baths and rough-hewn oak floors, but here was a rickety shower cubicle built by children from sticks, the heater *thunk*ing like a fairground generator, the water alternately freezing and scalding. Toiletries came not in small bottles but in sachets, which she had to tear with her teeth, like pub mayonnaise. 'Hair and Body Wash', it said, when surely it should be one or the other. Inside, washing-up liquid.

Back in the bedroom, she was presented with another problem: a distilled essence of farmyard silage as potent and concentrated as a nerve agent. She pulled on her best underwear and her third-best dress, but even with the window open, the smell was so acrid that it threatened to make her retch in her sleep. The source was easily traced to her boots, and she wondered if the pub might have a boot room but wasn't sure if such a thing existed or whether she'd just picked it up from *Downton Abbey*. She imagined the landlord glaring over his spectacles and decided to rinse the soles in the bathroom sink, cramming them under the tap, gouging at the ridges with twists of toilet paper. This stuff was as sticky as tar, the paper disintegrating at first touch so that in moments the basin was blocked and filled with a stew of fibrous, rotten matter the colour of turmeric. A cotton bud fared no better, buckling as if recoiling, and so she had to resort to the handle of her toothbrush before reaching into the filth, swirling with her finger telling herself, Don't touch your eyes, don't ever touch your face.

From Stickleback next door she heard Conrad's party music, and with renewed urgency, she hurled the boots into the shower cubicle and closed the door on them, scrubbed her hands and scoured the handle of her toothbrush but noticed that the filth was now spattered on the pale blue walls, like arterial blood (she felt like she knew which cow had done this, could identify the cow in a line-up) and if it was on the walls then it was on her clothes too. 'Let's goooo!' shouted Conrad, as she rubbed at her dress with the floor mat, but still the stench remained, was, if anything, worse now that it had been atomised and spritzed into the air, the bathroom the scene of a terrible crime.

This was the razzle-dazzle she brought down to dinner. The bar was suddenly busy with what's called 'an older crowd', hunched male backs in olive green, and she felt absurdly over-dressed in her small black dress, Audrey Hepburn addressing the National Farmers Union. She ordered a gin and tonic, a double, the glass as large as an astronaut's helmet, taking such a deep gulp that she almost sucked it on to her face. Time to summon up that metropolitan air. She wiped lipstick from the rim with her thumb. The rest of the group was already seated and as she approached, too far from the table, she shouted, 'I think I smell of cow shit,' effervescent, fascinating, an enigma to all.

Batter

He wondered why she was shouting about cow shit from across the bar. People were watching as she squeezed into the space left between Michael and Conrad. 'Hi, everyone! Sorry for swearing, Anthony. Promise me you'll never swear.' Had she been drinking in her room? 'The landlord says we have to order now,' she said, and they all squinted at the chalkboard, carb-heavy, everything with chips and peas. He heard Marnie ask about the fish of the day, as if it might be halibut or langoustine.

'Cod,' he said.

'Okay. Okay, cod and chips, I'll have that. Why not? Cod 'n' chips,' she said, giving it a little northern burr, just enough to make Michael think, *Don't do that*. They settled into conversation about all their aches and blisters and only Anthony was quiet, bemused as kids sometimes are when confronted with grown-ups' pub personas, their voices more strident, performances heightened. He remembered his own parents' nervous experiments with 'dinner parties', listening in with his brother and thinking, *Why are they talking like this?* Soon the food arrived, everything crisp and brown as autumn leaves, everyone laughing and chatting, and he felt pleased, as if this was somehow his achievement. On his left, he could feel Marnie flirting, her back tense, as if defusing a bomb. '"Pharmacist".

When did all the chemists become "pharmacists"?' she said, her voice too bright. 'Is that a recent thing?'

'I think so,' said Conrad, who had changed into a camouflage hoodie. 'It's definitely more common.'

'Like when the opticians all decided they were optometrists. Is pharmacy an American thing, d'you think? Like trick-or-treat?'

He noted Conrad's cornered smile, an audience member chosen by a magician. 'I think it's just . . . accurate. I studied pharmacy not chemistry, so . . .' Then, to change the subject, 'What did you study at uni, Marnie?'

'Oh, I didn't go.'

'You didn't go!' said Conrad, a little too shocked. 'Wow. Why not?'

Marnie shrugged. 'I wasn't clever enough.'

'She *was* clever enough,' said Cleo, slapping the table. 'She could have gone, as a mature student.'

'That's called an oxymoron,' said Marnie.

'I told her there were ways. If Neil hadn't stopped her—'

'Neil didn't *stop* me. I didn't want to, that's all.'

'That's a real shame,' said Conrad.

'Why is it a shame?' she said sharply.

'I don't know. All those experiences?'

'I had experiences,' she said, into her glass. 'At least I *think* I did, once, maybe twice. Yep, two experiences, I think. We'll let this one go, shall we?'

It seemed improbable that she wasn't clever enough. She was funny, and wasn't that just another kind of clever? Whether it was the fear of debt, a lack of confidence or exam technique, many of his smartest kids didn't go, one of his great frustrations as a teacher, and he thought he might say this to her. But he mustn't be pompous or teacherly and, besides, she'd already turned back to Conrad. What if the mythical Tessa had been sitting in her place? She was a triathlete so there were at least three things they could have discussed. He would have asked, 'Of the triathlon disciplines, which one is your favourite and which one is the most challenging?'

He was, he realised, devising lines of conversation for someone who wasn't there. Instead, here was Marnie, and though she inevitably twisted towards Conrad, her leg and bare arm pressed against Michael's. He thought how nice she looked in her cocktail dress, and as if he'd said this out loud, she turned to him suddenly and asked, 'How is your pie?'

'It's good. I mean, there's lumps in the gravy.'

'Lumps of *what*?'

'Some kind of granule, like instant coffee, but meaty. Would you like to . . . ?'

'It's tempting but I think no.'

He noticed that she had peeled back the batter on her fish, splaying it open to pick out the white flesh. 'Don't tell me you're not eating the batter.'

'Oh, you're not meant to eat the batter,' she said emphatically.

He laughed. 'Give over!'

'Give over what?'

'Who told you *that*?'

'I read it. The batter's only there to stop it falling apart in the fryer.'

'Don't be daft! Who says that?'

'*They* say it. It's true! The batter's just a container.'

'Yeah, like the pastry in a pie. You eat the pastry.'

'Yes . . .'

'Well, then. Batter's the best bit!'

'It's deep-fried flour—'

'With vinegar and salt!'

'Is this a northern thing? Are you playing the northern card?'

'I don't want to fall out with you over this,' he said, and she laughed.

'You're welcome to it. Please tuck into these succulent brown nuggets of lardy flour.' They smiled at each other, and after a while, she said, 'Seriously, though, *do* I smell of cow shit?'

And he leant towards her and was surprised when she leant in, her head suddenly on his shoulder. The air around her: vinegar and fat, gin and gravy granules and cheap shower gel. 'You smell very nice,' he said, meaning it.

Day Two:

ENNERDALE WATER TO BORROWDALE

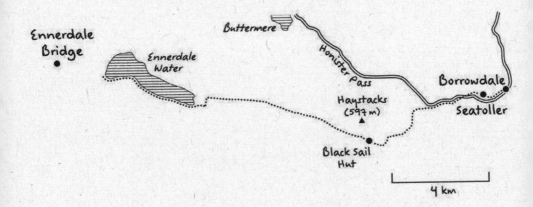

The After-party

The downpour began a little after four. She was used to the rattle of rain on slate roofs, even enjoyed the sound because she rarely stepped out into it, one of those Londoners who avoid rain as vampires avoid sunlight. Here on the surface of the great lake, the downpour sounded like a great, exasperated exhalation, as if even the rain was disappointed by all the rain.

She had been restless all night. The quaint inn creaked and groaned, and through thin walls real-ale drinkers snored and farted, fibre-glass duvets billowing like sails. A pint was an absurd quantity to drink but she'd played the game and drunk three, practically a bucket, her taut belly sloshing like a hot-water bottle. How could she drink so much yet feel so thirsty? The fat and the salt and the gin and the beer had drawn all the moisture from her body so she lay there, smacking her lips, feeling her breath go bad, trapped in a circular critique of her evening.

The brandy had been a mistake. When they'd called last orders he'd asked, 'One more?' then 'Shall we take it upstairs?' to the after-party in Stickleback, and soon she was propped against his padded headboard, a brandy snifter wedged into her cleavage. Yes, of the five in their party, they were definitely the coolest, cooler than the teenage maths whizz and his mum, way cooler than the geography teacher. Conrad had put on seductive music, a compilation of what she thought might be called slo-jams, and she'd felt like a teenager again, sneaking into a bedroom at a house party with a popular boy from the sixth form. Should she bounce on the bed, instigate a pillow fight? She'd already made a stupid joke about his camouflage hoody (*Whoa, where d'you go?*) and yet when she'd tried to talk meaningfully about life and relationships and whatever, he'd seemed distracted, changing the music, moving from bed to chair to bed, putting his clothes on hangers so that it was like being backstage with a model. At one point he'd dived on to the bed, lying next to her, head on hand (*oh, hello*) and she'd mirrored him and thought, *Might this be the moment?* But, fat-tongued and drunk, she'd peppered him with sloppy questions without responding properly to the answers, so that the exchange had the uneasy, one-sided feel of a red-carpet interview.

'So – do you wear pyjamas or . . . ?' She'd asked, brandy on her chin.

'Hm. Bit personal, Marns!'

Hm. She wasn't sure about *Marns*. 'I'm sorry, I'm just trying to paint a mental picture . . .' She squeezed her eyes tight.

'No, I do not wear pyjamas. I sleep *au naturel*.'

'Whoa, hang on, you sleep *outside*?' She opened her eyes, hoping to see him smile but he was moving on.

'How about you?'

'Depends. October to May I wear this white thing, from the M&S "Shroud" collection, big, like a decommissioned wedding marquee, then in summer if it's sultry, just this thong I found on the floor of a betting shop . . .'

Was this turning him on? It seemed not because he'd rolled off the bed to fiddle with charging cables, and soon after that she'd given up any hope of some grand seduction. *Past my bedtime, at midnight I turn back into a pumpkin, thanks for a fun night, oops, kiss on the ear. Goodnight.* Back in her own room she'd heard the murmur of Conrad's voice, low and earnest, probably a phone call to his ex, and she'd considered pressing her ear to the wall, perhaps with a glass like they do in movies. Why not? She'd already laughed him out of bed.

Jokes. The popular girl at school had once told her she was funny, one of those casual, half-meant compliments that can knock a life off-course: *You could model; You have a lovely singing voice; You are funny.* Her husband had said the same thing, back when he'd claimed to find funny women 'sexy'. But then he'd once said he'd liked her 'curves' too – his word, sometimes 'luscious curves' – and both had later joined the litany of things he'd grown to dislike, self-deprecation in particular, huffing and sighing at every joke. 'If you tell people you're crap,' he'd said, 'why shouldn't they believe you?' But if she couldn't laugh at herself and she couldn't laugh at him, what was she meant to laugh at? For a long time, she'd not laughed at all.

Long time ago. She was free of that now and free also to lie here at four and five and six, watching the battery warning flash on the smoke alarm, listening to the rain, finding hope in the notion that it rains more at night. Was it true? Why should that be? She would ask the geography teacher on the walk.

From seven a.m., new sounds, a dawn chorus of toilets flushing, the crack of productive coughs like small-arms fire; it was like living with trolls. Now the TVs were coming on, bad news through thin walls, and she reached for her laptop. It was too early for the sex clubs of LA and she'd made a vow to avoid social media while in nature but she thought perhaps she might do some online yoga in the gap between the wardrobe and the trouser press.

But now a new problem presented itself. In the night her ankles, knees and hips had somehow been welded into a single unit so that the whole lower half of her body was frozen, like one of those cheap plastic dolls that hinge at the shoulder and nowhere else. She swung her legs out of the bed and stumbled to the bathroom as if on stilts, sitting on the toilet with legs out straight ahead, rolling her neck where the bones had also been compacted from the weight of the rucksack so that she was horribly aware of each one, could even hear them grinding into each other, like walnuts squeezed in a fist. Standing again, she noticed that the skin on the soles of her feet seemed to have separated from the flesh, like baggy socks. Yoga was out of the question.

Instead, she stood at the window. Outside was like a room with heavy curtains drawn, the rain kicking up a mist from the lake so that it was impossible to tell where the water ended and the sky began. The sun must be up there somewhere but she saw only heavy swags of grey with no hope of brightness burning through. She had never quite lost the habit of taking the weather personally. If washing windows or leaving her umbrella at home could bring on the rain, what could she do to make the sun shine?

She would shrug off this self-pity but shrugging hurt and here it was, creeping in again like damp in the walls, the loneliness, present even in company. What had happened to the hope she'd felt in Euston station? Less than twenty-four hours later she felt the pull of home, secure and dry, with her books and radio and blankets, sure of what the day would hold. Through the walls she heard the eight a.m. headlines, though still nothing from Stickleback. They were due to set off at nine thirty: if she was quick she could eat breakfast alone. She showered, put on clothes as if dressing a mannequin, walked downstairs sideways, placing her feet gingerly one step at a time, like a marionette, to the bar, which smelt of beer and fish.

Of course he was there already, sitting at a corner table. She did not want to talk to him but it felt rude to sit elsewhere. Thankfully . . .

'You don't have to sit with me,' said Michael. 'It's too early to talk.'

'Oh. Really?' She was grateful and a little offended.

'I'm not very good in the mornings.'

'Me neither.' Spotting a compromise, she sat at the table diagonally opposite, easing herself in with a groan.

'How did you feel, waking up?'

'Like Gregor Samsa,' she said, a gamble, but he laughed.

'How was the private party?'

'Party?'

'In Stickleback?'

'Oh, I'm sorry, did we keep you awake?' For some reason, she did not want him to think Conrad's room had been a failure. Not a success either, whatever success meant. 'Pretty wild. Isle of Wight vibes.' He smiled and opened his individual box of cereal. 'You look like a giant.' He seemed confused. 'With your tiny box? Scale?'

'Oh. Yes. I see.'

'Fruit and Fibre,' she said, 'together at last!'

'Classic combination.'

'Like Lennon and McCartney.'

'By themselves, fine, but combined . . .'

'Yeah, who'd eat a bowl of something called just "Fibre"?'

He thought a moment. 'Well, in fairness I would eat that.'

She laughed. 'Yes, you would,' she said, as if she knew him. 'Anyway.'

'What are you going to . . . ?' He nodded towards the continental buffet.

'Oh.' She stood, scraping her chair. Orange juice the colour

87

of jaundice, a hazelnut yoghurt floating in a bowl of melted ice as if it had drowned there in the night. 'Ah, Paris,' she said. 'Well, I'm far too sophisticated for Frosties.'

'I won't tell anyone.'

'No. No, it's Fruit and Fibre for me too.'

He raised his miniature box in salute.

She sat and the landlord, an angry ghost, came and took her order: eggs and bacon, which, still queasy, she both wanted and dreaded. The rattle of her spoon in the bowl, the gargantuan crunch of her cereal. To mask it, she asked, 'What are you reading?'

He held up the book. 'It's about the changing face of sheep-farming.'

'Whoa, sheep-farming's changed its face?'

'I know! Again! You?'

She held up *Wuthering Heights*. 'D'you know it?'

'Only the theme tune.'

'That's got all the best bits. I *think* there are some sheep in it, if you want to—'

'I'm all right, thank you.'

'My second time. I read it when I was fifteen.'

'You love it?'

'Heathcliff's more of a dick than I remember. I'm rolling my eyes more than I did first time, but it's wild and northern.'

'Wrong side of the Pennines, I'm afraid.'

'It's all the same, though, isn't it? Once you're past Coventry.'

'Don't start. The batter was bad enough.'

Time passed, tap, crunch, tinkle. 'It's certainly wuthering outside today!' she said idiotically.

'I think technically wuthering means windy and there's no wind. So.'

'Thank you, Branwell.' He seemed to be eating his cooked

breakfast largely with his hands, folding a piece of bread like a sock puppet then using this to pinch a sausage and scoop up beans. She felt her stomach lurch and perhaps he heard it because he now unwrapped his knife and fork.

'I'm sorry. Manners. I've definitely let myself go. Too much time eating alone.'

'I know about that. At home I just trowel in the hummus,' and she mimed two scooping claws.

'Plates, eh?'

'Who needs 'em? I'm also a little hung-over.'

'Yeah, me too,' rubbing the top of his head.

'But we're still walking?'

'Of course! Well, I am.'

'Okay. Well, me too!'

'*Really*?' he said and, stung, she replied, 'Of course!'

'Well, visibility's bad but it's not windy. It's a clear path and we've got satnav, two satnavs, and you know what they say.'

A little time passed, chewing and swallowing. 'Go on.'

'There's no such thing as bad weather . . .'

Crunch, crunch. 'Go on.'

'. . . only unsuitable clothes.'

'Who says that?'

He thought a moment. 'The Norwegians?'

'Okay.' After a while, 'Okay, Norway, let's find out!'

'Personally, I don't mind the rain.'

'Of course *you* don't.'

'It's too foggy for views but you put your hood up and have this quiet little private world around you and you . . . carry it with you.'

'A cold, wet little private world.'

'It's not cold if you keep moving. Or you could call a taxi and go straight to the hotel.'

Did he think she wasn't up to it? 'Let's see how the others feel,' she said. Her breakfast arrived, the same brown hues of last night, even the eggs, and she ate what she could, then went up to get ready and to work out what to say to Conrad.

Rain Continued

In the shelter of the porch, Cleo read Conrad's text out loud. "'Sorry to bail but don't have right kit for rain and my head hurts bracket brandy exclamation mark. Will get taxi to next hotel and C U tonight.'"

Michael glanced at Marnie, who was pointedly adjusting the zips and buttons of her waterproofs. 'So much for sports psychology.'

'What a wimp,' said Cleo, directing the words at the room above, where presumably Conrad slept on. 'Never mind. We can still do this!'

'Yes! Yes, let's . . . go for it!' said Marnie, standing straight, shoulders back. But no one moved and still the water cascaded from the porch roof. It was like standing behind a waterfall and even Michael felt wary. A linear walk with a steep climb and a tricky descent, no way to abandon or shorten the route. He looked at Anthony, peering wide-eyed from his hood, and thought of those action movies, where frightened kids are urged to cross fraying rope bridges. 'Okay, here's the plan. We'll set off and if it's grim you can just keep going around the other side of the lake and be back here in an hour, dry off, get a taxi with Conrad. What do you think?' Anthony looked reassured and they all settled their rucksacks and stepped out.

He'd slept badly, kept awake initially by the sound of Conrad's seduction music and muffled flirting. Even through the wall, he recognised the cadence of Marnie's jokes and part of him had wanted to lean in to hear, while the teacher instinctively wanted to confiscate any booze and vapes. Conrad was quieter, constantly changing the music as if changing subject until a sudden silence made Michael wonder, Oh, God, are they kissing now? If they started having sex, he'd have to cough or stuff his ears, but then Marnie's voice was back and soon he heard her footsteps in the corridor. He felt a strange kind of relief, which he chose not to examine, drifting off until the rain woke him at four.

And still the rain fell. The trick to walking in heavy rain is to keep a straight back, because no one ever stayed dry by hunching their shoulders. Stride on defiantly. Soon the patter on his hood became a kind of white noise and he found himself approaching a fugue state – was that the phrase? – free from the churn of his thoughts. This happened sometimes on his solitary walks, on a Northumbrian beach or deep in a forest as the light faded, times where he might find a temporary peace of mind. In these moments, it was as if he were walking within some transparent bubble, like the clear jelly around the black dot in frogspawn. Then there were those other times, on some featureless fell, feet and fingers numb, profoundly alone, panic rising with miles to go, where he felt like a fugitive.

For the moment at least he was content in this little private world, checking now and then that his companions had not fallen too far behind, and after an hour the head of the lake was in sight. They squelched gingerly across a flood plain, a fine spot for a picnic but currently barely land at all, then gathered at a bridge where the river joined the lake, their shoulders hunched, faces pinched.

'So do you want to carry on or—?'

'Turn back,' shouted Anthony.

'Obviously we're turning back,' said Cleo.

'I think that's a good idea,' said Michael. 'Basically, you follow this path—'

'I'm staying with you,' said Marnie, 'if that's okay.'

'Really?' said Michael. Was she serious?

Cleo laughed. 'Don't be ridiculous. It's vile!'

'I didn't come all this way to sit in a hotel room. How far's the next hotel?'

'Twelve miles but—'

'Well, three miles an hour, we'll be there for lunch.'

'But the other side of a mountain, so . . .'

Marnie faltered, then blew the drop from the end of her nose. 'I've got boots. Let's . . . go for it!'

'Great. Great,' he said, and felt his dream of solitude collapse. It was easy to walk ahead of three people, much harder with just one. Cleo and Anthony were already heading off, dreaming of hot baths and dry socks, her arm tight around her son's shoulders as if squeezing the water from him. Michael and Marnie watched for a moment, then turned to look at each other through the tunnel of their hoods.

'You're sure?' he said.

'The sooner we start,' she said, 'the sooner we finish. Let's get it over with,' which, he thought, was not the point of walking at all.

Still Rain

She recognised the look he'd given her from boys picking teams at PE in school. *Oh. I've got you.* Well, tough luck, chunky knits. They were back on an asphalt road, the kind of terrain she liked, somewhere you could drive a black cab. It was also wide enough to walk two abreast so they fell into step, raising their voices to be heard above the clatter of rain.

'So, weather aside,' he said, 'how is it so far?'

'Very nice,' she said, but struggled to say more. She was not eloquent about landscape and thought of scenery as just that, a backdrop associated with nature documentaries or movies, so that the mist on the lake's black water suggested Arthur and Excalibur, while the great churning river to her right made her think of grizzly bears tossing salmon into the air.

'The River Liza,' said Michael, introducing them.

'Liza. I had a friend called Liza. I think more rivers should have normal names, kids I was at school with. The River Claire. The River Martin Fletcher. There's the Neil in Egypt.' She was wittering. Don't witter. 'The mighty Gemma Bostock, wending her way towards the sea . . .'

'This one doesn't go to the sea. It just feeds the lake.'

'Okay.'

'Classic ribbon lake.'

'I thought so too. Classic.'

They walked a little further. 'Sorry,' he said. 'It slips out sometimes. The geography. Like wind.'

She laughed. 'It's nice to learn new things. Remind me, your surname?'

'Bradshaw.'

'Classic teacher's name! I'm sure if you'd been my teacher . . .' she said, but the thought petered out. 'I remember as a kid we had this world atlas, huge, the size of a coffee-table, something I could only get out on very special occasions, like the record-player and the SodaStream. I remember it always made me feel a bit dizzy, there was so much of everything, all those vast empty spaces, either that or everything crammed in far too tightly. It was the only book that made me feel like that. A bit over-whelmed.'

'So what were you good at? At school.'

'Not much. Keeping my head down.'

'English, surely.'

'I was okay. Not great in exams. Just as I was getting the hang of it, it was over. Books were my TV, except I was *really* obsessed. "Go outside," Mum and Dad always said. I didn't see the point of outside. All that space and nowhere to sit down. Fresh air, it's a myth. It's the same air, no matter what they tell you.'

'No family walking holidays?'

'Country parks, you know, in the car, for ice-cream. We went outside but only so we could go to a different inside.'

'But look at you now!'

'Look at me now!'

'No such thing as bad weather.'

'Norway, I retract.'

'Hey,' he said, stopping suddenly, holding out his palm. 'Have you noticed?'

'Oh, my God,' she said, 'you're right.' The rain had not stopped but there was a change in its intensity, as if someone had complained about the noise. Tentatively, they lowered their hoods, like astronauts removing their helmets. Why not? She was already soaked, could feel a large wet patch on her back, the water making its way around into the lining of her sports bra so that there'd be two wet triangles on her sweatshirt, like a bikini on a Greek beach, and while her boots had yet to leak, the water was being drawn down through her socks, the skin beginning to rub. Only her trousers held out against the rain, trapping sweat inside so that it condensed on the fabric, like vapour on the lid of a casserole.

Still, she was determined to go on. Rather this than sit around, restless and bored, and besides, she wanted to reset the relationship with Conrad. If she stayed, she'd only spend money. She loved Cleo but, like many of her old friends, she took prosperity for granted, the shared restaurant bill, the taxi, the spontaneous train. Nothing was more humiliating than telling a friend, 'I can't afford it,' and since becoming freelance she could rarely afford anything. The single self-employed life gave her the freedom to fret at any time, at night in particular, and a great deal of her working day was spent writing passive-aggressive emails to finance departments, wondering if it might be at all possible, et cetera, or choreographing the movement of funds from credit card to overdraft to gas bill to rent.

She wondered: did Conrad realise she was . . . well, not poor but not secure? She appeared to maintain a stable metropolitan lifestyle, shelves crammed with books, neat clothes, a trip to the cinema now and then, but the cuffs of her winter coat were frayed, and the best part of her wardrobe dated from a Whistles sample sale in 2016. What would happen if, God forbid, the work dried up or there was a sudden unmanageable rent rise?

How long before AI could copy-edit *Twisted Night* in a nano-second? Her old work pension promised an income of two pounds twenty a week, and she furiously resented belonging to a generation whose future security depended on their parents' death, so that only orphans could afford a holiday.

All of these anxieties came garnished with rage, not least because of the disputed fifteen grand kept back from the sale of their flat, money that Neil held for 'legal expenses'. They'd argued about it the last time they'd spoken, two years ago now, Neil sighing and implying that, as a father, repaying the debt would somehow involve selling his offspring's shoes and toys. He would 'see what I can do', though it was 'not a good time'. Clearly the needs of a young family trumped the petty demands of a single woman and she'd not had the energy – the courage? – to ask again, though the subject always sent Cleo apoplectic with rage, directed as much at Marnie as Neil, *He's walking all over you, even now, little shit, get it back, get a lawyer*, forgetting that lawyers required payment to retrieve the money required to pay them.

Circular anxieties, ancient regrets, there wasn't a mountain in all England that could obscure them. She felt the rain breach her collar and prayed her laptop was still dry – she could never afford a new one. A thousand-pound loss versus the cost of a taxi ride: how many decisions had been tilted the wrong way by this kind of calculation?

Too gloomy to think about. The walk had turned into a trudge through acre after acre of lousy Christmas trees, in some areas the firs lying rotten and desolate as if trampled by some giant. On and on it went and she thought, *At least on a tread-mill you can watch pop videos*. The rain stiffened again and they put up their hoods, the path roughening and rising until they reached a small hut at the valley's end, mountains looming abruptly on every side, their peaks obscured by clouds. She was a spider in a bathtub, with no way out.

'So this is a cul-de-sac, yes?' she said. 'Is that the right term?'

He laughed. 'I suppose so. Except we're going to climb over and into the next valley.'

'Okay. Okay. Really?'

'I'm afraid so.'

'Climb? With ropes?'

'More of a clamber. We'll take it slowly. It'll be fine.'

'How high?'

'About six hundred metres.'

'You see, that means nothing to me.'

'So, less than a kilometre.'

'Obviously, but—'

'But vertically.' And he pointed into the air. 'It's a scramble, really. You'll need to eat something first.'

The hut was unoccupied so they sat on the bench outside, the water falling in a curtain from the eaves, steam rising off them, like boiled potatoes. Michael lowered his hood, drank coffee from a flask, ate his apple and named the peaks in his nice voice. At least she felt in safe hands.

But any relief from the rain felt horribly temporary and the banana she'd transported so carefully from the fruit bowl in Herne Hill had bruised and blackened. She fingered the sweet mush into her mouth. 'Costa Rica' said the sticky label. What was this banana doing here? What was she doing here?

He passed her the coffee cup and she raised it in a toast. 'To holidays!'

'Holidays!'

'You know,' she said, 'I've thought about it and I don't think I've ever in my whole life been this far away from another human being.'

'Well . . .'

'Except for you, of course,' she said, and nudged him with her elbow. As they sat and steamed in their temporary shelter, peering through the veil of rain at all that hidden majesty, she longed for a vision, the yellow light of a passing black cab.

Up the Down Escalator

Whether it was the altitude or a spiteful universe, this was when the rain began to fall in earnest, the path no longer apparent and replaced with a stream flowing parallel to the beck that splashed and gurgled first on their left, then on their right, as they jumped back and forth to find the easiest route.

But there was no easy route, and with every leap across the stream the weight on his back shoved his face into jagged rock or threatened to topple him over and down, and for the first time he wondered, What's the point, really, what's the point of this? No exorcism, no purging or clearing of the head, no sense of achievement. It wasn't even masochism, which was, he understood, supposed to contain an element of pleasure, just profound misery as the rain fell harder still, so that it felt like someone was trying to hose them from the mountain. No need to ask how Marnie was doing, shouting fuck and shit, fucking shit and shitting fucker, at the water and the rocks. He felt the old panic rise in his chest, a sense of dread, visions of broken bones and bleeding heads, and he told himself, as he might his students, Calm down, break the challenge into smaller tasks, twenty steps then twenty more. But when he squinted through stinging eyes the summit seemed no closer, so that it was like climbing up a down escalator on hands and knees, and now Marnie was directing her fury at him.

'You LIED to me!'

'How did I lie, Marnie? I said it was a climb!'

'I'm crawling on my hands and knees! This is grim, just so, so grim.'

'Nearly there! Keep going! Not long now!' But he was ageing with each step, wheezing, gasping, hips and knees complaining, simultaneously soaked in sweat and rain, and dehydrated from cheap bacon, exertion bringing bile into his mouth. Now he, too, was railing against the rocks and water, in milder terms, damn and blast and bugger, but with no less venom.

'You are such a liar, Bradshaw!' shouted Marnie.

They were above the cloud line now and would only know the summit when they got there, but even so. 'Just one more push, I swear,' he lied.

Inside the Cloud

For their honeymoon, they'd flown to New York, Marnie's first time, Neil generously allowing her the window seat in the premium economy cabin, though technically it was his on the boarding pass and you should always sit in your allocated seat. At twenty-five, long-haul air travel was a novelty and Marnie had pressed her forehead against the thick glass and marvelled at the clouds' solidity, the firmness of their lines against the blue. If you fell, would the clouds catch you? What was it like inside a cloud?

The answer, it transpired, was fucking shit and, no, a cloud wouldn't catch you because clouds were treacherous bastards and so were rocks and so was rain, and the mountain streams weren't babbling: they were taking the piss and so was everything outside, all of nature.

'Why am I doing this!' she bellowed into the rain. 'I'm not even sponsored!'

'Ha!' he barked. 'We're there! We made it!' Then, standing upright, 'Almost!' Even the mountain was a liar because there was a further crawl before she could finally stand upright, at which point a whole new bastard element introduced itself, a sharp and vicious wind, which slapped her wet clothes against her body and scoured her face with the scrapings of the freezer compartment.

'Is *this* wuthering, Mr Bradshaw? Are we wuthering *now*?'

'Yes, this is wuthering.'

'I'm getting consumption, I can feel it. Consumption in my lungs.'

'But look where we are!'

Nothing. She could see nothing and he was pointing into nothingness. 'There's Haystacks!' The grey of a sickbed sheet. 'Behind us, Great Gable and Green Gable' – the grey of old snow and dirty bathwater – 'and down there, in theory, is beautiful Buttermere!' The grey of a dirty shirt collar. 'And over there, you can see when the mist clears, that's Innominate Tarn where they scattered the ashes of Alfred Wainwright, the man who devised this walk.'

'Good!' she shouted. 'Good! I'm glad he's dead!'

'Marnie!' he said, a little shocked. 'Bit harsh.'

'Light grey, dark grey, black, grey and brown. It could be the Golden Gate Bridge out there, it could be the Bay of fucking Naples, we wouldn't know!'

'I didn't make it rain, Marnie!'

'Oh, no, it's never anyone's fault, is it?'

'Shall we head down? See how you feel at the hotel.'

'Oh, I know how I'll feel. Fucking . . . *furious*. Don't laugh at me!' she said, though she could feel herself on the verge of laughter too. 'Just get me down.'

He wiped the rain from the strange device in his hand, some kind of GPS, a prop from *Star Trek*, radiation levels rising, silicon storm approaching. 'This way!' he announced, pointing into the featureless grey, and now here was some whole new natural-world fuckery to deal with. The fell top was a plateau and the rain had soaked and submerged the path so that they were obliged to hop between small islands of spiked red weeds, Martian and treacherous and often turning out not to be islands at all, so that her new boots were plunged again and again into mud, the liquid quickly breaching the top, and this brought on a new storm of abuse.

'Fuck you, Countryfile!'

'What?'

'I don't like it here. People shouldn't even be up here.' She was squelching now, audibly squelching, her teeth rattling like joke-shop dentures as they hop-scotched along, her eyes boring into his back, resolving to be silent now. She'd seen this film before, the one where the neurotic city slicker is initiated into the ways of the wild by the taciturn, hard-handed adventurer, initially appalled then charmed by his simple ways. Well, screw that. She'd resist the cliché and show that she was just as steely, competent and capable as he was, which was exactly what happened in the movie too.

Only Cheating Yourself

Across the swamp, then a descent below the cloud line and now, with vision restored, they came upon a valley entirely different from the last, steep-sided, bleak and gunmetal grey, vast black lines carved into its flanks like tattoos. They'd made it over the top but the landscape was so stark that there seemed little to celebrate, the kind of place a location scout might propose as a hostile alien planet. Even its name sounded like science-fiction.

'Honister Pass,' he said.

'Very nice,' she said, without looking up.

'Well, look at it!'

'No,' she growled. 'I won't give it the satisfaction.'

'Look at all the slate!'

'We have slate in London, on roofs, where it belongs – it's flat and grey, like . . . like you, frankly, Michael.'

He decided that the hostility was playful, though perhaps a little harder-edged than he was used to. 'Oh, so you *don't* want to hear about the slate-mining communi—'

'Michael, I don't *care* – I *don't care* – I don't care if this valley was used to mine for slate or gold or fucking . . . toffee, I just want to get back. Okay?'

They joined another path, dead straight, slick and black. 'This used to be a working tramway back in the—'

'Okay, is it working now? Is there a tram that takes us to our hotel?'

'Not for one hundred and fifty years.'

'Then I do. Not. Care.'

The remains of a derelict building, neat stacks of slate on either side, marked the head of the path. 'These are the remains of the Drum House. Would you like to know why it's called the Drum House?'

'Michael, if you tell me why, I will push you down this hill.'

'Clearly it's not a *hill*.'

'Let's just — let's just get to the hotel. How much more of this?'

'Um, about ninety minutes?'

'Fuck! Fucking fucking fuck.'

'Maybe if you looked up, it'd go quicker.'

She narrowed her eyes. 'Oh, just go and . . . dry-stone a wall.'

They began to descend faster now, but the water sought the easiest path too, making the slate as slick and treacherous as ice, and when he offered his hand, she knocked it away. They shuffled down, each step a stubbed toe on a chest of drawers. 'Ow, ow, ow,' murmured Marnie, voice clenched with rage until, finally, the road, the tarmac felt luxurious beneath their feet.

The last dry part of his body had succumbed some time ago. Like falling into a swimming pool fully clothed, there was a kind of liberty in being so entirely wet and he'd long given up on his hood. Still, it seemed foolhardy to try to chat and they strode on down the valley, Marnie in the middle of the road as if daring someone to run her over. He heard the sound of an engine behind him and shouted, 'Look!'

Marnie's eyes widened. A vision, a small bus, the miracle of public transport and she began to laugh. 'Thank you, God!' It was almost upon them now and she began to search urgently for the nearest bus stop. 'Are you coming?'

'I think I'm going to walk.'

'But there's a *bus*, you idiot! A bus!'

'No, I'm fine.'

'But why?'

'I want to walk the whole way.'

'But look! Look around you. No one will ever know! I won't tell them!'

'I'll know.'

'But, look, it has a roof!'

'It's fine. You go ahead.' The driver was passing them now and Marnie was running or trying to run, the loose rucksack slapping against her back, shouting, 'Bus! Bus! Bus!' as if that was the bus's name. He watched as the driver took mercy and, without looking back, she used both hands to haul herself inside. He stood for a moment, feeling the cold rain run down his spine. Through the condensation in the back window he saw a shape that might have been Marnie taking a seat, then a pale circle that might have been her face, a hand banging on the glass, a finger writing in the steam, the words backwards, the bus already too far away to read the message.

Chattering

Conrad was at Reception, handing in his key card.

'Hi there!'

He turned and saw her and seemed shocked. 'My God, are you all right?'

'Just cold and wet. Are you—'

'Did you get rescued? Who did this to you?'

'Mr Bradshaw did this. Conrad, are you . . . checking out?'

'Ah. Yes. Yes, I am. I was about to write you a note. I need to get back for work.'

'I thought you had Mo-Monday off?'

'Yes, but it's a – it's a long drive and the weather's terrible and I don't have the kit, the boots and . . .' He stepped towards her, whispered, 'I can't stay in this hotel.' Then, in his normal voice, 'Also, I remembered I hate walking! Hey, do you need a blanket or a towel?'

'I'm fine. I'm going to d-drip dry.'

'But I've got your number off Cleo and we can meet in the Big Smoke, yes? Your teeth are actually chattering.'

'It's an . . . involuntary action.'

'I thought that only happened in cartoons.'

'No, no, that ha-happens.'

But he was eyeing the exit now. 'Anyway, the taxi's taking me back to wherever it was I left the car. Hope it's still there. It's an electric Audi.'

'Yes, you said.'

'You're very pale. Go to your room! Ask for a good one,' and here he stepped forward and put his arms loosely around her as if she were a dog that had just climbed out of a canal. 'I had fun with you,' he said.

'You certainly did,' she said. 'I'd better ch-check in now.'

'Of course. Of course. Have a great break!' He left without looking around and she squelched to the reception desk. The Wi-Fi password was wainwright2014.

In her room, she pulled off all her clothes and hurled them in great sodden lumps on to the bathroom floor, where they landed with a cartoon splat. Shivering, hair and skin still wet, she clambered into bed, punching the excess cushions to the floor, pulling the covers up to her chin and waiting for sensation to return. It was a large hotel, imposing from the gravel drive but over-lit and functional inside – meeting rooms, a cavernous breakfast hall, a conference hotel between conferences. Borrow-dale, the hotel information claimed, was the most beautiful valley in the country. Through the condensation on her window she saw rusty garden chairs huddled under a tarpaulin, a water-logged tennis court, nets trailing in the puddles. She thought, *I waxed my legs for this?*

Once feeling had returned, she padded to the bathroom, furiously twisting her clothes into plaits and squeezing grey water into the tub. It was true, she had not hit a conversational groove with Conrad, and had only found him attractive in a theoretical way, true also that they'd not really had a chance to open up (horrible phrase) beyond the superficial biographical stuff, though perhaps that might have come with time. But even if nothing had happened, it was humiliating to be abandoned like this – a bad date in front of a friend, in front of her godson! – and, once again, she was confronted by the gulf between expectation and reality, no sun on her face, no union with nature, no laughter with friends, no sex. No matter how carefully you packed your bag, there was no protection against this furious disappointment. Gathering up her tortured clothes, she arranged them on the radiators. A sign politely asked guests not to dry their clothes, but what else could she do? Blow on them?

At least the laptop had survived, and she returned to *Twisted Night*. A masked killer was murdering members of LA's sex-party community, but she was distracted by her feet. The friction of the wet socks had rubbed the dead city skin so that it was flaking off in grey worms like the rubbings of a pencil eraser and she picked at the stuff, appalled, and began to feel better. At least she had the pleasure of the cancelled plan. No performance tonight, no brandy-fuelled clowning, just her feet and then dinner with an old friend. Michael too, though she didn't feel the need to perform for him. Was that good or bad? Never mind. The new skin beneath the dead stuff was as shiny as the white under the shell of a hard-boiled egg and this was by far the best time she'd had all day.

Her phone bleeped, a text from Cleo.

Are you alive? There's a POOL! Meet you in the hot tub in 20

She texted back –

Work to do. Also no costume!

– though even as she pressed send, she knew this would not be permitted.

They sell them at Reception. See you in 15

Bathers

Michael stood in a pool of water at the reception desk, staring at the screen of his phone. An old model, far from waterproof, he tried not to look at the thing while walking, which meant that Natasha's message might have been sitting there all day.

'Sir?'

He looked up.

'Your key.'

'All right, yes, thank you, great.'

It was the first he'd heard from his wife in months, and he felt irrationally embarrassed about his appearance, soaked, exhausted, hair pasted down, dripping on to the carpet of a mid-range conference hotel. He should get to his room, get warm and dry, read the message there.

'You made it!' It was Marnie, tugging on the belt of her dressing-gown, slapping towards him in disposable slippers. 'You look like an amphibian, making its first tentative steps . . .'

'How's your consumption?'

'It's all right. I had a tincture for my palsy. I still carry a great hatred for you in my heart but, no, all good.'

'And do you have a sense of achievement?'

She patted the pockets of the dressing-gown. 'Nope. Nothing. Nothing at all, though I did want to apologise to you for all the shouting.'

'That's fine. I was shouting too.'

'But not at me.'

'No, it was grim. I'm not just saying this, but you can really swear.'

'Ah, thank you. Still, I'm sorry for being rude about Alfred Wainwright.'

'Well, he's not around, so,' he glanced towards his phone, 'no harm done.'

'I'll leave you. We're going for a swim, if you want to get wet again.'

'Ah, no, thank you.'

'There's a hot tub, though that's not necessarily an incentive.'

'I don't have my bathers.'

'The bathers that were crocheted by your Edwardian governess?'

'"Trunks"?'

'No, that's worse.' She turned to the receptionist. 'What would you call them?'

'Men's? Swimming? Costume?'

But he had a text message, from Natasha. 'I'm sorry, I have to . . . I'll see you in the bar? For a drink?'

'Sure,' she said, and to his back, 'Oh, Conrad ran off by the way. He said goodbye, sorry to miss you. Then he ran off.'

He turned. 'Okay. That's a shame. But we're still hanging on, Marnie!' he said, opening his wife's message as he went. 'We're still here!'

Chlorine

The pool occupied a flimsy half cylinder, like a polytunnel used to grow lettuce in winter. On the wall, a mural of palm trees and an immense piña colada seemed to jeer at the mossy brown-ness beyond the glass, now misted with condensation, its metal frame dotted with rust. No hibiscus or coconut oil, instead the smell was of old towels and chlorine, but at least they had it to themselves. In the pool, Anthony held on to the edge and idly splashed his legs while Cleo's head protruded from a great meringue in the hot tub. 'Come on in!' she shouted.

Marnie shrugged off her dressing-grown and slapped along the pool's edge, stiff-legged, flat-footed, the flayed soles of her feet too sensitive. If Conrad had stayed, perhaps they'd have pushed each other in, splashed about. Perhaps it was just as well he'd left. There's a particular intimacy in seeing someone in their swimming costume, and the one she'd bought from Reception was solemn and modest, a swimming costume you could wear to a funeral, but even so she tugged at the bottom edge to pull it down further as she climbed into the foam.

'What do you think of the luxury spa?' said Cleo.

'Club Tropicana. But with pints. I like this,' said Marnie, patting at the suds, streaked with a tideline of unmentionable grey, like old snow. She closed her eyes, listened to the churn of the water pump and after a while . . .

'I'm sorry Conrad had to go,' said Cleo.

'I don't mind,' said Marnie, crisp and casual.

'Work, long drive and all that,' said Cleo. 'He said he loved meeting you.' Marnie groaned. 'He did! He told me!'

'Hence the squeal of tyres.'

'And he's going to call you in London. He realised this wasn't for him.' Marnie said nothing, just pushed the foam away from her face. 'So, how was it?' asked Cleo, and Marnie told her about the rain, the mud, the climb.

'But how was Michael?' said Cleo.

'He was nice. Quite quiet. I mean, we couldn't talk much because the rain was so loud, and I was shouting and swearing at him, but he seemed like a nice man.'

'He is a nice man,' said Cleo.

'He is,' said Marnie, 'very nice,' and fell silent, because niceness was something that was both rare and also hard to talk about.

'There's a lot going on,' said Cleo, meaningfully. 'A lot.'

Marnie opened her eyes. 'We didn't really talk personally.'

'You should. It would do him good to talk to someone, I think.'

'About what?' said Marnie.

'But the thing is Anthony and me are heading home tomorrow morning,' said Cleo, and Marnie pushed the foam into her face.

'We're meant to be walking for three days!'

'But the rain, and it's so far, and Anthony's been invited to this paintball party—'

'So what do I do? My ticket's from Penrith on Tuesday!'

'The hotel's still booked. It's very posh. Stay on!'

'What – with a stranger?'

'He's not a stranger now. And it's not like you're sharing a room.'

'I wanted to see you. I came to spend time with *you*!'

'Okay, drive back to York with us. We'll talk in the car.'

'This is so typical, Cleo, you bully me into coming away—'

'Hang on! "Bully"?'

'Always "You need to get out more! You're lonely! It's time to get back on the horse—"'

'That's not bullying, that's worrying.'

'Well, stop, please, I beg you, stop worrying about me!'

'Caring, then. You're a brilliant woman. I think you're a brilliant woman and it sends me crazy that you don't . . . think more of yourself and get out there.'

'Out where? Out here?'

'Anywhere outside your flat! You never used to be like that. Friends say they don't hear from you, they don't see you, you're always cancelling. It's a long time since Neil . . .'

'So why bring him up?'

'Because he was so bad for you, so, so bad – he completely killed your confidence . . .'

'Please, can you just . . . stop interfering?'

They lapsed into silence, listening to the motor. 'Cleo, I'm very happy on my own. I mean, look!' And here she scooped up a handful of the suds and placed them on her head. Cleo smiled but said nothing and their eyes drifted to the pool, where Anthony was swimming slow, easy lengths.

'It was a mistake to bring him, I think. He gets very bored.'

Marnie felt another pulse of indignation and thought, *Who cares what a kid wants*? When she went on holiday with her parents, her boredom was taken for granted. But her case – that a kid's opinion should count for less, his childhood should be more like her own – was a hard, mean line to argue in a hot tub. It was difficult, too, to sulk off when covered with foam but she did her best, dripping dirty suds, like a poorly rinsed roasting tin.

She was a good swimmer. In the marriage and its aftermath, she'd used water as a kind of punch-bag and, sure enough, after a few lengths of the pool, she began to feel better. Silly to spoil this last night in a sulk. Diving, skimming the pool's bottom, she saw the back of Anthony's skinny legs batting at the water and, touched by the sight, she swam in his direction, approaching underwater like a shark, grabbing his ankles. Even with her head underwater, she could hear his shriek.

'Sorry! I'm sorry! I was just coming to say hi!'

Anthony, wide-eyed, was clutching at the pool's edge.

'What's going on?' Cleo shouted from the foam.

'Nothing, I was just – it was a joke!'

'You pulled me under!'

'I did not! Don't split on me, Anthony, I was saying hi. Just hi. It's fine!' she shouted across to Cleo, who resubmerged. Marnie pinched the water from her nose. 'I saw you swimming earlier. You're very good.'

'I'm not. I'm really bad.'

'Not at all. Show me! Show me your stroke.'

'Too tired now.'

'Okay. Don't fancy the hot tub?'

He wrinkled his nose. 'Hot tubs are for old people.'

She laughed. 'No, you're right. It's because you're not filthy and tense. Give it time.' They were silent for a while, forearms resting along the edge of the pool. 'Give it time.' The awkwardness of open conversation with adults was something she took for granted, but it should be easier with children. They'd once been close, taking him for holidays in London after her divorce, and if anything had marred those occasions it was the parents' presumption of envy, as if Cleo were loaning her a rare and much-loved toy to play with for a while, as long as she handed it back afterwards. She'd loved him without coveting him and had hoped that this would last, but soon he'd be deep into his teens and she'd be just another grown-up, ridiculous and embarrassing, someone to avoid at social events.

'I've not been a very good godmother these last few years, have I?' she said. 'I think I got out of the habit of seeing people, your mum and dad and friends, and then it was hard to go back in, like starting a new school or something. Which is crazy, when you're thirty-eight.' Why was she saying this out loud? Anthony's eyes stayed fixed ahead. 'But I love seeing you growing up, everyone so proud. And if you ever want to call for a chat or come and stay in London again . . . I know the flat's small but—'

'Yeah. Okay, I'd like that,' he said.

'Really?'

'Yes. I used to love it there, your flat.'

'Oh. Well, great. Let's do it! We can go to Forbidden Planet, go to the movies.'

'Cool.'

She had a sudden sentimental urge to grab his head and kiss his lovely spotted brow, but he was already underwater and she felt his cool, skinny body brush against her legs as he pushed off, skimming the bottom all the way to the far end of the pool.

Hopeallswell

Hi! A little bird tells me you're walking coast to coast. Wow!
Hopeallswell x

There was not much to go on. The 'little bird' was Cleo. His
wife hoped all was well, meaning, he imagined, that she hoped
all was well.

Still, it was something. Since Christmas, their main source
of communication had come through the streaming accounts
they still shared, a strangely intimate diary of the period drama
she'd watched back-to-back, the arty film she'd abandoned. It
was a diary written in code – should he worry about the serial
killer documentaries? If she was watching sit-coms, was she
happy or sad? – and in return, he curated his own viewing
history, going easy on the zombies and the erotica, watching
documentaries about deep-sea life and vulcanology. If he's
watching *Master and Commander*, she'd think, he must be fine.

Occasionally she'd get in touch to see how things were with
the house. She had left quickly, promising to return for the rest
of her possessions when she had her own place but he'd rather
she'd disappeared completely than left him in that half state.
She was everywhere at home, in the furniture and the pictures
on the wall, the plates from their wedding list, the brush still
matted with her hair, the roller she used to remove lint from her
skirt (that swift, sweeping motion down, the twist in her hips),

a tube of Canesten that he couldn't bring himself to throw away. Two people had lived there, but it was hard to spot his influence, and even his watch had come from Nat, simple and elegant, a present for his fortieth. How many times a day did he look at his watch? He couldn't tell the time without her. Without her, he ate standing up. Dust gathered in the empty fruit bowl. He ran the dishwasher once a week and watched TV, but it was always too quiet, no floorboards creaking, the air still, every room a spare room. He'd once returned from school to find an estate agent showing a young couple around their ideal family home with room to expand, and the sense of seeing his former self was enough to send him back to his car, marking homework there until they were gone. The house was a show-home for a life that had escaped them, and he wanted both to be rid of it and for things to be just as they'd been before.

For now, the anonymity of this three-star hotel room was almost a relief. He tossed the phone on to the bed and took in his surroundings, still standing in his sopping clothes, which he peeled off now, grimacing, then sitting on the edge of the bed to read it again. Hopeallswell, like a village in the Dales. What was there to say in return?

His eye snagged on an earlier exchange.

Let's leave it for a while. It's too much

The closing line from a flurry of dialogue, the post-mortem of a terrible phone call in which she'd revealed that she'd been on a few dates, early days, very casual, a colleague, Frank. Strange how you could hear a name all your life, only for it to take on some unexpected significance, so that he could hear it now only with a sneer. This *Frank* was a fellow English teacher, and he pictured the two of them lying head to toe on the sofa, quoting Wilfred Owen, chatting about *An Inspector Calls*. Are you moving in? he'd asked, and she'd said certainly not, early days, very casual, that terrible phrase *I just thought you should know*. He'd heard the teacherly tone in her voice and in return he'd been snappy and graceless, asking banal questions about the new job, the village, her parents' health, straining for politeness. The clichés of the end of a marriage were in the air – *no regrets, we had a good time, let's move on but stay in touch* – but there *were* regrets and terrible times and where could he move on to? They'd talked over each other, misheard or misunderstood, he'd clammed up, she'd felt obliged to fill the gaps, and it was all so different from the ease they'd once had, as if the phone was cutting out.

They'd resorted to the slow motion of texts, her thoughtful, kind messages stacked in grey boxes on the left, his terse blue monosyllables on the right, yes, no, not yet, I will, a visual representation of his petulant withdrawal. Awful to see it transcribed now, this bitter little two-hander, and he knew that if he pulled the screen down with his thumb, there'd be more, bare and bitter exchanges about solicitors and direct debits and forms that needed signing, then I miss you, I hate this too, please respond. Anger, confusion, admin.

He put the phone down once again. Why now? She must know that he'd be passing nearby in a few days' time. Did she want to meet up? The message was meagre but also impossible to ignore, like catching the eye of someone you used to know on the street. Respond or keep walking?

He growled, dug his hands into his hair and used it to pull himself upright then set about untangling the sopping mass of clothes. A sign on the radiator politely asked guests not to dry their clothes so he arranged them on hangers on the shower rail. He removed his watch and put it face down by the basin. On its back, 'To Mike, all my love always'. Hardly anyone called him Mike.

He smiled experimentally in the mirror, once, twice, in the same way you might test a car's brakes before a steep descent. At least he wouldn't have to think about what to wear.

Vinegar

She went down to the bar in her second-best dress. In *Twisted Night*, the detective had been seduced by the main suspect, in a hot tub, coincidentally, though less heavily chlorinated. Close-reading erotica had left her feeling vampy and seductive and so she wore the black dress with red roses, a widow suspected of murdering her husband. Conrad would be on the M6 by now but that was his loss, and there was no reason why she shouldn't prowl the Wainwright Bar for snacks and good times. Tuesday, a sign declared, was pie night. There would be a choice of eight pies. Beneath the sign, Michael, in yesterday's shirt, was looking at his Ordnance Survey maps. On the speakers, an eighties mix, 'Sweet Dreams' by Eurythmics.

'Sweet dreams *are* made of this,' she said.

He looked up. 'Sorry?'

She indicated. 'I didn't even know there were eight different types of pie.'

He turned to look at the sign. 'I guess,' he said, 'that they're including savoury pies and puddings, so—'

'You see, that's why you're in education,' she said. 'Do you want a drink?' He indicated his full pint. 'Snacks? Small pie?' He was fine, and she walked towards the bar, imagining his eyes on her or perhaps the maps. Conceptually, the room was an incoherent mix of old English button-down chairs and

modular airport furniture but she didn't care: she felt flirty and
provocative, leaning across the bar, arranging her hair to make
it fall just so as the young man listed all the flavours of crisps
and, whether it was the soft-porn or swimming, she was
reminded of the erotic ambience of even poorly reviewed conference hotels. Her first night with Neil had been in a place like
this, a team-building exercise in the Cotswolds, constructing
bridges with planks and oil drums as elaborate foreplay, every
look and touch charged, until later that night, after the karaoke,
a text with his room number. The way her heart had raced.
Afterwards, they'd lain in bed and laughed about it: was this
team-building? Maybe best if she didn't tell anyone . . .

'And to drink?'

She wanted a vodka martini, very dry with a twist, but the
house ales were Shepherd's Finger and Peaty Glen. She ordered a
gin and tonic and – why not? – a bag of chardonnay vinegar
crisps, crinkle cut, carrying her glass by the rim, like a coupe of
champagne, the crisps held lightly in one armpit, *Wuthering
Heights* in the other. Michael had his head down so she settled
at a nearby table and tried to read but it seemed as if Frankie
Goes to Hollywood were telling Heathcliff to *relax* and so—

'What's the route like tomorrow?'

He looked up, alarmed. 'Are you walking with me?'

'No, don't worry, I'm done with walking. I'm heading back
to York with them.'

'That's a shame. I don't think it's going to rain. Patterdale's
two valleys over so that's two climbs, but not like today . . .
You okay?'

She was puckering her lips. 'Wow. These crisps are *incredibly*
acidic. Do you want one?'

'Uh, no. Lots of streams to cross but the descent into
Grasmere will be—'

'Ow!' She slapped the flat of her hand on the table. 'It feels like a manufacturing fault. I think my mouth might be bleeding.'

'So if they're faulty—'

'—like battery acid—'

'—and you're bleeding, perhaps you should stop eating them.'

She laughed. 'Don't be ridiculous. Go on.'

'The thing is, in the afternoon you have to do it all again, up over five hundred metres to Grisedale Tarn . . .'

She could feel her interest leaching away. 'How was it last time?'

'I've never done it before. I'm just reading the map.'

'Show me,' she said, joining him, 'how to read a map.'

She knew perfectly well how to read a map but it was fun to see his enthusiasm, and she found herself stealing little glances as he talked about contour lines, the difference between footpath and bridleway, and how to estimate time with the joint of a thumb. It was all fantastically boring, of course, or rather the subject was boring but the speaker was not. She liked his voice, reassuring, the kind of voice used to sell funeral plans on afternoon TV ('savoury pies and puddings'). She liked his profile too, handsome in an old-fashioned way, someone from a sepia photograph whose only mistress is the sea, and it was pleasant to sit and sip her gin, their hips and elbows touching, distracted only by the ulcers on her tongue.

'What does this mean? "Here be dragons . . ."'

'I'm boring you, aren't I?'

'You're not. Really, you're not.'

A moment, and here were Cleo and Anthony. She scraped her chair away.

Because this was a three-star hotel, the pies came garnished with bracelets of green pepper and old-fashioned cress. Marnie had resolved not to sulk about the early departures, so they talked about school and teased Anthony gently for his braininess. Cleo ruffled his hair, kissed his head, stroked his arm in the extravagantly maternal way she sometimes used to demonstrate their closeness and modernity, and Marnie thought that, though she loved them very much, there were times when she wanted to flip the table over. Being with other families sometimes felt like indoctrination, as if she were attending a symposium on what family life could be. Here's what you might have had if you'd made better choices, here's where you might have poured your love. Again, the presumption of envy galled her more than envy itself. She had her moments but there was much about being child-free that she cherished. Was it any wonder that she'd withdrawn, when so often her friends behaved with the showy self-satisfaction of a wealthy family who've invited the poor cousin for Christmas?

Did Michael feel this too? Perhaps they should have talked about that rather than contour lines. For the moment they ate factory-made desserts piled high with aerosol cream, and then the boys went to play pool, leaving the two friends together, turning their glasses.

'D'you think you'll see him again?' asked Cleo.

'Conrad? He said he'd call but—'

'Or you could call him.'

'I do believe,' said Marnie, sipping her drink, 'etiquette requires it is the prerogative of the person who *fled*, rather than the person who is fled *from*—'

'He didn't *flee*. And you're doing it again.'

'What?'

'You know what.' There was a shout from the pool table as Anthony made some improbable shot and Michael reeled with mock indignation. They were comfortable together, Michael at ease, unpatronising, Anthony visibly fond.

'Can I ask – and I'm not interested – but can I ask, why didn't you think I'd get on with Michael?'

'Um, well, he can be quite serious, reserved.'

'I can be serious. I can talk to reserved people.'

'But messed-up, you know, had a bit of a breakdown, had to take some time off, and the separation's hard.'

'But even so . . .'

'I don't know, I thought you might like someone a bit more London, more outgoing, I thought it would do you good to have fun for a change.'

'I do have fun.'

'Sorting out your cutlery drawer.'

'I have fun!'

'You barely left your flat for three years!'

'No one did! It was against the law!'

'Not for three years, and it started well before that.'

'So what about the woman who was going to come? What did she have?'

'Tessa? I don't know, she was more outdoorsy.'

'I can be outdoorsy! Christ, just because I can't name trees. I *can* name trees by the way.'

'You can tell if it's a tree.'

'More than that! And we can talk. We actually get along quite well. He's funny, isn't he? He has a sense of humour?'

'He's . . . wry.'

'Wry. Well, wry's good, I can work with that.'

'Great. Well, go for it! Dive in!'

'I'm not going to "dive in"! I just wanted to check, is there anything . . . wrong?'

'No!' said Cleo. 'I really don't think there is,' and Marnie was reassured, though she wished it had been said with more conviction.

Day Three:

BORROWDALE, GRASMERE, GLENRIDDING

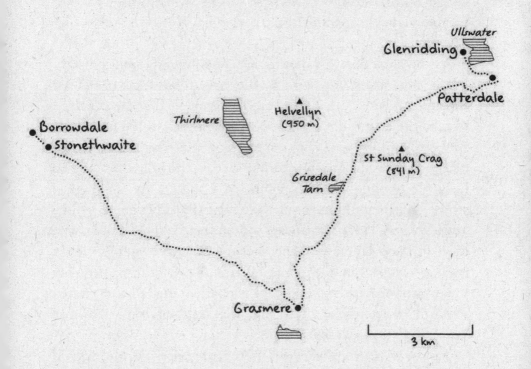

The Vow of Silence

Deep sleep. He had forgotten what a wild pleasure it was, and he found himself in high spirits, alone in the vast breakfast room. The kitchen had prepared a packed lunch, there was coffee in his flask, and it was all so wholesome and old-fashioned that he might have carried it in a spotted handkerchief at the end of a stick.

As the crow flew, his destination was just nine miles distant but he was not a crow and would have to zigzag for at least seventeen miles, more if the weather brightened and he decided to take the high route. There was mist in the air, the becks and waterfalls still flowing with the force of yesterday's rain, and he had to stop frequently to clamber across the gills that crossed his path, plotting a route on slippery boulders and submerged stones, finding the momentum to swing to the other bank, willing himself light. There was always a point between his foot leaving the bank and landing on the slick black rock, when he felt a twist of panic, yet each time he found his footing, climbing steadily towards Lining Crag, looking back at the valley, saturated with all the potential of spring, the scent of wet earth and bruised leaves, a garden after heavy rain.

This was better, wasn't it? In the presence of others, he'd been too concerned with their welfare and happiness, what to say and how to be. Now he could return to the original project, the thinking-through, the walking-off. Apart from bar staff and receptionists, he would not speak to another human being for eight days and, expressed like this, he felt a certain trepidation. 'I understand you might want time to think,' Cleo had said, 'but why not just pay someone to lock you in their garage for a week?'

'The views, Cleo!'

'Views aren't people. Lakes and rivers, they're just things to point at. Besides, the two aren't mutually exclusive. I remember when you *liked* other people.'

'I do, in moderation.'

'Hm. Well, at some point you're going to have to let someone in.' It was all too sombre for a last night. 'Hey, Michael,' she'd said, clutching his elbow, 'let me in!' and they'd laughed. 'Well, not me, but someone.'

'Hey, did you tell Nat I was doing this?'

'Not her, though.'

'I don't mind, I just wondered.'

'You know I can't talk to you about Nat. I was talking about someone new.'

'Bit too old for that now, I think.'

'You are forty-two!'

Forty-two, product of six times seven, technically middle-aged but very much the beginning of that decade, and wasn't forty-two a special number? Better still, if you subtracted child-hood – another sixteen, no, eighteen years – then he was only twenty-four years into his adult life, and with this combination of arithmetic and numerology, he tricked himself into temporary youth, hopping from rock to rock, only losing momentum on the final scramble up to Grasmere Common. On the horizon, he could see a dot of red, the woolly hat of another walker, and he began to accelerate so that he might pass with the minimum of conversation. *Heading to Grasmere?* or *Might brighten up later!*, the kind of remark that's a prophylactic against interest or engagement. But as he got nearer, he recognised the stance, doubled over and apparently calling the mountain a bastard. There was no way around and, besides, she'd seen him and now stood grinning at the summit, as if she'd pulled off some terrific practical joke.

He should have been annoyed but was not, not quite. He could postpone the vow of silence for a few miles more.

Dorothy Wordsworth

Through the village, over a stone bridge, along the river path, the air misty and muffled as if the valley had not quite woken either. She was aware of the sound of her own breathing, unfamiliar birdsong, water dripping and spattering, everything reeking of petrichor, and when nature's symphony got boring, she put in her earbuds and listened to a podcast. It felt sacrilegious, listening to cynical urban voices among all this beauty but there was no one here to judge or make her twist her head to look at some side-blown tree or unusual rock, and she felt a sense of self-containment, contentment even.

The plan had formed in the night, writhing and fidgeting in an unfamiliar bed at the thought of the day ahead. The taxi back to St Bees would feel like surrender, and then there was the long drive to York, the demands from Cleo that she change her life. Hardly a holiday, and surely there was a better way to spend the day. Online maps were plentiful and she'd screen-grabbed these and emailed them to her phone. Overcast but brighter later, a 20 per cent chance of rain. Seventeen miles seemed a lot even on flat ground, three thumbs at least, but wouldn't it be funny to beat Michael to it, to be waiting in the hotel bar in Patterdale? *Yes, yes, tricky ground coming down into Easedale but fine views over Eagle's Crag*, or whatever it was these people said to each other. She'd showered, pulled on stiff clothes, stashed the free shortbread in case of emergency. In the dim breakfast room, she'd eaten a large bowl of tinned grapefruit segments, a sachet of crispbread, pale strawberries as hard as apples, typing a text one-handed to Cleo.

Am walking, go without me! Talk soon and thank you x

At Reception she'd laced her boots excessively tightly as if preparing for amputation, settled the red beanie on her head and hung her compass around her neck like a St Christopher.

Inevitably the self-satisfaction couldn't last. Hopping over streams began to lose its Christopher Robin charm as they became more treacherous, and she was aware of small dramas starting inside her boots, toes rubbing in new ways, the beginning of a blister, a toenail digging into flesh. The battery on her phone was draining and she imagined explaining to Mountain Rescue that she'd lost her way because of podcasts. Gasping, cursing at the top of the ascent, she checked her map. Half a thumb. Resentfully, she looked back at the view, recognised the solitary figure and found herself unexpectedly pleased. Choosing a comfortable boulder, she braced her feet across the path, removed the hat and adjusted her hair. There was plenty of time to come up with a witty greeting but . . .

'Fancy meeting you here!' she said.

Through gasps, he managed, 'Quite a coincidence.'

'I was going to jump out on you, like a dandy highwayman. Steal your Thermos and your granola bars.'

'Your wine gums or your life!'

'Hang on, you've got wine gums?'

He looked to the sky. 'Not necessarily,' he said, mock-innocent, and they stood for a moment, just smiling until 'I thought you were going home.'

'Yes, couldn't face it. And it's against my religion to let a hotel room go to waste. But I don't want to disturb you, if you're communing with nature.'

'No, no, I'll commune with you.'

'We could walk a small distance apart, like we've had a row.'

'No need. Unless you're still angry with me.'

'No, no. I've forgiven you.'

'Okay. Let's see how we get on.'

There was a momentary scuffle as they arranged themselves on the narrow path. 'Is it the same as the Underground? Should I stand on the right?' and then they were walking side by side.

'I like this,' he said, indicating the large compass that dangled uselessly around her neck.

'This? That's for getting the lid off beer bottles,' she said, miming it, then holding the compass up to her ear like a mobile phone. 'Hello? Hello? No reception!' and that, she thought, was quite enough mime for now.

'How are you navigating?'

'Sun, moon, stars. No, I sent the map to my phone. I thought I might beat you there,' she said. 'But no chance.'

'How was it, walking by yourself?'

'Takes some getting used to. I mean, if I walk alone in London I usually have my keys bunched in my hand but here, well, you're still a little nervy but at least you'd hear them coming. Except I was listening to podcasts. Is that allowed? Or do the National Trust hurl you off Helvellyn?'

'I think you should do whatever you want.'

'I mean, I like nature, but there's a lot of it. I bet even William Wordsworth, every now and then, thought it was all a bit much. I bet there were times when he and Dorothy must have been like, well, we've seen the chaffinches and the beavers and the shady bower, now tell me your top five favourite pageants.'

133

He laughed again and she realised how much she enjoyed making him laugh. 'Top five satirical engravings,' he said.

'Yeah, top five Odes about Revolutionary France. Dorothy, tell me your top five symptoms of syphilis.'

'Or gout.'

'Pray, William, tell me your most embarrassing experience on laudanum.'

'I'm sceptical Wordsworth ever wrote about beavers, though.'

'I'm sure he did. It's an easy rhyme for one thing.'

'Their house is in Grasmere if you want to pop in.'

'No, I'm okay. I love reading. I'll read anything but I've never really got poetry. Fiction's just there, but poetry you have to seek out and there's always this voice in my head saying, *Oh, look at you, with your little slim volume.* I understand the words individually but it doesn't go in, just sits on the top. I remember reading that one about Tintern Abbey at school but it went over my head, all that stuff about ecstasy.'

'The sublime.'

'Exactly, the sublime. Is it the same as "outdoorsy"?'

'I think it's more than that. Do you get the sublime in London?'

'You do but only in certain postcodes. It's like school catchment areas, pushes prices up. I'm still not sure what it is, though.'

'Well, I'm a geography teacher so not my brief. But we did learn "Daffodils" at school and I remember the ending. Something-something the bliss of solitude, something "heart with pleasure fills and dances with the daffodils". And I think that's the sublime. A heart filled with pleasure.'

'There's a man who definitely wouldn't listen to a podcast.'

'Maybe it changes when you get older. You put a kid in the most exquisite place, clear sky, mountains, wild seas, and they still can't wrench their mind off the phone or the spot that's coming up on their chin or the boy they fancy. But you get to a certain age . . .'

'And you think about what?'

'I don't know. Time passing, mortality, your place in things, how insignificant you are.'

'Me? Specifically me?'

'Yes, just you.'

'It does sound a bit depressing.'

'Or the antidote to depression. At least, that's the theory.'

'Does it work?'

He thought for a moment. 'We'll find out,' and she thought she might pursue this, but it didn't seem the time. Instead they took in the view. The last of the mist had gone now and they could see the Easedale valley opening before them, a long, gentle ascent, the route following the gill to a patchwork of baize-green fields, the edges of a town. Above them the sky still hung heavy and low but there was a suggestion of the sun, like a torch shone through a blanket.

'See, that's my problem. I'm still thinking about the spot on my chin.'

'And the boy you fancy?'

'Not any more,' and she thought he might pursue this too, but they began to walk again.

'How old are you, Marnie? If you don't mind me . . .'

'I'm thirty-eight.'

'*Really?*'

'Because I'm such a young gazelle? I actually don't mind looking the age I am.'

'Perhaps I'm not a very good judge. Unless it's deep time. If you were a mountain range . . .'

'Ninety billion years, you say?'

'Because you don't look a day over seventy-five billion.'

'Well, that's the special creams,' she said, and thought, *Listen to us, sparking away*. 'How old are you?'

'Forty-two,' he said.

'Can I just say you absolutely do look *at least* forty-two.'

'Thank you!'

'That's all right. We both look like what we are.' It was true, he did look a little careworn, though it was galling that men could get away with that stuff. No one would ever say, 'Wow, she looked careworn last night.' Perhaps this was what he was going for, pleasingly unkempt, though it was hard to imagine him going for anything deliberately. Beards, for instance, were meant to be metropolitan, and Michael looked like someone who'd spent a year filming puffins in the Hebrides.

'Well, maybe it will all kick in when you're forty,' he said.

'The depression?'

'A love of nature. And gardening.'

'I don't have a garden. I've had a little cactus for years but I honestly can't tell if it's dead or not. And I've got two window boxes but they're like little dioramas of no man's land.'

'No thoughts of moving to a small farm, then?'

'Absolutely not. I'd top myself, first wet afternoon. Neighbour would come around with a hotpot or some wild garlic and I'd be gone.'

'You're a city girl.'

'Oh, I don't particularly like the city either.'

'But this isn't so terrible, is it?'

They paused a moment. The path was firmer and wider now, the lake visible between the trees, the end of the morning's walk in sight. If it had been a finer day, this would have been spectacular but even so . . . 'Is this,' she said, 'is this the sublime?'

'Does your heart with pleasure fill?'

'It's very pretty,' she said, and took a photo with her phone.

From the fells to their right they heard the sound of a horn, a rising note, corny and absurd, like something from Robin Hood. 'What's that?' and as they stopped to look, three figures in flat caps strode over the crest, walking sticks in hand. 'Sheep farmers? Are they herding sheep?' The horn sounded once again and then the most extraordinary sight.

Dogs, a pack of dogs, fifty or sixty began to pour over the crest of the hill. Instinctively, she felt the city-dwellers' fear of trespass, as if she was being hunted down, and she held on to Michael's arm as the hounds rushed towards them. Sixty, seventy dogs of all shapes and sizes, joining the path then pouring in a torrent until they were upon them, then moving on, indifferent, followed down the hill by figures with whistles and sticks, a neat little brass horn, almost a toy, in the woman's hand. The valley was alive with dogs, as if pouring out from secret tunnels, and she couldn't help but laugh, there were so many, hounds and terriers and lurchers, some shaggy and scrappy, some sleek, all unnervingly silent as they streamed around their legs, urged on by the farmers, who also passed them now, sure-footed and imperious in leather boots and tweed. Marnie stood still until the last of a hundred dogs had passed and then they looked at each other and began to laugh. 'Honestly,' she said, 'the countryside, it's fucking *mad*.'

Stegosaur

Paths became bridleways, lanes became village streets, with tourist coaches parked in front of tea-rooms. He thought he might lose her to the gift shops selling gingerbread and postcards of daffodils but they decided to keep going. Too many tourists, they agreed, without being entirely sure of how they differed. Instead they saw a pub, whitewashed and quaint. 'Thirsty,' she croaked, rubbing her throat.

The bar was dark and cosy, and they chose between things like Goatherd's Moone and Olde Thumb and Foggie Moss. 'These beers need proofreading,' she said, tapping the pumps, and they touched glasses and drank, then found a table near the fire. For a while they checked their phones and sipped their drinks – nothing from Natasha – until they caught each other's eye. 'Tell me about your work,' he said.

'Really? It's very boring.'

'I don't think so. You proofread.'

'Copy-edit. Though proofreading's part of it.'

'What's the difference?'

'Proofreading is "You misspelled 'instantaneously'", copy-editing is "Why not say 'instantly'?" Other things too, tabs and paragraphing and consistency but mainly it's making sure the writer's saying what they mean to say.'

'Like marking homework.'

'I realise how dull it sounds.'

'No, I like marking homework. Really. Hang on,' he said, and got more drinks. When he returned, she'd produced her laptop.

'Okay, I shouldn't really show you this . . .' She turned it towards him.

He scanned the document. The fire crackled. 'Wow,' he said.

'I know!'

'It's not like marking homework at *all*.'

'I should hope not.'

'I wouldn't know where to start.'

'Hot stuff, isn't it? But give it a go. Have you been to a Hollywood swingers' club?'

'Not for . . . *ages*.'

'As a lay reader then, tell me what you see.'

He scanned the text. 'Well, the commas—'

'The commas are the *least* of my worries.'

'I've never seen this spelt with two *t*s before.'

'Yep.'

'And I'm not sure of the logistics.'

'Exactly, because she's sitting down here but suddenly he's behind her and—'

'So how is he—'

'Exactly.'

'And I'm not sure this makes sense.'

'It is quite startling. With adjectives, the conventional order is opinion, size, age, shape, colour. You don't learn that, you just know – it's "the lovely little old round red robin" – but she's gone size, size, colour, size and it's not even the right colour.'

'Repetition of "thrashing"?'

'Yep.'

'I don't think I'd do any of this in a hot tub.'

'That's a health-and-safety issue but I agree.'

'And do you find, when you're working on something like this, do you . . .'

'Get involved? No, I'm like a surgeon, steely objectivity.'

'I must admit,' he said, 'I *am* sort of gripped.'

'As indeed is he,' she said, and closed the lid. 'Mr Bradshaw, you look like if you pulled at your collar steam would come out.'

'Well, that's the booze,' he said, and looked into the bottom of his glass. Some of the worst times with Natasha had followed the second bottle of wine, the alcohol no longer loosening them into affection or silliness, but making them sullen and argumentative. After her departure, he'd caught himself stumbling on the stairs or waking, wretched and confused, on the sofa at three in the morning. But this felt like younger days, almost like being a student, and he realised he had accidentally been lulled into enjoying himself. The fire was warm, Marnie looked great in the orange light, eyes wide with mischief as she suggested they have one more. 'Very refreshing,' she said, finishing the third, and they both started to laugh.

After the twilight of the snug, even this overcast day made him squint, as if stepping out of a cinema into daytime. 'It is very bright,' he said, over-enunciating, and this made them laugh too. More than bright, the combination of fresh air, exertion and alcohol created an almost hallucinogenic effect and the Grisedale Pass now seemed primeval, as if a stegosaur might come trundling over the brow of Great Rigg. 'I feel quite stoned,' he said, and Marnie gripped his arm.

'Me too! Let's sweat it out. Race you!' and she began to sprint, the rucksack flopping from side to side. 'I'm auditioning for the SAS!' she shouted.

'I don't think the SAS call it an audition,' he said, and they had to stop because they were laughing so hard as she speculated on what an SAS audition might involve. 'Night march with a forty-pound backpack, song from a show, then jungle training. Jazz-dance and then they beat the shit out of you.'

They played a game in which Michael called out the names of geographical features from the map and Marnie had to decide which were made-up, which were real. Nethermost Pike! Catbells! Hoghouse Platter! Cold Kaller! Dollywagon! Craggy Crag! Some walkers passed, a white-haired older couple outpacing them. 'Hello, there,' said the man, in a Scottish accent.

'Hello there,' Michael replied, in the same voice, and after another ten metres they started to laugh again. Is this what the punks had felt like? 'We're bad hikers!' said Michael.

'So bad,' said Marnie, and he thought how much he liked her, how pleased he was that their paths had crossed, *literally* crossed! If they'd had another drink, perhaps he might even have told her this.

He was simultaneously drunk and acting drunk, a kid reeling after a sip of ginger ale, with the particular sensation of being both inside and outside himself, finding everything silly and joyful and hilarious, and at the same time thinking, *You idiot, stop this now.* Could he ever have the first without the second, stop watching over himself? *I'll pretend I didn't see that, put it out, big day tomorrow.* Perhaps another drink would quieten that voice. Perhaps when they got to the hotel they should go straight to the bar. They were on holiday after all. Perhaps she might even stay on for a day or two.

Ridiculous idea. At Grisedale Tarn they walked to the shore. 'Maybe we should swim,' he said, 'to sober up,' and they tested the icy black water with fingertips.

'I think that would kill me,' she said.

'Or make you stronger,' he said.

'No, it would just kill me. But you go, knock yourself out.'

'Not today. But we *are* going to swim before the walk's over,' he said, except that she was going home tomorrow, so how could that be?

They walked on. If he'd been alone and sober, he'd have climbed a fell, St Sunday Crag or even Helvellyn, with its tourist horde, the Madame Tussaud's of mountains but Marnie was visibly wilting. 'I can't see any hotels.'

'Two hours,' he said, and she groaned. 'Okay, I'm going to let you into a secret. I think I know you well enough now.'

'Ooh, this sounds juicy,' she said, poking him with a finger.

'It *is* juicy, but we need to be sitting down.' They found two boulders, facing each other across the narrow path and he opened his rucksack. 'This will help your energy.'

'Is it methamphetamine?'

'No, it's better than that,' he said, and began to dig into the top layer until he found . . . 'Fresh socks.'

'Oh. I'm not sure that *is* better.'

'Trust me, just change your socks. It's like getting a new pair of feet.'

She blew air up at her forehead and reached for her rucksack. 'I can't pretend I don't feel a bit let down.'

'Try it. I think you'll like it.'

They began to undo their boots, as if getting ready for bed, and it felt vaguely provocative, feet exposed to daylight. 'Look at this,' she said. 'A glimpse behind the curtain. Men's feet are bizarre, aren't they? Massive great things.'

'They're perfectly normal feet.'

'No wonder foot fetishists are all straight men. Look at you with your flapping great yeti feet, look at the hair on your toes.'

'Hey. You can talk.'

'Oh, I know, they're gross,' and she stretched out her legs, bridging the path and resting her bare feet, one, two, on his knees. 'The guy in the shop made me swear to cut my nails but look at this one. Look at this hairy toe, Rasputin here.'

He looked. They were pale and damp, sore on the knuckle of the toes, with just the remnants of chipped red nail varnish still visible. 'Like vacuum-packed trotters,' she said, though he found he very much wanted to take one in each hand and hold on to them, his thumbs pressed into the arches. A moment passed. She took her feet back and they began to pull on fresh socks.

'Can I ask you a question?' she said. 'If you're walking for ten days, how come you're travelling so light?'

'I'm scared to tell you.'

'I'm unshockable.'

'Okay. Three pairs of pants, three pairs of socks, and I wash them every night in the hand-basin. In rotation.'

She shook her head thoughtfully. 'Okay. Okay.'

'Have I shocked you?'

'No, I'm just . . . Why does that make me feel so *sad*? Just this deep and elemental sadness.'

He laughed. 'It is a little bleak.'

'It's the phrase "wash them in rotation".'

'Hey, life on the road.'

'Bit like Jack Reacher.'

'He does that too?'

'But for different reasons. He's an ex-military vigilante, you're a member of the Ramblers Association.'

'*Ex*-member.'

'Because you killed a man?'

'You're funny, but I'm the one with the lighter rucksack so who's laughing?'

'That is true. I've got twelve pairs of pants in here, for three nights.'

'Why?'

'I don't know. Maybe I worried I might shit myself four times a day.'

'Has that ever happened?'

'Not since my honeymoon.' Their boots were back on now. She stood and bent her knees, bouncing experimentally on her feet, trying them out. 'It's a miracle!'

They set off, and as they descended into the next valley the cloud began to break up into smaller floes, revealing the first blue for days, and it began to feel as if they were their own procession, as if there might be crowds waiting for them at the end, cheering.

The Wedding Salmon

Clouds parting to reveal blue sky, Marnie wondered where she'd seen this effect before and realised it was the opening credits of *The Simpsons*. She did not want to seem facetious and instead said, 'That's why they call it sky blue,' so it was fair to presume she wasn't sober yet.

After a while, 'That didn't really happen on my honeymoon,' she said. 'That was a joke.'

'Good to know.'

'I mean everything else went wrong, but not that.'

'What went wrong?' he said.

'Quicker to say what went right. I don't know, the whole thing was a mistake.'

'The honeymoon or the marriage?'

'Both.'

'You don't have to talk about it if you don't—'

'Oh, I don't mind. My main memory of the honeymoon, the wedding day too, was thinking, Well, this is a *very* bad idea. He knew it too, we both did, we just couldn't quite bring ourselves to say it, especially after we'd spent all that money. Even on the honeymoon, there was this running commentary on how much everything cost, like we were on a meter. His background was accounting, though he liked to call it "finance", so he was good with sums. We flew premium economy as a treat and I knew how much every inch of leg-room cost, pounds per nautical mile. We had cocktails in the Rainbow Room, chinked glasses and he said, "That's three quid a sip. Enjoy!" Then we had a massive row about whether a burger is technically a type of sandwich, so that was romantic too, walking down Fifth Avenue while someone shrieks, "Define sandwich! Define sandwich!"'

'It's not a sandwich.'

'Exactly, thank you, Michael! Anyway.'

'How long were you together?'

'Married nearly three years, which is more than you get for manslaughter. Together three before that.'

'And you met?'

'At work. This was when I used to go to an office. You know those big billboards at roundabouts and train stations? We sold those. I got sent there when I was working as a temp, a receptionist, and they asked me to stay on. It was all right. Some nice people. Neil, my ex, used to act like he was Don Draper or something. That was the role he played. Nice suits, sometimes with a little waistcoat, always very neat, very confident, always talking about lunches with clients, what the right site could do for their business. He couldn't pass a billboard without telling you how many impressions per day, how much it cost, the virtues of digital over paper. You'd go through Piccadilly Circus and, I swear, you'd want to throw yourself under the thirty-eight bus. I shouldn't be mean. I married him and we did have fun, to begin with.'

'Was he . . . ?'

'Attractive? In a cheesy way, the least popular member of a boy band. He was quite flashy and confident, posher than me, eight years older, and it was nice to be . . . I don't know, swept along by that, to begin with anyway. I used to think, Why me?

146

Why not choose someone more confident and sexy and brash? I thought it was romantic to be asking that, but it turned out he was asking exactly the same question. "Actually, you've got a point."'

'So how did you get together?'

'Well, he used to flirt, sitting on my desk every morning, really cheesy stuff, Bond and Moneypenny, gross really. And sometimes we used to go for lunch. That was a thrill. He was the first man I ever saw eat sushi – this was 2006 – and I thought it was just . . . mind-blowing. I think he thought he was educating me, not books but, you know, being a man-about-town in a very minor men's-magazine sort of way, espresso martinis and poker and tickets to see *Stomp*, I mean the glamour. There was this woman in human resources who fancied him and hated me, *really* hated me, a real bully, texting me at night, criticising my work, and he used to flirt with her too, he flirted with everyone, but then we went on this office team-building thing in the Cotswolds and we got off with each other, secretly, sneaking into his room. That was the start of it. And I was so thrilled, you know, to be picked, which is not quite the same thing as love but is part of it. He wants *me*! The first year was so exciting, snogging in the stationery cupboard and the lift, pretending to say goodbye then meeting up, real Romeo and Juliet stuff. That was the best part, when it was us against the world. And the sex too, I suppose, lots of sex, pardon me.'

'That's all right.'

'I mean we did *every*thing. By which I mean all three.'

'All three?' he said, and here she made a series of hand gestures, a kind of obscene hand-jive. 'Yep,' he said. 'That is everything.'

'I don't even think we were breaking any rules but we thought it would be better that way. Or he did. "Best not tell." But then someone said something to someone and it was all out in the open and that was when it got really horrible. This woman, human resources, was furious, *furious*, blaming me for stuff, ignoring me, hinting that maybe I'd be happier somewhere else, and he *still* flirted with her. So I started to get really unhappy, losing sleep, getting depressed, and that was when I started looking for a change. I didn't have a degree but I'd always read so much and so quickly, best part of my day, reading on the train, two, three books a week, and I was quite good at fixing the copy and the letters and the marketing material, better than my bosses. So I did a course in my spare time, wrote to all these publishers and editors and got a few trial jobs. And then I resigned. Became self-employed.'

'And all this time . . .'

'We were going out. He was nice. He encouraged me, partly, I realise now, because he wanted me out of the office but we were quite happy for a while. Moved in. Got a lot of cheap furniture, an espresso machine, and when our lives were too tangled up, got engaged. That's when I should have paused, really, because no one was pleased, I mean *no one*, not really. It's like we'd announced that we were going to, I don't know, start a camel farm together – everyone frowned and smiled at the same time and said, "Good for you," but you could tell they all thought, *Fucking hell, a* camel *farm, that's a terrible idea.* The only one who straight out said don't do it was Cleo. She always hated him, thought he was naff, a charm boy, not even that charming, with his little waistcoats. She came to our flat once, only once, and we had this big expensively framed poster as you walked in, for *Moonraker*, and she looked at me and her eyes said, "Pack your bags and *go*." She was right, of course, she's always right, as you know.

'In a weird kind of way, I was rebelling. Cleo kept saying,

148

"You don't have to do this, wait," but I was twenty-five, it's not unheard of, and that whole thing of waiting until you're thirty-five, it just seemed a bit . . . posh. And I wasn't a high-flyer exactly but he was, we were doing all right. My parents liked him, my mum anyway. *His* parents thought he was marrying the maid, but they never said it. We'd talked about kids in a year or two, he wanted to be a dad, had dad fantasies, thought it would mellow him. Why wait?

'But I think I knew. And the wedding, that was a challenge. I mean I would have *loved* to be jilted. Miss Havisham, that was the *dream*. The service was horrible – the indifference in that room – the speeches were horrible. The best man told this long, awful story about Neil pissing his pants in junior school assembly. Complete. Silence. Then my husband got up and talked about it a bit more, like pissing his pants was the biggest thing that had ever happened, like he'd done two things in his life, pissed his pants and got married, and then he just went on and on about how expensive the wedding was. Joking but also very much *not* joking. I don't want to sound like an egomaniac but it was *my* wedding day, I thought I'd at least get a mention. You know, a cameo. We had to cut the cake early because everyone was leaving, couldn't get out of there fast enough. By the time we did our first dance, I swear, there were about nine people. The best man had to tell the caterers to stop stacking chairs until the song had finished. Blushing bride? I was *mortified*. And the volume of leftover salmon. He made us take it home in bags to put in our freezer. It's traditional, I know, to keep a slice of the wedding cake but not the main course. We lived on it for years, like we were in a nuclear bunker. What's for dinner? Oh, great, the wedding salmon. Hey, this mountain's nice. What is this mountain?'

'Helvellyn.'

'Ah. There she is. Little bit of snow on top, it's a good look, it works. Are mountains "she"?'

'I think so. Mountains, boats and rivers.'

'She looks good for her age. Which is?'

'About five hundred million years. But the honeymoon?'

'Ah, the honeymoon. I think that's when we realised. It was such hard work, trying to keep him upbeat, keep it light, keep it sexy, and you could feel the enthusiasm just . . . leaching away. We went out to the Statue of Liberty and he said it was smaller than he expected and so was the Empire State and so was the hotel room and so was the marriage.

'Anyway. We gave it a go, but he kept putting off having kids, which was suspicious, and it was as if . . . You know that thing when you're watching a film that you're not really enjoying and the other person doesn't like it either, but you've paid for the rental, you're halfway through, you sort of want to know what happens and, besides, there's nothing else on. But really you're just waiting for someone to say, "Can we stop this? I *hate* it." And neither of us did. Some people sit like that for their whole lives together. Waiting for it to pick up, waiting for a good bit. We were lucky in that respect. It could have gone on longer.'

'But you drifted apart.'

'Well, not *drifted* exactly. He was fucking Human Resources, so unless he *drifted* into fucking her . . .'

'Ah. Okay. The one who—'

'Yep.'

'How did you find out?'

'Oh, she told me. She wasn't going to let *that* opportunity slide. I got a text, like it was birthday cake in the tea-room. "Hi, Marnie, how are you? Just giving you the heads-up."'

'Well, I'm sorry.'

'Oh, I don't mind. I can laugh now. Look!' She bared her

teeth. 'She got her *Stomp* tickets, and I got some stories out of it. An encyclopaedic knowledge of the Bond movies. Maybe two good years and less than half the flat. He still owes me fifteen grand, the bastard.'

'Well, you must get it back.'

'That's what Cleo says. I think in his mind it's like I cancelled at short notice so he's keeping the deposit. Anyway. All my friends were very nice – "You're better out of it", "His loss", all that stuff. "Go, girl!" Of course, as soon as we'd celebrated the divorce, they all went off to get married. It's like I'd just got off this terrible rollercoaster, covered in my own vomit, going, "Don't do *that*, it's *awful*," and they all said, "No, no, we'll be fine, we're going to have a different experience, bye, goodbye." And for the most part they have. I hardly see them now. So. Lucky them, I suppose.'

'And do you regret . . . ?'

'Go on.'

'Not having kids?'

'With him? Not with him, but . . . That's a big one: I'll tell you what I do feel . . .' She hesitated. 'I suppose the main thing I feel now, and I want you to remember I've had a drink or two, is that I would have liked to have loved someone. You know, mutually, and for a period of time, and at that time of life, when you've got so much of it. Love, not salmon. I think I'd have been good at it. That's what I wanted, and I did try, really. But he was the wrong . . . I don't know . . . I was going to say object of affection, but he was just an object. It was a bad investment. I should have put it somewhere else.'

'Maybe you will.'

'Well, I've spent it now. I'm too jaded, too old. Me and Helvellyn. At this time of life, a relationship, it feels like starting a book halfway through. And presenting yourself to a stranger like that, not even your whole self – because who wants that? – but the self you think they'll like, thinking about what you say and how you dress and what your face is doing. Honestly, the self-consciousness is so great I'd get sucked up by it, like a black hole eating itself. And who wants a date with a black hole?'

'How would you split the bill?'

'When they've eaten *everything*.'

'I hope you don't feel like that right now.'

'No, but this is different, this is just conversation. But down there . . .' She gestured to where she thought London might be. 'Why put yourself through that? I'm very happy alone. Do what I want, watch, eat, read, listen to what I want, sleep. Now. Shall we abruptly change the subject?'

'Only if you want to.'

'I do. Here's my question. Are we nearly there yet?'

'We are! Fifteen minutes.'

'Oh. Really? I could have walked further.'

'You see? New socks.'

'New socks. Powered on by the sound of my own voice. Now you've got to tell me your origin story. In revenge. What happened with you and . . .'

'Natasha? That, I'm afraid, is what in an exam we'd call a sixteen-marker.'

'Maybe another time.'

'Maybe over dinner. Shall we have dinner, when we get there?'

'Sure. I'd like that.'

'We'll sober up and then we'll start drinking again.'

So they walked into the wooded valley, the last rags of cloud breaking up and evaporating like steam on a mirror. The stories we tell about ourselves are never neutral: they're shaped and structured to create an impression, and Marnie hoped she'd not gone too awry. But she was surprised that recalling misery had not made her miserable. The opposite was true and though later, sober, she might regret saying so much, she was happy to abide in the pleasant wooziness of the afternoon, the low spring light, the various birds beginning their evening session in what she still thought of as the drivetime slot. For the moment she felt content, not because she'd spoken but because she'd been listened to.

And this feeling persisted until later, on the driveway to the grand hotel at the edge of Ullswater, where the strange thing happened.

They had paused for a moment at the hotel gates and he'd taken her gently by the arm so that they were facing each other. 'Can I just tell you . . . ?' he said, then exhaled as if exasperated. 'I've been wanting to do this ever since I first saw you at the station,' and he put his hands on her shoulders and pulled her towards him, and instinctively she closed her eyes, lifted her chin, put her head to one side.

Hôtel du Lac

'Can I just tell you I've been wanting to do this ever since I first saw you at the station,' he said, and began to adjust the straps on her rucksack. 'It's sending me *crazy*. It's throwing you off-balance for one thing, swinging free like that . . .'

Why had she closed her eyes?

'. . . and you want the weight on your hips, not your shoulders.'

And frowning now, why was she frowning?

'May I?' he asked, and she licked her lips and nodded, and he undid the plastic belt buckle across her clavicle and reached down for the other buckle at her waist, pulling it tighter. 'Bit late in the day but . . . there. What do you think?'

Her smile seemed tighter too. 'That's so much better!' She rolled her shoulders. 'It's a bit like being properly fitted for a bra,' she said, which seemed a strange thing to say but perhaps they were both still a little drunk.

They walked side by side along the gravel driveway, straight-backed, like teenagers preparing to get into a nightclub. The hotel was from the 1920s, flat-fronted, painted an expensive creamy white with a lush green lawn that rolled down to the shores of Ullswater. Wooden jetty, tasteful lawn furniture, even an artist's easel set up to face the lake, and a woman in a loose white shift dress and sunhat, crouching and dabbing.

'This is posh,' he said, aware now of his mud-spattered trousers, his sticky, beery mouth, the salt and sweat stiffening his skin.

'Too posh for us,' she said. 'We're going to be asked to sleep in the gazebo.'

More than posh, it was romantic, extravagantly so, a honeymoon hotel or weekend retreat for new lovers. 'Don't stare,' said Marnie, 'but I think that's someone from the Bloomsbury Group.' The woman at the easel was waving with her paintbrush, and as he waved back, he caught the smell of his armpits.

'I actually stink.'

'It'd be funny to go up and look at her easel and it's just a big cock and balls.'

'Beer and sweat. I really don't think they're going to let us in here.'

'We's just as good as any toff,' said Marnie. 'Anyway, the rooms are paid for.'

'Are we going to have to eat here?'

'Well, I'm not walking anywhere. But listen, if you want dinner alone . . .'

Did he? 'No, we should definitely have dinner. I'd like that.'

'Me too.'

They waited at Reception: oak panels, parquet floors, a single white lily in a chemistry beaker. Sade's 'Smooth Operator' whispered from the speakers. Suddenly he held up a finger. 'Did you hear that?'

'What?'

'Sade. She just sang "coast to coast"!'

'She did not.'

'No, she did. It's in the chorus,' and he sang the melody.

'"Smooth Operator" is *not* a song about rambling.'

'I know!'

'She's singing about LA to Chicago.'

'Okay, but I would point out that Chicago is not on the maritime coast.'

'It's a stop on the way to Key Largo. Anyway, you can tell her yourself.'

The receptionist, hair scraped back, glided towards them in rose-gold blouse and high-waisted tan trousers. 'Can I help you?'

'We have a reservation.'

'Certainly. The name is?'

'Walsh.'

'And Bradshaw.'

'Two rooms.'

Marnie was in Shelley, Michael in Keats. 'They're just opposite each other,' said the receptionist, meaningfully, and she pointed out the bar and the library, the terrace for cream teas, a leaflet of romantic walks, a menu of spa treatments and facials, which they could do alone or together. The Wi-Fi code was romanticwordsworth, all lower case.

They climbed the wide wooden stairs, Marnie reading the leaflet as they went. 'Hot stone massage?'

'At least I'd be able to name the stone.'

'Yep. Feels like . . . Is that my old friend . . . basalt?'

In the corridor, they stood on opposite sides, rucksacks brushing. 'Ready?' said Marnie, and they opened their doors at the same time. Keats was even worse than he'd expected: four-poster bed, fresh flowers with a heavy perfume, dark velvety wallpaper, as if the furniture and fittings were all conspiring in some grand act of seduction, and perhaps this was Cleo's last joke. Perhaps if Conrad had stuck around, perhaps if Tessa the triathlete had stayed the course . . .

'Let me see your room.' Marnie was squeezing past him. 'What a dump. What's your view?'

'The mountains.'

'I got the lake.'

'Do you want the mountains?'

'No, I'll muddle through.'

'Four-poster bed?'

'Oh, yes. Big double-ended bath. Really, if we ever get married again . . .'

'We'll know where to come,' he said, and there was a silence.

'Great! So. It's five now. Shall we do our own thing? I'll do some work and we'll meet at seven thirty?'

'Sounds good,' he said and, somewhat awkwardly, she punched him lightly on the shoulder.

'Today. That was fun,' and she was gone.

His mind had become snagged on 'Smooth Operator', murmuring to a bossa-nova rhythm as he pulled off his boots, the lyrics tweaked to reference various long-distance national trails. *Coast to coast, star-ting out in Cumbria/Pen-nine Way/ Up the York-shire coast to Northumbria/Eleven days.* Hot water roared into the immense high-sided copper bathtub as he tried to give a name to his behaviour and was forced to accept that he was flirting. Skittishness did not come naturally to him but where was the harm? God knows, it had been a while. He examined the complimentary toiletries and with a chef's flourish added Black Pepper and Rosemary bath foam to the torrent. He climbed in, held his nose and submerged himself entirely.

More soberly, he thought back to their conversation. He was not an expert in human nature but he knew that humour could sometimes mask deep hurt, and he hoped he'd reacted appropriately and sympathetically, if only by listening. The main thing was that she had confided, that such confidences were a kind of gift and that he should probably offer up something in return. It might do him good to speak about these difficult last years to someone he liked, though he would need another drink and low lighting. The single-shirt policy only worked if he was alone, and there was nowhere in Patterdale to shop for fashion. Maybe if he ironed it and wore it with the sleeves rolled down or put his olive-green sweatshirt on top. Maybe if the restaurant was candle-lit, she wouldn't notice.

The water was starting to cool. He contemplated masturbating but worried that the high-sided copper bath might clang out like a mighty old bell, his elbow the clapper, dong, dong, dong, echoing far across the valley, bringing the farmers running across the fields as if a barn was on fire. He'd refrain just in case, but in case of what?

In Shelley

The tub was high-sided beaten copper, as large and imposing as the Ark of the Covenant, and clearly built for two. With no other body present Marnie was obliged to brace herself with knees against the sides, like a sweep trying not to tumble down a chimney, struggling to keep her phone dry while she texted back and forth to Cleo.

How's the hotel?

Ridiculous. Thank you.

When did you arrive?

Just now. Walked!

! With M?

Yes

Then, to change the subject, she typed –

It must be very expensive. What do I owe you?

Nothing. Monday out of season. Our treat.

Should she argue? She decided not, and typed –

Thank you

– and dropped the phone on to a towel. Sober now, here was that unease. She was pleased that she could put on a show but it was still a show and if, God forbid, she'd been handed the transcript of her account, the edit would require a mess of additions and deletions, corrections and clarifications. The facts were largely sound but nothing in her glib, flippant account had conveyed the pain of pretending her wedding had been the best day of her life, her marriage anything but a mistake. She had not lied except about the most important thing: how it had all felt.

And then there were the omissions. God knows, she didn't care about how Neil came across and, if anything, she'd been too kind, omitting his spite, the cutting remarks, the endless undermining. But neither had she mentioned the love she'd once had for him or the sexual spark that had been real enough, intoxicating even. No mention either of the way this had soured, so that he seemed to dislike her precisely for the things he'd once desired, her hopes of a family stalling and fading, sex disappearing along with those hopes, her sexual confidence too. Six years now.

Running parallel to the reality of her marriage was a phantom version of her twenties in which she'd been more ambitious, studied, travelled, taken risks, said yes. When she thought of her younger self, which she did too often perhaps, she felt a small part compassion but a larger part anger, as if she were banging on a thick glass wall. And yet to talk honestly about those regrets and humiliations to someone she barely knew would be awful, excruciating, like crying in a supermarket. No one wanted to be confronted with that much honesty on an afternoon's walk, but to turn it into tired anecdote was scarcely better.

And now she felt dishonest. Only one phrase was new. *I would have liked to have loved someone.* It felt conceited to declare that you had something to give and yet this was the truest thing she'd said, and also the most embarrassing. That would be her note in the margin of the transcript: 'Too much?' Now that she was sober, the remark made her gasp out loud. 'Glah,' she said, let go of the sides of the bath with her knees and slid below the water and, through the submarine depths, heard her phone vibrate again. A coda from Cleo –

Just make the most of it. Have fun! X

This seemed like an admonition. Home tomorrow, snap out of it. She rose from the water, clambered out of the high tub as if climbing a five-bar gate, dried herself and caught her reflection in the free-standing mirror, tensed some muscles and inspected herself, front and side and behind, pushing her shoulders back, pouting slightly. It was fanciful to think three days of exertion had made a difference and perhaps it was a trick of the soft evening light, but she didn't mind the way she looked, steam-cleaned, rosy like an Impressionist postcard she'd once had, a woman drying herself after a bath. If she were able to replicate this exact lighting set-up, carry it around with her, she might be all right. Or perhaps she should knock on Michael's door. *Hey, check this out.* Instead, she pulled on the dressing-gown, went to the window. Make the most of it, Cleo had said, so she looked at the lake very, very hard.

On the bed, she laid out the most glamorous of her three dresses, one arm kinked at the elbow, shoes on the floor, to gauge how she might look if surprised by a steam-roller on the way to a date. Not that this was a date. The bath had left her light-headed and she collapsed next to the empty dress and opened her laptop.

She had an hour to work but the font seemed to have changed to wingdings. Instead she looked online at the restaurant's menu and decided what she'd order. Nice wine, pleasant conversation, potted shrimp, something with a *jus*. The four-poster took on the snug quality of a childhood den built beneath the dinner table. She set her phone alarm for twenty minutes, dropping it by her head. It slipped into a crevasse in the mountain range of pillows as she fell into a deep sleep that would last for nearly three hours.

Model's Own

Taking his book, he went down early and sat on a bench by Ullswater. He knew that Marnie's room overlooked the lake so there was a certain amount of display to this literal beard-stroking, his eyes barely grazing the page. Many years ago, when he'd first arrived at school, he'd taken care to be seen reading in the staffroom, books from Natasha's syllabus, Orwell and Steinbeck held high, because surely this was what an English teacher would want to chat about in her spare time, totalitarianism and the alfalfa in *Of Mice and Men*.

But it had worked, it had made an impression, and now here he was, at it again, legs crossed, posturing with a book. Juvenile really, this ostentatious soulfulness, but it was a beautiful evening and this would be his last night in the Lakes. Soon he'd be crossing the great plateau of Westmorland alone and he'd earned this opportunity to walk the shore thoughtfully, book under his arm, hands behind his back, as if presenting a documentary on the Wars of the Roses.

At seven thirty he went indoors, the French windows open to the still bright evening. He'd cleaned his boots and folded down the cuff of his trousers, but even so he felt bumptious and loud as he clomped into the dining room. A waiter approached, all in black, slim and sleek as an eel, and it was suddenly as if he were at a checkpoint, attempting to cross the border with false papers. If Marnie were here, he'd sail through.

'Table for two, please.' The waiter's gaze flicked over his shoulder. 'She's on her way down. But before I sit, I wonder, this sounds eccentric but . . . I feel a little underdressed.'

The tie that the waiter retrieved from lost property didn't quite go with his porridge shirt. Thin and glossy it was the only Prada item he'd ever worn and his collar was too soft and frayed to hold it in place, but it was a good joke. He ordered a bottle of white wine, third on the list, to impress. The menu was in English but still required translation. *Jus*, he knew, was thin gravy and he'd had *smears* on his plates at home, but what was *gnudi*, what was the *dukkah* that came with the duck? He rehearsed jokes in his head and scratched at his beard with both hands where it met his collar, as if he were his own dog.

'Is Sir ready to order?'

Sir was what the kids called him. It was nearly eight. 'A few more minutes?' The room was dimming, the candlelight illuminating the empty chair just so. There were three other couples in the room, none of them walkers, all lost in a pre-erotic reverie, and he wondered if he should remove the tie now. Perhaps she was working or watching TV or having an early night. He might text her but didn't have her number. Should he try her door? He felt a keen sense of disappointment, like someone who has brought a cake to a party but lost the address, like someone who's been stood up on a date.

'Actually I will order if that's okay.'

The lovers watched him eat alone. First came an amuse-bouche, compliments of the chef, a tiny glass of green froth that tasted like frozen peas blended with cream and was exactly that. Salmon came in five ways, which seemed a lot, five pink piles with an unnatural plastic sheen like display sushi. If Marnie were here, he could refer back to her salmon story, perhaps that would be a way into talking about Natasha. For now, he sipped his wine and tried to balance his book against the salt and pepper, but that wouldn't work so he simply ate, chewing or rather letting the fish dissolve on his tongue like a lozenge as he stared into space, face set in the expression of someone who has tripped on a paving stone but is incorporating it into their walk. If Marnie were here, they could have ranked each of the five ways. Do it. In reverse order, foam, smoked, confit, skin tuille, mousse. Eat more slowly, he told himself, or there'll be nothing to do. He had only really expected to eat food that could be held in a folded slice of bread and it felt silly to eat so lavishly alone, a yokel at the court of the Sun King. Between bites, he laid down his fork and looked at his phone. Natasha's text. **Hopeallswell.** It was a short drive from her parents' house to Richmond on the far side of the Dales. He'd be there in four days.

His main course arrived, his third consecutive pie but deconstructed here, the shredded beef stacked in a sticky brown cylinder on the opposite side of the plate from the casing, as if the meat had argued with the pastry. There'd been a craze at school for novelty erasers in the shape of food, and that was what the carrots looked like, sculpted, perfect. The gravy came in an espresso cup, two teaspoons of meaty treacle. Lovers wanted something light before they made their way upstairs, but he could eat all this in four bites, which meant he would have to leave seven minutes between each bite if he didn't want to be in bed before nine. Perhaps he should let Natasha know he was passing. The lovers drifted off in pairs and as they cleared his plate, he began to draft a text.

All IS well. In fact I'll be near you Friday

And now Marnie clattered into the dining room and he stood sharply, knocking the table, stuffing the phone into his pocket, pressing the tie to his chest. She looked both elegant and frantic, as if rushing for the lifeboats, apologising from halfway across the room.

'I am so, so sorry.'

'It's fine.'

'I didn't feel the phone vibrate, so many fucking *cushions*.'

'Really, I don't—'

'Why didn't you come and knock?'

'I thought you might want a quiet—'

'No! That's drinking at lunchtime for you. I was wiped out!' She scraped the chair and sat, and he noticed that, although she looked wonderful, the lipstick didn't quite match the edge of her lips, as if she'd applied it while running downstairs.

'I don't mind.'

'Well, I do! It's our last night,' she said then, as if correcting herself. 'Also, I'm *starving*. What's the food like?'

'Delicious but very small portions.'

'Yes, that's what I feared.' He poured her wine and was struck by the lightness of the bottle – he must have drunk three-quarters of it himself – just as the waiter arrived with his pudding. 'Hello there,' she said, gripping his arm. 'I wonder, can you tell me, what is the *biggest* thing on the menu?'

'I'm so sorry, the kitchen's closed.'

'No! Oh, God, really?' She peered at Michael's plate.

'Chocolate seven ways,' he said, offering it to her.

'I'll need more than seven.'

'I could bring you a cheese selection?'

'Yes, please, but don't select. If you've got a wheel of some-thing, that's great, roll it in. And lots of bread, thank you, sorry, thank you,' and she drank the wine down thirstily.

'So,' he said.

'So.' She was here now but he felt the evening had escaped them, too tired and tongue-tied for skittishness, drunk but without the fun of the day. She hadn't even noticed the tie.

'So,' he said, once more. 'What's the plan for tomorrow?'

'Oh, I'm just going to hang out here, strip the breakfast bar. I might even have a massage. I mean no one's touched the small of my back since, I don't know, the London Olympics but if I *pay* someone . . . Maybe I can get a late checkout. Taxi's at five and I'll be back in London by nine. Ready-meal, TV, *ennui*.' Her cheese arrived, cold from the fridge, and they managed another half an hour of conversation but the waiter was loitering, resentful of this slow Monday, out of season. 'He is literally tapping his watch,' said Marnie, and they caved. They climbed the stairs, groaning at their shared aches and pains, then stood at their doors.

'Hey, Keats, I'm sorry about tonight,' she said.

'That's all right, Shelley.'

'I talk at you all day and then it's your turn and—'

'Really, you've not missed anything.'

'But thank you for today. It was actually fun. Not like those other hell days.'

'Careful, you'll get a taste for it.'

'I wouldn't go that far. Well. Goodnight.'

'Goodnight. And if I don't see you in the morning – goodbye.'

'Goodbye. If you're ever down in London . . .'

'Or up in York.'

'And I forgot to say, I like this by the way,' she said, stepping forward so suddenly that he stepped back into his door. She tugged at the bottom of his tie.

'Ah, this old thing? I borrowed it.'

'Not model's own? It doesn't quite match the shirt but I appreciate the effort.'

'Prada.'

'Prada! You should steal it.'

'Use it as a belt.'

'Well, it makes a real difference.' She looked at him appraisingly. 'You've got it going on. What happened? Did you wipe down your trousers with a damp cloth?'

'I think it's what the kids call a glow-up,' he said, resting his chin on the palm of his hand. She laughed and put her hand on his arm, and he thought how nice it felt to make someone laugh again.

'You see, you *can* be funny,' she said.

'You sound surprised,' he said, wrenching the tie over his head, catching his ear.

'Cleo said you were "wry".'

'Oh, God, did she?'

'Merely wry. At least it wasn't whimsical.'

'No one wants that.' He was wrapping the tie around his hand, like a boxer bandaging his knuckles. A moment passed and then he said, or found himself saying, 'It's going to be a beautiful day tomorrow. Sunny all day, no wind. And it's the highest part of the walk, eight hundred metres to Kidsty Pike but gentle, a slow, gentle climb, then around Haweswater, and you'll have walked the whole of the Lakes, west to east. Just rearrange your taxi to pick you up in town, we can easily make it there by five. You can catch the same train home.'

As he spoke she watched him, her head to one side and he felt his conviction slip. 'Well. You don't have to decide now. Just meet me in Reception if you—'

'No,' she said, 'I'd like that,' and she turned and opened her bedroom door.

Day Four:

GLENRIDDING TO SHAP

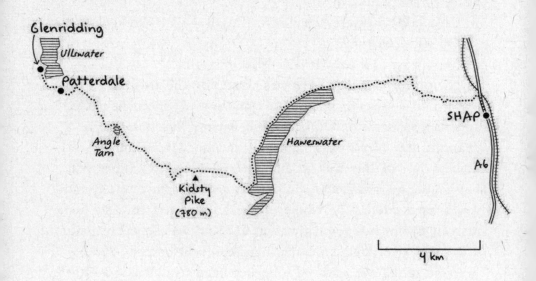

Cat/Cow

She woke up early and in a different country, Switzerland, perhaps, or the north Italian lakes. She'd never seen those places but had read novels in which characters retreat to mountain sanatoriums to recover from doomed love affairs or a hard war. The bright, gaudy turquoise of the sky gave a clarity to water that yesterday had seemed leaden and sinister, an ocean on a distant planet. Now it sparkled and you might row a boat, perhaps even swim in it, not now but soon. Perhaps she ought to stay in the hotel today, live out her sanatorium fantasies.

But she'd spent too long in rooms and the mountains looked inviting too, to the extent that this was possible. The deep aches had subsided, and she felt as if she could sprint up them, so by way of warm-up, she opened her laptop and balanced it on the bed for online yoga. The crush she'd developed on her instructor was probably the most significant relationship of the last two years. Marnie had been cynical at first, but the instructor was so perky and upbeat, so encouraging and sincere, that she'd succumbed and now laughed along with her goofy jokes and wondered how she'd smell, of lemongrass and orchids, toothpaste, a light, zinc-free deodorant. It had taken a while to overcome her nerves, but now they talked quite comfortably, both laughing at the more demanding holds.

'You're joking!' said Marnie, to the screen.

'You can do it! Three more breaths!'

'I can't!'

'Two, one. Okay, let's meet in down-dog.'

'Okay, meet you there!' There was definitely something going on yet it could never work. The yoga instructor lived in a world of floor-to-ceiling windows, expensive rugs, beeswax candles the size of a cake tin and she'd be secretly horrified by Marnie's moth-eaten Ikea rug, the Tupperware cheese tubs she used as yoga bricks, the unwashed polka-dot leggings, holed in the gusset, frayed to translucence across the buttocks. 'Breathe the love in,' she said, but at times the instructor's serenity could seem like aloofness, as if she didn't know of Marnie's existence, something that was literally true.

No, she wasn't feeling it today. Too hungry, too stiff, too distracted, too excited, she abandoned the session. Would she feel lop-sided all day, wobbling like a pub table? Never mind. She packed and limped downstairs, ate a sanatorium breakfast, rearranged her taxi then waited in Reception, the doors open to the blazing morning, bleaching the outside, like an over-exposed photograph.

Michael, when he appeared, looked hung-over and puffy, smiling with a wince. 'Morning!' she said, and they gave each other a small hug. (*This is new*, she thought, a development, the small hug, though she noted, too, that he hunched forward slightly so as not to press against her breasts, as if leaning over a fireplace.) He insisted on paying for dinner, returning the tie to the receptionist, thank you, goodbye, we'll come again, and they stepped out into the glare. In the village, the tourists were getting ready to join the queue to climb Helvellyn but she felt as if they were the true pioneers, crossing the river, then following a clear path that climbed but not dramatically, no more than the ramp at a supermarket. They walked and talked, so at ease that when they finally remembered to look back the valley seemed like an expensive wooden toy, painted blocks on green felt around a cellophane lake. How had they made it so high without noticing?

Now they began to notice, the path steepening, the sun blazing unobstructed. She'd not been abroad, not felt the sun on her skin like this for years and it was bliss but exhausting too. By mid-morning, they were rationing water, which felt melodramatic but exciting, and then another landmark as Michael sat on a boulder, took off his boots and started to unzip his trousers at the knee.

'I feel like I'm seeing things no woman should see.'

'Is it too provocative?'

'It's like those tearaway trousers that strippers wear and yet not like that at all.'

'Ta-da!' He stood in his long shorts.

'Hot pants!'

'Is it too much?'

'What happened to that guy in long trousers?'

'Oh, he's gone.' On they climbed, Marnie stealing glances at his shins, no, his calves, calves at the back. The singular of 'calves', was it 'calf' or 'calve'? Either way, they distracted her on the climb to Angle Tarn, where she and Michael rested. The lake was beautiful, a series of bays and peninsulas, even a pair of cartoon islands, and she knew there would be a reason why it looked like this rather than a simple circle but didn't ask in case he told her. Instead, they lay near the shore, silent, eyes closed, heads cricked against rucksacks to face the sun. *Another landmark*, she thought, this ease in silence, and it occurred to her how far they'd travelled in just three days. This kind of concentrated company was not without its perils, and she was still unsure what this *was*, a question that had cost her some sleep and was as unfamiliar to her as the sun on her face. For the moment it was pleasant to lie still and silent, watching the lightshow on her eyelids.

'My head hurts,' he said. 'I shouldn't drink alone.'

'Me neither. During lockdown it was a real problem. Little treat at six-oh-three on a Tuesday. All those treats.'

'Oh, me too. In the house, going insane. When I was with Nat, it made sense, eating together, watching a movie, but getting pissed on your own . . .'

'Chatting to the radio, bumping into furniture. People talk about mystery bruises, but it was either the coffee-table or the chest of drawers, so where's the mystery?'

'Do you worry about it?'

'Drinking alone? I did. But I do everything alone so . . .'

'And you don't mind?'

'The drinking? When it got out of hand, I stopped. Most Tuesdays I'm sober.'

'Very sensible.'

'You should see me alone on a Friday night.'

'If I saw you,' he said, 'you wouldn't be alone.' She kept her eyes closed.

They fell into silence, the light burning orange on her eyelids, the heat becoming sinister and radioactive. 'I'm going back with a tan,' she said, 'or burns.' Time passed, the sun like a hot hand pressing down on her face, sweat beading on her chest and forehead. She drifted into sleep, until a sudden skittering of stones startled her.

'Hm?' she mumbled. 'Are we leaving?'

'Stay asleep,' he whispered. 'I'm going for a swim.'

Now she was awake.

Wild

'Not swimming exactly,' he said, 'a dip. A plunge.'

She was sitting now. 'Don't do it!'

'It's Scandinavian. I have to get rid of this hangover. Go back to sleep.'

'But if I sleep who'll call the ambulance?' He laughed, though the thought had crossed his mind. 'Seriously, Michael, that's melted snow.' There was still a frosting of the stuff on the highest peaks, but he was already heading towards the tarn.

'I think I can do it!' he shouted, pulling his T-shirt off over his head. He'd read articles about this, the thrill, the cleansing power of the cold plunge, a liquid defibrillator for the heart, the mind, the blood, the libido. Sweating in the sun, it had seemed like a thrilling idea and the shorts were around his knees while he was still unlacing his boots, noting the way his stomach concertinaed when he bent over, adjusting it accordingly. 'You might want to avert your eyes,' he shouted, without turning, but if he tensed every muscle and kept his back to Marnie, he might be all right. Willing his shoulders broader, he piled his clothes on a boulder beneath his boots and attempted to stride purposefully over spikes of grass and sedge. At the water's gravelled shore, he dabbled his fingers in the water.

'Why are you *doing* that?' shouted Marnie, laughter in her voice. 'Do you think it might be *warm*?'

The sun was burning his shoulders but no amount of heat would make this anything other than excruciating, and even as his toes touched the water the blood was roaring in his ears, his heart rapping at his sternum in a rhythmic *bad idea bad idea bad idea*. The water was silver-tinged and viscous, like gin from an ice box, and he bent, scooped it up, dribbled it on to his neck and felt it burn, felt his bowels contract, as if they were clambering up into his ribcage, pursued by his genitals. So much for showing off. Bravado long gone, it was a perfect vignette of mid-life crisis and yet there was no way out of it now, no choice but to fall forwards into the acid bath. He could no longer feel his feet. What if they snapped off at the ankles? Behind him he could hear Marnie scrambling down the bank. Was she going to push him in? He would count to three then go before she had the chance. He exhaled, quick short breaths, one two three four five six seven . . .

'This is so stupid,' she said, and he turned and laughed. Marnie was standing beside him in black underwear, arms folded across her chest, shoulders hunched, her skin pale and mottled except for a bib of pink where she'd caught the sun. 'I can't let you die alone.' He allowed himself only a schoolboy's glance, but he thought that she looked magnificent. Instinctively he folded his arms too and attempted to tense every muscle in his body simultaneously.

'Okay. So how do we do this?' she asked.

'I suppose we just count to three and go.'

'I can't dive.'

'Just sort of fall forward, like a felled tree.'

'Head under?'

'I think so.'

'So, completely submerged?'

'Otherwise there's no point. It'll hurt but like a slap, just for a second.'

'Slaps hurt for a long time. Also, I really don't want to be slapped.'

'But then it will feel amazing, high, like a drug.'

'Couldn't we try to find some drugs?'

'This will be a natural high.'

'Or a low, a natural low.'

'Let's find out.'

'Okay.'

'Okay.'

'What is that bird? Over there, curved beak.'

'Don't change the subject, Marnie. Are you ready?'

Together, they counted, 'One . . . two . . . three!'

Neither of them moved.

'It's a curlew,' he said.

'Okay, let's go again,' she said. 'One . . . two . . . three.'

Again, neither of them moved.

'I really can't feel my toes now,' she said.

'Let's get a little further out,' he said, and they shuffled forward on stone feet until their ankles were submerged.

'Okay, let's go again. Ready?'

'One . . . two . . .'

'Count backwards.'

'D'you think that's the problem, the order of the numbers?'

'It's the only thing stopping me. Three, two, one and then we go.'

'On "go"?'

'Go on "go".'

Together they chanted – 'Three, two, one, go' – but still they remained.

'Okay, let's not count at all,' she said. 'Let's just go. Let's just go together! Seize the moment. Let's do it. Do it! Seize it!' and she took his hand. 'Are you ready? Now!'

'Now!'

'No . . . now!'

'Let's gooooooo . . . NOW!'

'Okay, this time, no excuses. We go . . . now!'

'Now!'

'Now. No, now!'

'I think we're being too nice about it,' she said, after a while. 'I think we should just—' and suddenly she tried to swing him around by his hand, twisting his wrist – 'Ow!' and he stumbled, jabbing the soles of his feet on the gravel but grabbing her other arm and pulling her towards him so that for a moment her whole body was pressed against his, her hand on his hip, laughing and shrieking. He felt iced water splash the back of his thighs, pure ice, so he lunged forward, taking her with him, his hand on her bra strap and then on her lower back, long enough to feel the softness above her hip, damp with sweat, his thigh between her legs and they stood there for a moment, braced against each other, his chin on her shoulder, like exhausted dancers. Once again, he had the sensation of being outside the moment, observing and judging and shaking his head, and wasn't it better to be only inside? How was that achieved? 'Don't fight it, Michael,' she whispered in his ear, her voice low and breathless. 'You know you want it. It'll be nice when you're in, I promise,' and he contemplated jumping in if only to staunch an erection. Another sudden lunge and he almost surrendered and let himself go, almost, almost.

But he pushed back, and now they were locked like deer with their antlers entangled. A second passed, another, with just the sound of their panting as they stood in four inches of water, foreheads touching, hands high on each other's arms. 'The art of sumo,' she said, and he felt her breath on his face, her morning coffee, glanced down and thought of the word 'bosom', which made him laugh. He looked up saw that she was watching his face, smiling and—

'Good morning!'

The voice came from the path and they looked up. Two white-haired walkers, a man and a woman, the couple who'd passed them yesterday, drunk from the pub. 'Hello there!' he shouted, letting go of Marnie.

'Wee bit cold for a dip, don't you think?' The woman, that Scottish accent.

'*I* want to,' she said, curling over and folding her arms, 'but he keeps stopping me.'

'Well, rather you than me!' laughed the man, and they walked on towards the summit, laughing good-naturedly, raising a stick goodbye while Marnie and Michael stood, suddenly self-aware like Adam and Eve.

'I think,' said Marnie, 'that we have to accept the fact that neither of us is ever going into that water.'

'I think,' he said, 'that we should get dressed and pretend this didn't happen.'

'My honeymoon again!' She smiled a little weakly, and he hobbled back to his pile. Marnie's clothes were a little further off and he glanced as she walked away, rearranging her underwear, brushing at the back of her thighs with her fingertips, the kind of gesture he would remember forever. He felt a surge of something that quickened his heart, like the water but warm, and a few minutes later they were back on the path. 'Well, that was exhilarating,' she said.

'Nothing gets the blood going,' he said, 'like the failure to do something.'

'Remember,' she said, 'that sometimes the bravest thing you can do is chicken out,' and he chose to believe that she was right.

On Not Learning Portuguese

There was rarely anything spontaneous about her spontaneity. Calculations were required; an evaluation of her underwear (black, matching, Kevlar), how the act might be taken (open-minded and appealing or deranged and desperate). In retrospect, it felt a little forced and ill-judged, and perhaps Michael felt it, too, because the rest of the morning passed uneventfully, in the sense that neither of them got undressed again.

And yet she felt sure that something was happening. Here it was, the curiosity she thought she'd lost, and she wanted to know everything about him and tell him everything, or almost everything, so much so that she'd checked the map last night for other railway lines across their path. There was a station in Kirkby Stephen, they'd be there on Wednesday, another in Northallerton, if she held out until Friday.

I'm sorry, I've got to get back for . . . There was no honest way to finish the sentence. No human would miss her, and no pet would suffer; her cactus would abide in its zombie state; she'd miss no meeting, skip no dates, disappoint no one whatsoever. There was work, of course, but she still had the weekend if she did twelve-hour days. It would be nice to use a familiar toilet but her most pressing commitment was to an open packet of feta that would need to be eaten by Thursday, and she couldn't let her decisions be swayed by half a block of brined cheese.

The fact remained: if she blinked off the face of the earth, no one in London would notice for several weeks, and it was this absence of a reason to leave that was the greatest reason to stay. Only Michael would miss her.

Was that true? Each approach he made came paired with a nervous withdrawal, like someone returning to a sputtering firework. Was her company a pleasant surprise or was she the party guest who won't go home? If only there was something humans could do, a system of mutually comprehended sounds and gestures to express thoughts and feelings. She remembered a short story she'd read as a kid, by Roald Dahl, about a machine that can pick up the screams of trees and roses when they're cut, and maybe that was what honest, direct communication would be like: the mowing of a lawn, too much to bear. In the absence of straight talk, they'd have to persevere with irony, hints and double meanings; the brush of a hand, looks and smiles and wrestling in their underwear. Jane Austen stuff.

Thankfully, there was natural beauty to distract them, waving its arms, shouting, 'Over here! Look at me!' The peaks were all around them now, outlined sharply against each other, like old-fashioned theatre flats. They walked a ridge, still a climb but not too arduous, the ground easy-going, short, tough grass like office carpet, until they were standing at a viewpoint, a rocky crown, toothed like battlements, the kind of place you might go to summon dragons.

'This is it. Kidsty Pike. Nearly eight hundred metres,' he said, breathless, 'our highest point.' Her train left Penrith at 18.23.

'Incredible,' she said, hoping this would cover it, and thought that if the Sainsbury's at Euston was closed, she'd go to the Tesco near Brockwell Park, open until midnight. 'Back there is Helvellyn,' he was saying, 'the valley where we came from.' She'd get milk and eggs and bread, toilet roll, some soup to microwave. 'That's Rampsgill Head, that's High Street, that's Place Fell . . .' And now he was naming things, pikes and gables and edges, and she allowed herself to watch him. He was not unappealing like this. Even when the content was dull, its conveyance had a kind of animation that was not unattractive, and there it was again, the double negative. If she saw it in a manuscript, she'd query it. A note in the margin: just use 'attractive'.

'You okay?' he said.

'Just, you know, taking it in. It's very attractive.'

'And it's literally all downhill from here. Well, except for the Pennines. At least you're saved that.'

'Thank *God*. So. Where now?'

'Down there to Haweswater, along the river, over the fields in time for your train. We should head off. You okay?'

'Fine. Just suddenly, I'm running for a train again.'

'Plenty of time. No need to run.' And they began the descent, the gentle slope turning into a clamber down through rocks like a derelict staircase, so that it was hard to talk, to retrieve the intimacy they'd had yesterday, time falling away until they began to skirt the shores of another lake.

'Except it's a reservoir.'

'What's the difference?'

'Artificial. There was a lake here but much smaller and there was a village, Mardale Green, which the army blew up, a pub, a church. They dug up the bodies and moved them, then flooded it all. When the water's low, you can see the remains. The village, not the bodies. A drowned village.'

'That's creepy.'

'I mean cities need water, so you've got to have reservoirs but they're not the same. No natural shores or beaches, just tidemarks. The water levels go up and down so plants don't grow in the same way.'

'Can I ask you something?'

'Of course.'

'Say if it's too personal. It is quite personal, the most personal really.'

'Okay. Go on.'

'Why didn't you have kids?'

The question landed as the path narrowed and she could no longer see his expression. 'I'm sorry if it's annoying. When people ask me, I get annoyed. There's nothing that's less someone else's business, so I've probably annoyed you too, but we started talking about it and didn't finish.'

'No, I don't mind.'

'Hang on,' she said, 'let me . . .' The path was opening up again and she ran to his side. 'Go on.'

'Okay. Well. We did want to. I don't think we ever needed to talk about it, just took it for granted, and the years went by and it didn't happen, and by the time we found out what was wrong . . . I'm going to have to talk about my sperm here, there's no way round it.'

'That's fine.'

'It seemed I had a low sperm count, plus low motility, so we tried to address that and it didn't work and we were about to go to the next stage. You know, catch one in a jar. Things got in the way. She needed a break, time apart, to think. And that's where we are. Or were. She moved out eighteen months ago now.'

'And how do you feel about it?'

'Not being a father?'

'So far.'

'So far. I don't know. I'm pretty sad, if I'm honest, but it's tangled up with sadness about the marriage going wrong and other things and it's, well, it's a tangle.'

'A tangle. I understand. I'm sorry.'

'It's okay.'

'Do you get annoyed, when people ask?'

He thought for a moment. 'I think what annoys me more is pity. And caution. You sense this embarrassment with parents. You know, "Don't mention the kids, hide them in the cupboard", like they're expecting you to burst into tears. Either that or they're all over them. I mean, I love Cleo—'

'I love her too but—'

'You know what I mean.'

'I do. I get that all the time, or I used to, when I used to see my friends and their babies, the way they'd look at me, like "Sorry about this, but isn't she gorgeous?" Little pinched, rueful smiles. "You can hold her but you mustn't abduct her."'

'And I understand the dilemma, they want to celebrate what they've got—'

'They're only being sensitive.'

'But the sensitivity is insensitive.'

'You don't want it to be taboo.'

'But that doesn't mean you want to talk about it either.'

'And it makes it hard. For everyone.'

'It does,' he said. 'It does.' She was talking too much and resolved to listen but the next thing he said was 'How do you feel about it?'

'Being child-free?'

'So far.'

'Well, I'm thirty-eight, so I suppose if I'm quick . . . But I don't know. There's the obvious problem, but even if I was dating, a single woman in her late thirties must be in want of a child. I'm just a giant walking red flag.'

'I'm sure that needn't always be the case.'

'You don't think so? I could see the fear in Conrad's eyes,

revving his engine. Can you rev an electric car? Anyway, you'd have to have the conversation, wouldn't you? It's hard to keep it light with that in the air, and there's always this assumption . . .' She stopped for a moment, took a breath. 'Sometimes I feel sad, sometimes I feel I ought to be sadder. I wanted it, still do sometimes, but it's not *all* I want. I mean there are definitely – stupid word – triggers and I'll feel this . . . surge of, not regret exactly, just something here, a squeeze,' and she placed one hand at the top of her chest. 'But it's an ache, not a pain, and I don't stare into playgrounds, I don't fondle baby shoes, I just wonder about it. Sometimes you'll see someone with their kid and there'll be some little gesture, a hand on a face, a moment of connection and I think, Well, I'd have liked that, it must feel nice, shame that probably won't happen now. But then I see some little brat screaming on the bus and I think, Well, maybe not. Maybe I'm good.'

He was silent for a moment. 'I always liked the idea of carrying a kid on my shoulders. I know that sounds strange . . .'

'No, I understand.'

'. . . but the way they sit up there, the fit, like a saddle. Just always seemed comfortable.'

'Shall *I* get on to your shoulders, Michael?'

'Maybe later.'

'I don't mean to be facetious . . .'

'It's fine.'

'. . . but I don't feel simply sad. I'm fucking angry too, that I wasted so much time on the wrong person. Soon as we got married, he did everything he could to avoid it, everything. What was *that* about? Or when friends used to say or imply that they were *jealous*, lucky you, all that freedom, all that sleep, that kind of thing? "You can have a lie-in, Marnie, you can be hung-over all the time, you can smoke crack, no one gives a fuck." It's true I do have time and freedom and I love it, sometimes. But the notion that I should be "making the most of it", travelling the world or out every night, there's a kind of tyranny in that too, that life has to be *full*, like your life's a hole that you have to keep filling, a leaky bucket, and not just fulfilled but *seen* to be fulfilled. "You don't have kids, why can't you speak Portuguese?" Do I have to have hobbies and projects and lovers? Do I have to excel? Can't I just be happy, or unhappy, just mess about and read and waste time and be unfulfilled by myself?'

'You could take up hiking,' he said.

'Maybe that's the answer. Hiking and Portuguese.' They walked on a little. 'I used to have more friends. And I liked them a lot and I think they liked me.'

'I'm sure they did.'

'Maybe, but then they all went off and got these very particular lives, my male friends too, and I started to feel as if I was the one who was alone. Like in a gang, you've got the clever one, the wild one, the funny one, and the one who's alone, just that, only that. The one without. No one wants to be defined by the thing you don't have, whether it's a kid or a partner, and people are *obsessed*, especially people in a relationship. You'll be out somewhere and people you've barely met will ask you, "Are you seeing someone? Do you want to? Are you on dating apps, sex apps?" Oh, they love asking *that*, married men especially, living vicariously. "Do you have sex with strangers? Pass the olives." It's very . . . intrusive. Part of me understands, you're getting to know someone and it's either that or "What do you do for a living?" But it does get . . . exhausting.'

'Of course, you know the solution.'

'Never, ever go outside. Yes, I've been trying it but that doesn't work either. It's a cycle, isn't it, a trap? You're not with someone, so best not be with anyone.'

'You get lonely.'

'There it is. The forbidden word, you get lonely,' she said and thought, *My God, I've said it out loud.*

'I know that feeling,' he said, 'quite well,' and they walked on.

She worried that she had asked him the question and answered it herself so she resolved to stay quiet so that he might speak. Instead, he made bland remarks about the view, birds, trees, polite but artificially bright, as if they'd had an argument rather than whatever that had been. When the silence got too much, she said, 'I've got that last-day-of-the-holiday feeling. You're still away but you might as well be at home.'

'I know what you mean.' The lake, too, was coming to an end, squared off by a brutish grey barrier, like the wall of a prison, conifers peering over the top. 'Want to see something interesting?'

'I worry when you say that, because it's often quite dull.'

'This,' he said, pointing to the wall, 'is the world's very first hollow concrete buttress dam.'

'I present to the jury exhibit A.'

'Look at it! It's magnificent.'

'It's certainly a lot of concrete.'

'You're like my year-tens. You can be very cruel.'

'I'm sorry. You're right, it's the best – again?'

'Hollow concrete buttress . . .'

'Concrete buttress dam in the world.' Another silence, then she said, 'Of course, if we'd had kids, we probably wouldn't get to see things like this.'

There was a moment before he laughed. 'Do you want to take a photograph of it?' he said.

'No, a photo won't get the magic. Unless . . .' She was

reaching for her phone and it occurred to her how intimate, how significant it was, to take someone's photograph for the first time and add them to your library, like a book that you've read or at least started reading. Why else use the word 'library'? The morning embrace, the nude wrestling, now the photograph. The order was off but the point remained: she wanted to see his face when he wasn't around. 'Stay there. Smile.'

'But if I stand here you won't get the dam.'

'Look this way.' She took the photo. 'And now . . .' She stood next to him, fumbling with the screen, his arm across her shoulders as stiff as a milkmaid's yoke, the camera too close, the image too fish-eyed to flatter either of them but too late to abandon now. 'Okay. Say, I don't know . . . "buttress".'

'Buttress.'

They peered at the photograph. 'Well, at least we've got clothes on. Shall I delete that now or send it to you to delete?'

'I'm not deleting it,' he said. 'That's my screensaver.'

'Except I don't have your number.'

They exchanged numbers. 'Is there a landline?' he asked.

'Yes, West Dulwich two five two. Why d'you need my landline, Nana?'

'What's wrong with landlines?'

'So you can send me a telegram?'

'Oh, what – so you're too cool and metropolitan to use a landline?'

They walked on. A village, a river, one field, then another, the Lakes long gone now, the change in landscape so abrupt that it was like stepping from the kitchen to the living room. Their destination, the town of Shap, was in sight when he said, 'Tomorrow's limestone country. A completely different terrain, easier-going, Westmorland then the Eden Valley. It's going to be really lovely, the day after too, crossing into the Dales, much softer and greener.'

'Go on.'

'Well, if you can bear it, you could call your taxi-driver, miss this train and get one in Kirkby Stephen or even Northallerton. A day, a couple of days more. Only if you want to. Give it some thought,' he said.

Part Three

THE DALES

—

*Also men fall into two classes – those who forget views
and those who remember them, even in small rooms*

E. M. Forster, *A Room with a View*

The Black Dog

Almost immediately he felt as if he'd made a mistake.

With no expectation, he had spent three days in the company of a nice new human being and now he was going to ruin it by wanting more. Like one last drink or coffee after dinner, like missing the last bus, a good time was going to be ruined by wild excess. Almost as soon as she cancelled her taxi, the walk had become dull and wearying, the conversation self-conscious and stilted and now, in the afternoon gloom of the terrible pub, that sense of folly deepened. The Black Dog was the name Churchill gave to his depression and perhaps this was where he'd got the idea: the immense TV showing Australian horse-racing, the smell of bleach, the urinals visible from the bar. 'Perfectly okay,' the online reviews had raved, 'but not some-where to linger.' Was there an extra spare room? Of course, because everyone else was at the two nice pubs or the B&B on the main street. Standing at the bar, waiting for the keys, he felt as if he was handing himself in at a police station.

'Last night was the honeymoon,' whispered Marnie. 'This is the messy divorce.'

On his own, this would have been fine but even a masochist wants a clean towel, and in company it was excruciating. 'You might still catch your train,' he said.

'No, I like it. I like the sound the carpet makes,' and she

tapped her foot and hummed 'Hotel California' as the bartender returned, slapping the keys on to the bar like a wager. Was there Wi-Fi? There was not. Michael took room three and gave Marnie room one in the hope this might be the best.

They climbed the stairs. 'Do you think it's haunted?'

'The ghosts of hygiene inspectors.'

'I can't believe the rooms don't have a theme.'

'Plagues of Egypt.'

'Horsemen of the Apocalypse.'

'Fungal infections. I'm in Impetigo, you've got Ringworm.'

But he wondered if her sense of humour would survive the night. An overhead bulb, wood-patterned vinyl flooring, a greasy black duvet, a view of the railway line. 'Room one oh one,' she said.

'Shall we do a runner?' he whispered, aware of the thinness of the walls.

'It's fine. There's a desk and chair, I can work. Just as long as your room isn't sumptuous.'

It was not sumptuous. Alone again, he sat heavily on the single bed, its mattress made from torn cardboard sewn into a sack. To kill time, he called his parents. Mum was helping out at church and he spoke to Dad, a conversation that would allow him to unpack at the same time.

'. . . up over Grisedale to Patterdale.'

'Know it well.'

'Then up past Angle Tarn to Kidsty Pike.'

'There's a nicer way.'

'But that's the way I did it, so.'

And on it went, his father telling him all the ways in which he might have done it better until Michael said, 'Then it'll be Richmond and over the Moors.'

'Richmond's near Natasha, yes?'

And only now did Michael pay attention. 'Well. Quite near.'

'Will you see her?'

'I don't know, Dad. She's been in touch but probably not.'

'She's been in touch?'

'Just to say hello.'

'To see you?'

'It's best if we don't.'

'Well. If you do—'

'There's no reason to.'

'If you do, send our love.'

There was a silence. He'd heard the change in his father's voice, an uncharacteristic softness that he might have responded to. 'I will if I see her,' he said briskly. 'I've got to go.'

'And you're on your own.'

Too much trouble to explain, too confusing. 'I am,' said Michael.

'And you're all right on your own.' It was not a question, and he didn't want any answer except 'I am. I like it. Tell Mum I called.'

'Righto.'

Michael hung up while the receiver was still pressed to his father's ear. Every call was like this, a role-played recreation of the frustrations of his youth, the instructions and corrections, the inability to discuss anything in a direct way. He hoped he'd not inherited his father's reticence. If he'd had his own son, he would have endeavoured to be different.

But he thought back to that afternoon's conversation, the way he'd resorted to silence and platitude when he might, for instance, have said what it was like to want children of your own and to teach, to be presented with this parade of kids at their best and worst, year after year, their parents too, complacent, incompetent or absent, taking it all for granted, how he wanted to shake them and say, *Look, look what you've got!* He didn't trust himself to express any of this out loud but surely there had to be a mode of conversation between therapy and trivia. He'd found it in the past, with Natasha.

There she is. As if he'd summoned up a spectre, the room began to vibrate, the key rattling in the wardrobe door, the light-bulb swinging as the southbound express train tore by. He waited for it to pass, then checked his phone. No texts, no further messages but he mustn't think about that, must wrench himself back into the moment, try to be present with someone in the here and now, though ideally not here, and not quite now.

The Cannibal in the Wardrobe

Almost immediately she felt as if she'd made a mistake.

She'd been greedy, overreached herself and now here was a room far more desolate than the one awaiting her in London. She felt vibrations, heard the growing roar and the clang of rails and, through her grimy uPVC window, watched as her train hammered past, the 18.23 to Euston, carriage H, seat 23, so close that if she opened her window she might leap on to the roof, clamber between the carriages, wrench open the door and take her place. But the window didn't open and so she returned to work, bringing order and consistency to an orgy in a bungalow at the Beverly Hills Hotel. There were an improbable number of 'beautiful' penises, even for a suite, breasts so relentlessly 'high' that they were practically shoulders. The book was fantasy, of course, and a normal body would have been as out of place there as a colliery brass band, but even so she wondered if it was possible to eroticise the unremarkable bodies of the no-longer-young, mottled and veined, past a prime they'd never known they'd had. Inevitably she thought of her own scene by the tarn, how much she'd liked the way he'd looked, the way he'd looked at her. It was embarrassing but only partly so, and she wondered, What if we'd stayed a second night in that nice hotel?

But nothing sensual or romantic had ever happened in the

Black Dog, could ever happen, and now she was saddled with the cost of another train ticket. Back to work. She wondered about the phrase 'lavish bungalow'. She was sure that Beverly Hills had bungalows, but so did her aunty Pat. She looked up a synonym for 'girth', sighed and closed the lid.

Melancholy was creeping in, the kind of distilled, high-grade sadness found under a bus shelter in a rainy seaside town. How could she shake it off? A shower would leave her feeling dirty, and while online yoga might restore balance, she was wary of putting her face near the floor. What was Michael doing? As if in answer, she heard his door open, hurling herself across the room so swiftly that she had to wait a beat before answering the knock.

'I don't want to interrupt the party,' said Michael, 'but do you—'

'Yes!' she shouted, never more grateful. 'Yes! Yes, please,' and she left without bothering to change out of her boots.

They walked back towards the main street, pleased to be outside again, talking in normal voices. 'Sorry about this.'

'Oh, it's fine,' she said. 'It's the first *Psycho*-themed hotel I've stayed in, that's all. The bed's okay, I just feel like I'm being watched through a peephole by someone masturbating in the wardrobe. A cannibal probably.'

'That's why I thought we should eat out.'

'I agree. I don't want to find a hank of someone's hair in a pie.'

'Shepherd's pie!' he said, and he looked so pleased with himself.

'Very good,' she said.

They found a chippy, bright and lively, with condensation on the windows and Formica tables. Michael said it was 'notorious with hikers', though Marnie wondered if 'notorious' was the right word. Cagoules and heavy boots, and trekking poles by the door, like a ski lodge. They slid into a red vinyl booth, finally facing each other, and she was reminded of the kind of cheap place teenagers go on first dates, struggling to spin the single course out past thirty minutes. Nick's Big Easy Diner on Bromley High Street with Sean Hayward in 1998. A more innocent time, though this seemed innocent too. While Michael looked at the menu, Marnie looked around. She had long given up hope of encountering anyone young or cool on the journey. The website designers, the cinematographers and war reporters were all somewhere other than in this chippy on a midweek night. Here were the retirees determined to stay active, old school pals meeting up in middle age, long-married couples bickering over itineraries.

'Too late for the Early-bird Special,' said Michael.

'Too young to die.'

'Hm?'

'I was just thinking this is the worst place in England to score MDMA.'

'But the best place for scampi and a buttered roll.'

'All those waterproofs. If the sprinklers go off, no one will even notice.'

'D'you realise we're probably the coolest people in the room?'

'"We"?'

'Is this the landline thing again?'

'But you're right, there's a definite buzz.'

'They're excited about the switch to limestone pavement in the morning.'

'Hang on, it's paved?'

'It's a geological term, natural landform, distinctive, exposed white slabs—'

'Coolest person in the room, you say?'

'Actually, these guys are cooler,' and he nodded towards an elderly couple, dapper and spry, the man in knitted tie and tweed jacket, the woman in neat cardigan and a pinafore dress, laughing and kissing as they waited to be seated. 'They look like fun.'

'Why do old people kiss like that?' she said. 'Like goldfish, over-puckering,' and she demonstrated. 'Old people and kids with puppies.'

'I think it's nice.'

'Ah, do you, Michael, do you? It's fine, but when I'm old I'm going to kiss normally. None of this pouty face-pulling, like they're sucking at a straw.'

'By the way, you may have noticed—'

'Are you changing the subject?'

'Yes. On top of the socks, I only brought one shirt.'

'I *did* notice that.'

'I apologise. I thought, well, I'm alone, two hours a night, nine nights, eighteen hours, no one's going to see me.'

'You don't have to justify your low standards to me, Michael.'

'It's not low standards, I just thought I'd be invisible.'

'It's fine, just stay over there.'

'It's not even a nice shirt.'

'I like it – it really pops. I have a tea-towel in that fabric.'

'Absorbency, it's what you need in a shirt. And if you look closely . . .' he tugged at the shoulder '. . . it's got these fine black criss-cross lines on it.'

'Detailing! A graph-paper shirt. Even your clothes are like homework.'

'It allows me to chart the course of the evening.'

'Where are we right now?'

'It's an exponential curve.'

'But going up or down?'

'We'll find out. If you want to sit in another booth . . .'

'Too late. Look out,' and her eyes flicked to the elderly couple, the kissers, approaching now. 'Don't let them talk us into any perverted mind-games.'

'Mind if we . . . ?' said the man.

'Please, do,' said Michael and they shuffled dutifully down the bench. After a moment, the lady, small and stylish, white-haired and bright-eyed, put her hand on Michael's arm. 'It's nice to see you both with your clothes on,' she said, in an Edinburgh accent, and they began to laugh.

'Oh, God, it was you!' said Marnie.

'Sorry about that,' said Michael.

'Oh, not at all. We found it most amusing.'

'Did you make it into the water?' said the man.

'I wanted to,' said Michael. 'She stopped me.'

'Oh, is that right?' said Marnie.

'We chickened out, I'm afraid.'

'Aye, very wise,' said the man. 'I think it would have killed you.'

'Almost certainly.'

'Are you walking all the way across?' said the woman.

'He is,' said Marnie. 'I'm not.'

'Well, we'll have to race you,' said the man. 'How many days?'

And Michael told them. They ordered and then lapsed into the old familiar conversation, high-level versus low-level, weather forecasts, the state of their feet, the genteel boastfulness of *How far are you going?* It was both dull and comforting, like the sound of a radio through a wall. The food arrived, delicious, they agreed, and Marnie accepted that she would not talk to Michael after all. Instead, she sat quietly and took him in, charming and plausibly interested in things that were surely of interest to no one, so that giving him up for the night felt generous, like lending an umbrella that you wanted for yourself. She thought, too, of the last time the four of them had been together, his leg between hers, his hand on her hip. Oh, he was the nice young man *now* but what if she lifted her foot, put it between his legs, and pressed there, watching his face? But that wouldn't work with her boots on and so, with an effort, she tuned in. They were talking about the best sock/boot combination, and she thought, *Okay, well, that's enough of that.*

'So, what are your names?'

They were Brian and Barbara from Morningside and they were meeting their two sons and their daughter-in-law tomorrow to walk for a day or two. They'd been married for forty-two years, for as long as Michael had been alive! 'Are you from around here?' asked Brian.

'I live in York, Marnie's up in London. "Up" or "down"?'

'Seems like "down" to me,' said Marnie.

'Ah, London,' said Barbara, darkly. 'Does that make this difficult?'

'Sorry, what?'

'The long-distance relationship.'

'We're just friends,' said Michael.

'It looked a little more than that to me,' said Barbara, twinkling.

'But have you seen the way she eats her fish?' said Michael, changing the subject and they all three teased her for a while. She didn't mind, let them have their fun, but the generosity was gone. She wanted Michael back, and she felt the same petulant impatience she'd known as a small child at the shops when her mum would stop to chat to dull old people.

Marnie's phone bleeped and, in revenge, she allowed herself to pick it up. A text read, Hey. You should be back in London by now. Hope it got better. I feel bad about leaving. Want to go for a drink and I'll explain? No walking required! Maybe this weekend? Conrad xxx

I feel bad. Well, that was something. She grinned, half wanting Michael to notice, and sure enough, 'What's that?'

'Oh, just a little message,' and she flashed it at Michael, a subliminal glimpse.

'A date?'

'Uh-huh.' She was aware that Brian and Barbara were watching them.

'Well. There you go. Are you going to say yes?'

'Not now. I'm still annoyed. Got to toy with him a little first. Cat with a mouse. Let the games commence!'

'Well, I'm pleased,' said Michael and soon after that, they said their goodbyes and headed out, the village in darkness now, the road sinister.

'We could go on to the pub for a drink,' she said, but the moment had passed. Cars drove past. After a while, she said, 'Nothing happened, by the way. With Conrad.'

'Maybe that's what he wants to talk to you about.'

'Wouldn't have thought so.'

'Well, I think you should.'

'Go for it?' She shrugged. Outside the Black Dog, she hesitated once again, dreading her room, but he had closed down. 'I should go,' she said. 'I've got that guy waiting in the wardrobe . . .'

'Of course. Big day tomorrow. A twenty-miler!'

'And you've still got to zip your booty shorts back together.'

'That's true.' He insisted on paying for her room in advance, then said he'd have one more drink, which he carried to a small table, and she left him to sit in the light of the big TV, watching the snooker alone.

Day Five:

SHAP TO KIRKBY STEPHEN

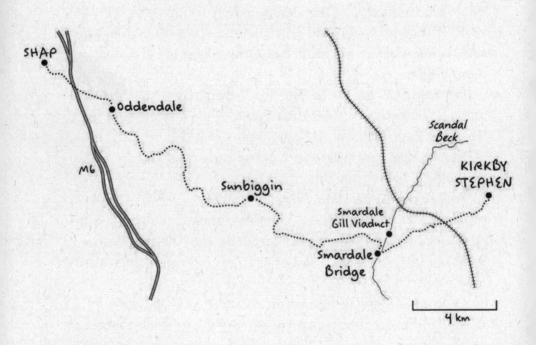

Random Shuffle

They fled early, leaving their keys on the bar towel and sneaking away like truants. The Black Dog's full English sounded sinister so they bought snacks, fruit and juice from the local shop and set off through back-streets to the railway bridge, pausing to watch the London train thundering beneath them.

'I promise it will be worth your while,' said Michael.

'I'm not worried.' She took the carton of orange juice and rotated her palm on the plastic spout.

'Did you just wipe the top with your hand?'

She laughed, surprised. 'I did!'

'Why?'

'I don't know, I think there's just something about being with you that makes me feel like I'm on a school trip. Also, I don't want your lurgy.'

'"Lurgy".'

'It's science, Michael, look it up.'

'Oh, so the palm of your hand's cleaner than my mouth?'

'It was till I got your lurgy all over it. Do kids still say "lurgy"?'

'Er, no. You could have just sky-ed it.'

'What's sky-ing it?'

'Pouring it into your mouth without touching. So it doesn't get lipsed-up.'

'That's impossible.'

'Try it.'

'All right, I'm going to sky it, so it doesn't get *lipsed-up*.'

'Go on.'

'Here goes.' She rolled her shoulders, licked her lips, raised the carton and, for a moment, the sky-ing went well, the juice arcing into her mouth until she began to laugh at her own success, spattering the tarmac, wiping her chin with the back of her hand.

The railway line, then the motorway, six lanes of rush-hour traffic. In the months following the assault, he'd found himself prone to feelings of panic around busy roads, a conviction that something terrible was about to happen. At its worst, absurdly, he'd been unable to ride a bicycle because he no longer believed that the forward momentum would be enough to keep him upright. Why wouldn't he be slammed into the pavement? These feelings were less frequent now but he felt an echo of it over the motorway, the nausea, the tightening between the shoulders, as if concrete was inadequate. It was that feeling of being too far from shore, the foot searching for the sand, and he pushed the sensation down. He definitely had the blues this morning – Nat's phrase – and they had a long day ahead of them, but they were soon in the wild again, crossing the moorland with a new set of mountains ahead, improbably distant, the Pennines.

'What's that?' she said.

Lines of white rock were breaking through the scrubby grass, like exposed vertebra. '*That* is limestone pavement! You see, the way it erodes into squares, these lines, like—'

'Pavement. Yes, I see.'

They looked, and after a while, he said, 'D'you think maybe I oversold it?'

She laughed and he felt hopeful again. 'No, it's very nice. Like a rockery.'

'Exactly. Nature's rockery.' He worried that she regretted staying on. The landscape was, to his eye, lovely but less varied than the Lakes, and seven hours was a long time to talk to anyone, even someone he liked very much.

'You can listen to a podcast, if you like.'

'No, I'm good.'

'Or music. It's a long way to go, I won't mind.'

She thought for a moment. 'I have an idea,' she said. 'Do you have headphones, wireless headphones?' He did. 'And your phone?'

For a moment he felt nervous (**Hopeallswell**), then turned his back so that she could retrieve it from his rucksack.

'Why do you keep it in here?'

'So it's out of reach.'

'But then how do you look at it?'

'It's not a problem.'

'Are you *very* online, Michael?'

'What do you think, Marnie?'

'I don't know. Maybe you're big on the dark web. Never mind. Now. What's the PIN? I'm not going to look at your sexts, I promise.'

'1981.'

'The year you were born? Really?'

'Plus one.'

'Ingenious. Okay, here's what we're going to do. We're going to listen to each other's music, all the songs on shuffle, and I'm going to hold on to your phone and you're going to have mine, so no skipping, no censoring. Just the real you.' She held out one of her earbuds, which he took and glanced at briefly. 'Are you worried about my lurgy?'

'I'm more worried about mine.'

'I don't care, look . . .' She made a show of screwing his bud deep into her ear and he wondered if this was a kind of flirting too. 'There. Now. Let's start. You first. Pick me a good one. At random.'

He looked at the screen of her phone. Music. Songs. Shuffle. Play. Female voices, talking to all the girls on the block.

'Black Magic' by Little Mix (2015)

Michael grimaced. 'Really?'

'You can't take your earphones out!'

'But the song of the skylark!'

'This is a classic pop song – you must know it.'

'From school discos. It's not in my collection.'

'But don't you want to know what it is that makes the boys want more?'

'Is it some sort of secret potion?'

'It is! It is. Like in *A Midsummer Night's Dream*.'

'But if the potion is the only reason they're in love—'

'You're worried it's not real love? Because it's not based on chat?'

'I'd certainly be uncomfortable in a relationship—'

'—with one of Little Mix—'

'—with anyone, if it was based on deception.'

'Maybe that's the subtext . . .'

'Subtext.'

'Ssh! I love this bit, when the song fades out and the singer does all these runs and high notes,' and here she sang a little example. 'Are you nervous, in case you can't follow that?'

'I'm not embarrassed by anything in my collection.'

'I'll be the judge of that,' she said. 'Let's spin the wheel,' and Marnie pressed play. Strumming guitars, a melody, the sound of flutes . . .

'El Condor Pasa (If I Could)' by Simon & Garfunkel (1970)

'Well, this is instantly depressing.'

'It's not my favourite of their songs,' he said.

'A sparrow or a snail. It's a tough one, isn't it? I mean hammer, nail, you're going to be the hammer.'

'I suppose they mean is it better to be passive or aggressive.'

'Why not both?'

'Much better. I haven't heard this song for twenty years. I mean it's on there, but I don't remember listening to it. School assemblies, that's where we heard it. One of the teachers had Simon and Garfunkel's *Greatest Hits* and every day we'd leave the hall to one of the songs. Nine-year-olds filing out to "Bridge Over Troubled Water".'

'Is there going to be a lot of classic rock, Michael?'

'There is a little bit. I'm sorry.'

'No, I like it. It's very short, isn't it? I need to rescue this party. Press play.'

Silence. They frowned, straining to hear.

'What is this?' he whispered.

'Don't know. Turn it up.' And now a noise like the roar of a waterfall. 'Oh, I know what this is,' she said. 'This is my brown noise.'

'What's that?'

'It's like white noise but browner. It helps me sleep sometimes.'

'It's really disturbing.'

'I know! I like this bit . . . here it comes . . .'

'How can you sleep to this? It's like the end of the world.'

'I find it comforting. But I think you can skip the rest.'

'You said no skipping.'

'Fine, but it is eight hours long!'

'Okay, just one skip.'

'Do you think I should take it off my Big Party Playlist?'

'I think you should never listen to it again.' He tapped fast forward and now they heard the strum of an electric guitar.

'Don't Speak' by No Doubt (1996)

'Oh, God,' she said, 'this song . . .'

'It's highs and lows, isn't it, your collection?'

'If I start to cry here—'

'Light and shade, it's a rollercoaster.'

'I'm serious. This was my first break-up song, year ten, Sean Hayward. I listened to it on a loop and we'd only gone out once. Nick's Big Easy Diner.'

'Big Nick's Easy Diner.'

'Easy Nick's Big Diner. Except there was nothing easy about it.'

'What did you have?'

'Sean had sticky ribs and a baked potato. I had the jumbo shrimp cocktail, because I wanted to impress.'

'Seafood.'

'I know, quite bold in landlocked Bromley. Then we went to see *Deep Impact*. I was having all these fantasies about me and Sean Hayward surviving a tidal wave together and we walked out and he dumped me.'

'I'm sorry.'

''S okay.'

'Did you really feel like you were losing a best friend?'

'Like the song. I thought I was *dying*. Of course, everyone else thought it was really funny but when you're fourteen, my God, that stuff. Didn't you have that?'

'Paula Mattis. But that was later, seventeen. Still, heart-breaking.'

'If only we'd had some kind of magic potion.'

'Exactly.'

'A break-up at that age, it has a kind of quality to it, like you've learnt it from a song. Course you'd die rather than admit it and it *is* agony but it's also an impression of agony. Your life's over but, you know, give it a couple of weeks. I liked the innocence of that. With Neil, it was mainly about paperwork and money and the shame of telling people. Not heartbreak, shame. Was it like that for you?'

'No. No, that was heartbreak.'

'Was it? Oh. I'm sorry.'

'I like this guitar solo.'

'You're changing the subject.'

'Yep.'

'Fair enough. If you want to tell me not to speak—'

'Don't speak! No, you can speak.'

'The song's got quiet but don't be fooled, it's going to get loud again.'

'Do you think when he hears this song, what'sisname—'

'Sean Hayward?'

'—on the radio or through an open window, he stops. Looks up. Thinks . . .' Michael rubbed his chin, looked skywards '. . . Where *are* you, Marnie Walsh?'

She laughed. 'Absolutely one hundred per cent *no*.'

'I bet he does. I bet he thinks you were real good.'

'Okay, your turn. I hope this lightens the mood.'

'Pull Up To The Bumper' by Grace Jones (1981)

'Mr Bradshaw, you dark horse. I had you down as sea shanties.'

'I love this. Definitely one of my top five songs about driving.'

'Quite bad driving.'

'There's no justification for getting that close, even in traffic.'

'Though, if you read between the lines, it's not really about driving.'

'No?'

'It's about *parking*.'

'It's *the* parking song.'

'Reversing around a corner.'

'It's the big shop car-park song.'

'Exactly. Even so, I'm surprised to find it on here.'

'Actually, I think it's Natasha's.'

'It's not going to make you cry, is it? Because this is a really weird song to cry to.'

'No, it's on a playlist called Sunday Afternoon Barbecue Vibes or something.'

'Yes, that's very much what Grace Jones was going for, geography teacher's back garden, bank-holiday Monday.'

They walked a little further.

'We don't *have* to use this as a catalyst to talk about sex if you don't want to.'

'Good, because my memory's not that great.' They walked on.

'But it's been a while?' she said.

'Yes.'

'Yeah, me too.'

'How long?'

'You say first.'

'No, you go.'

'Okay,' she said, 'on three we'll hold up fingers.'

'Okay. One . . . two . . . three and—'

Michael held up two fingers, Marnie four.

'Only two?' she said. 'You nympho!'

'Out of control.'

'I really miss it.'

'Christ, me too.' They walked a little further.

'But tell me – what are you like as a *driver*, Michael?'

'Is it time for a new song?'

'I mean do you keep two cars' distance or . . . ?'

'I think it's very hard to assess yourself.'

'But if you had to.'

'I think people I've driven with would say I'm responsive to the road, but not *too* cautious.'

'Hm. Feel a bit queasy now. Put the brown noise back on.'

'It's fading out. Shall we have something else?'

'Okay. This one's mine. Let's see. Spin the wheel!'

'No Limit' by 2 Unlimited (1993)

'Oh, God, no!' she shouted. 'Turn it off!'

'I'm sorry, I'm afraid I can't, the rules.'

'This isn't even mine! Seriously, Michael, turn it off.'

'I like it. I think it's catchy.'

She made a grab for the phone. 'It doesn't count!'

'It's got a strong beat.'

'Look, I'm taking my earpiece out. I refuse to listen.'

'It's on your phone!'

'It's Neil's! It's not even mine. It's Neil's!'

He immediately pressed stop and they walked on, registering their surroundings once again, the great expanse of moorland, not silence but birdsong, the crunch of their boots.

'Sorry,' she said. 'Slight overreaction there. I thought I'd got rid of all his shitty music. I sat there and went through and purged it all but that one must have snuck through. Sneaked? Snuck.'

'Is that what he liked?'

'Not even good techno or house, just shitty poppy stuff, hyperactive kids' music. God, he had terrible taste. Ask him his favourite lyric, he'd say it's probably "Techno, techno, techno." If he'd had his way, first dance at our wedding would have been "Pump Up The Jam".' Michael laughed and she managed to smile. 'Sorry. Can you do me a favour? Can you delete it?'

'Okay.' He stopped for a moment, scrolled and swiped it from the library. 'There. All gone. Do you think you should have another go?'

'If you don't mind,' she said, and he pressed play again. A moment, and then a piano playing the chords to a Christmas song.

'Joni. That's better.'

'I know this song.'

'Bit of a cliché, having "Blue" on there.'

'I like it.'

'Course you do. It's classic rock.'

'I like the bit where she shouts, "Techno, techno, techno,"' he said, and they walked for the rest of the song, listening.

'Here Comes the Sun' by The Beatles (1969)

'I *knew* it,' she said, 'I knew there'd be Beatles.'

'Everyone likes the Beatles.'

'Men more than women, I think.'

'Is that true?'

'The Beatles and George Orwell and *The Shawshank Redemption*.'

'I do like all of those things.'

'And that's fine. It's a kind of fantasy, isn't it? Being in a band, being one of the four basic personality types. You're all John or George or Paul or Ringo. It's music, but also this dream of male friendship.'

'Maybe.'

'Do you have friends like that?'

He thought a moment. 'Not really. Or I used to. Less so now.'

'You broke up the band.'

'Not formally, just more . . .' He paused for a moment, making a decision. 'I don't know if Cleo told you. I had this . . . well, I can't really call it a fight. I got beaten-up, really badly, in the street.'

'She said you'd been in hospital.'

'I was. I was for a while. I don't want to go into it but when I came out I was a bit . . . shaky. Not just physically, but nervous, around people, crowds, the kids at school. I still get it a bit. Not this second—'

'Well, that's good to know.'

'—but it comes and goes. The point is I had these mates, male friends, some from work, and we used to play football every week, a kick-about, middle-aged men laughing at each other, and when I was all better, I went back. And everyone was so *nice*. "Are you okay? You look well." And there was no tackling and no shouting and all these pats on the back every time I touched the ball, well done, mate, well done, and it was quite touching really, everyone being so thoughtful. But it didn't feel right. So I stopped going.'

'You were upset because they weren't meaner.'

'No, it was just . . .' He hesitated here because there was another scene, immediately after that match, where he'd sat in the car park, hands over his face, shoulders shaking, without quite knowing why. 'It wasn't the same.'

'Might you go back?'

'Maybe. But as a pal not a fucking . . . mental patient. So.'

The F-word was a mistake. The teacher in his head told him, *Hey, no need for that*. It was melodramatic and self-pitying and he was keen to move on. She must have sensed this too because she asked, 'So you're working on solo material now?'

'I'm back in the studio.'

'Forming Wings?'

'Oh, I'm not sure I'm Paul.'

'So which one are you? Of the four basic personality types.'

'I don't know. You tell me.'

She looked at his face, as if this might help. 'George, I think.'

'Really? Doesn't everyone want to be John?'

'The Pauls all want to be Johns and the Johns are generally

unbearable. The Ringos are nice enough and fun. But a George is the classiest option. Trust me,' she said, 'a George is the thing to be,' and he felt satisfied with that. 'Right. What's next?'

A-choo

The game carried them across Westmorland, past places with blunt and peppery names, like Ravenstonedale, Nettle Hill and Orton Scar, each song providing a vignette, so that by the time the scenery began to change, she knew about his Sunday school, his best meal and his worst hangover, the cousins in Dublin, piano lessons, his first crush and his voting history, each story inconsequential in itself but adding detail, as if increasing the resolution of a photograph. Such conversation always carried with it the danger of a sudden derailment – even quite late in her marriage, Neil could startle her with Strong Views on corporal punishment or some cruel school anecdote – but she found that she liked Michael's picture more as it accumulated detail. There were no political upsets, he was principled but not pompous, and she even liked most of the music, though she found herself unable to separate it from his domestic past: this was the soundtrack to his life with Natasha and she was struck by the strange intimacy of listening to another couple's music, the songs they'd cooked and eaten and made love to, as if she'd been caught going through their cupboards. There must have been associations he would rather not share. Certainly she was editing her own copy as she went (*Six years is too much. Try four.*) For the most part, the conversation was frivolous and self-conscious, like an episode of a short-lived podcast, but she told herself that this was fine, that conversation, like music, could serve different purposes, in this case distraction from vast distances.

Eventually the moors began to soften and buckle, then suddenly descend into a valley, like the crease in a book. They were approaching Eden, Michael said, and there was something of a paradise about the view from Smardale Gill, a great long-legged viaduct braced across the valley, an idealised landscape from an eighteenth-century painting.

'Go on, then,' she said. 'I know you want to.'

'What?'

'Tell me about viaducts.'

He laughed. 'It's a railway bridge.' Then, without catching her eye, 'Are you getting the train tonight?'

'One more day?' she said, watching him. 'If that's all right with you.'

'No, I'd like that. You'll get to cross the Pennines. See the Dales. And you did bring twelve pairs of pants, so . . .'

'Will I get to see the shirt again?'

'What choice do I have?'

'Okay. One more day and I'll leave you.' They climbed the valley's flank and she felt they'd found their rhythm now, in every sense. Her feet and knees and shoulders no longer complained, smiling no longer felt unnatural and she'd abandoned her private language too, fwa and petah, flu-ah and cha-ha. She no longer fretted when they fell silent, though also thought there was a conversation that must be had. She felt the pressure of it building and a certain pleasure in this pressure, like the tickle of a suppressed sneeze. The trick would be not to sneeze in his face.

Fields, farmyards, the backs of houses, the high street. After the moors, the town seemed a metropolis of Methodist church halls and Co-ops and bakeries. The pub where Michael was staying was full or perhaps he just wanted to save her from another Black Dog, but a series of phone calls won her a coveted room in 'the best B&B in the Eden Valley'. A B&B, she feared, was like staying with a great-aunt you'd never met, but Sunnyview Lodge was large and handsome, with a neat privet hedge and stained-glass transom, and there was something courtly and old-fashioned about being dropped off at the door like this.

'I feel like a war-time refugee,' she said. 'With my London ways.'

'Shall I pick you up at seven?'

Being picked up: it *was* courtly and old-fashioned, and she had a momentary worry that it might not be proper, a single young lady out after dark with a gentleman caller. This costume-drama atmosphere persisted as she was shown to her room – 'Boots off, if you don't mind' – by a landlady with a perm like a mauve moped helmet, prematurely familiar so that Marnie was instantly 'my love' and 'my darling'. There was a guest lounge with maps and guides, a full English breakfast, of course, and, in the Lavender Suite, a fireplace, a pale pink candlewick bedspread, a cast-iron bed frame, which had escaped being melted down to make Spitfires. 'No guests,' the landlady said, but there was a complimentary bottle of home-made sloe gin tied with a bow, home-made shortbread in a biscuit barrel, a selection of teas . . .

And suddenly she was alone in 1942. Only the rumble of lorries on the main road broke the illusion. Marnie boiled the kettle, charged her devices, lay on her bed and heard the bedsprings creak, wrenching her mind around to *Twisted Night*, which felt more forbidden than ever, as illicit as a copy of *Lady Chatterley's Lover*.

The Auld Shillelagh

It was Curry Club Night in the Auld Shillelagh.

'That's exciting,' she said, 'a private members' club.'

'I'm amazed we got in,' he said, and it was true. The pub was already busy, so the only seats they could find were at the back, a wooden booth, candle-lit and cosy, far from the small stage. Michael's bedroom was directly above their heads, a long, bare, converted corridor but nice enough, and taking their seats, he had the feeling that they were in the right place. 'It's like we've got into Studio 54,' said Marnie, who had worked through her rota of three dresses and was wearing his favourite, from the second night, the one with the roses. *His favourite*. Good God.

Confusingly, it was also Country and Western Night, a local band, guitar and keyboards, fiddle and, propped against the piano, a washboard for later. Peroxided hair piled high, waist-coated and mascaraed, the singer was growling 'Walkin' After Midnight' to a semi-circle of locals, who tapped their thighs on the one and three. Rogan Josh and Patsy Cline in an Irish pub in Cumbria; Michael felt at home but he was less sure about Marnie. He had never lived in London, had no desire to do so and knew, too, that it wasn't all bento boxes in high-glass towers, but he very much wanted her to be happy here. Glancing back from the bar, he saw her straining to read *Wuthering Heights* by candlelight and noted, too, how nice she looked, a little make-up, hair washed, roses on her dress. What would an observer presume? That it was a date, that they were married? A couple on a night out, kids with the babysitter. Was that plausible?

And where would he be without her? He imagined a parallel evening, finding somewhere quiet, drinking alone with his book and phone and thoughts. That wasn't so bad either and he still felt the pull of solitude, but he'd grown sceptical of his ability to make conversation with himself, unsurprised, unamused, unchallenged, caught in familiar rhythms, like bouncing a tennis ball off a wall. Conversation had its challenges and risks, but for now it was preferable to being alone. Plenty of opportunity for that.

She was looking right at him. She smiled.

And now she was looking to the side, standing, then laughing, pointing towards the bar. It was the couple from the chip shop, Brian and Barbara, turning to wave. He smiled back, mimed a glass, mouthed, 'Can I get you?' but they shook their heads and indicated others, a family group, who were joining them, pulling up chairs, shaking Marnie's hand, and she glanced at him over Brian's shoulder, a wide-eyed, hostage look.

And so he lost her again, instead spending the night with Brian and Barbara's two sons, Stewart and Donald, and new daughter-in-law Amelia, hearing all about their honeymoon and how they'd met, where they were staying in town, the weather, the food, where to find the best curry in Edinburgh and Leeds and York, mortgages, the bloody Tories, Scottish nationalism and roast potatoes and squirrel-proof bird-feeders, and every now and then he'd glance at Marnie, chin on hand, candle-lit, a good guest at a stranger's wedding and sometimes they'd catch each other's eye and she'd send a look that seemed to say, he thought, *Stay there, wait, just wait.*

Hours passed, the music getting louder and more raucous, and it was only when it was his turn to go to the bar that he realised how drunk he was, far drunker than he'd been for many years, perhaps ever. So what? He was having *fun* again and it wasn't nearly as bad as he remembered. He squeezed through the crowd, strangers smiling and clapping him on the shoulder as if he were going to collect an award rather than the next round. At the bar, he found himself experimenting with focus, letting it drift in and out as he stared at the spirits – they were on whiskies now, God help them – and the band was playing an old Hank Williams song, 'Hey Good Looking', a song he knew without ever consciously listening to it, the kind of simple, silly song his father liked and he had a sentimental memory of Dad singing along to it on the radio, a Sunday afternoon in the late eighties. A hand, warm and slightly damp, was taking his own. 'Hello, good-looking,' said Marnie. 'I thought I'd come and help you.'

'I'm sorry, I thought it would be just us.'

'I don't mind. Well, I do a bit.'

He was confused for a moment. 'I'm having trouble getting served.'

'No rush. Let's just wait.'

And it was fun to stand, holding her hand down at his side as if it were a secret, eyes forward but sensing her smile. He ordered, and the band announced their last song. And it was fun, more than fun, to tap glasses and feel the whisky's burn, then turn to the band as they played 'Crazy', the old Patsy Cline song. It was what a New Year's Eve ought to be but never is, sentimental and munificent, full of hope and generalised love. Marnie had taken his hand once again, their forearms touching along their length as the crowd danced in front of them, elderly couples mostly, the men in plaid shirts and bootlace ties, and it seemed easy and natural to slip in among them, Marnie's arm around his waist, his chin on her head, sending up the dancing but taking it seriously too. *Crazy for feeling so lonely . . .*

But the song was no length at all and they still had drinks to deliver, so they lifted the tumblers high, fingers dipped carelessly into the liquid and squeezed back through the crowd, who were cheering now, for the band or for the two of them. 'Ah, God bless you both,' said Brian, a great grin on his red face, raising his glass in a toast.

'The pair of you,' said Barbara, 'you lovely people,' and now Marnie was whispering into his ear with whisky breath.

'Walk me home, Mikey,' she said.

He laughed. 'Absolutely no one calls me Mikey.'

'D'you mind?'

'Not at all.'

'So walk me home, Mikey.'

'I will,' he said, 'I will.'

Greetings from Viaduct Country

The sting of cold air was not enough to sober them up as they walked back through the town, arms linked. She was aware of her dress sticking to her back with sweat, the dampness suddenly chilling so that she had no choice really but to press close to Michael, so that he tripped and laughed and had no choice but to hold on to her in return and this was how they staggered back, drunks from a silent movie. It seemed very important to think and speak clearly and also impossible to do so, and 'I loved Curry Club!' was all she could manage.

'I loved it too!' he offered in return, so at least they were as bad as each other.

And then they were outside Sunnyview Lodge and from somewhere came an overwhelming urge, some sublimated desire, to push him into the privet hedge. 'Bush push!' she shouted, and he looked a bit surprised but rebounded and tried to push her into the bush in return, and then they were wrestling again, the second time in two days. 'Ssh!' she said.

'You started it!' he hissed. 'You pushed me in the bush!' and she gave him a shove and it was Jane Austen time again.

And then they were at the gate. 'I should get back,' he said, 'late night,' and she peered at her watch.

'Mikey,' she said, 'it is precisely nine forty-five,' and they both started to laugh and before he could stop, 'There's a kettle in my room. And some sloe gin!'

'Gin and whisky,' he said.

'Feelin' frisky,' she said, and yet despite this he followed her up the path.

'Ssh!' She opened the door as quietly as possible. From the guest lounge came the sound of the TV and she beckoned him to the stairs, which they climbed on tiptoe as if she were sneaking a boy into her room, which she was, she was actually doing that: that was the thing she was doing. Halfway up the stairs they gave up on silence and bounded up, shedding privet, and into the Lavender Suite, where she closed the door and, weirdly, bolted it, though thankfully he didn't seem to notice.

'This is nice!' said Michael, as she hurried to pick up discarded clothes and underwear, jamming them into the open top of her rucksack. The big light was on, a 100-watt bulb in a tasselled shade, but it seemed a little too brazen to turn on the bedside lights, so to distract him . . .

'Check out my biscuit barrel,' she said, and he did so, lifting the lid while she fixed the lighting.

'Very swanky,' he said, 'this will certainly keep your cookies fresh' and they were laughing again, and she was reminded of those times when she used to work with other human beings whom she liked and got on with and sometimes they'd go on trips or on the annual team-building weekend and rush back to someone's hotel room, how illicit and fun that was, all squeezing into a room with nowhere to sit except the bed, raiding the mini-bar, smoking out of windows, getting complaints from Reception. That was how she'd got together with Neil, but forget Neil, he is not Neil.

'We need some choons!' she said, but the radiogram was tuned to Radio 4 and a discussion of the Dead Sea Scrolls. 'Let's get this party halted!' she said, though Michael was bopping his head and biting his lip. 'You can't dance to the Dead Sea Scrolls. Retune!' and while he pressed the buttons cluelessly, she found the sloe gin, in its tall green bottle tied with a ribbon. 'It's a secret potion!' she said, and began to sing 'Black Magic' while the radio cycled through jazz and classical and the weather forecast, another lovely day in the north-east but make the most of it because . . . She opened the sloe gin with her teeth and spat the tiny cork across the room, like a pirate, swigged it, delicious, like cough medicine, and flopped on to the bed, the springs in the frame clanging like a bin lorry. 'D'you want a glass?' she said, offering him the potion. 'Or a teacup?'

''S okay,' he replied, and took a swig, winced and placed it carefully on the bedside table.

And then they were both on the bed. There were too many pillows. Their heads were crooked up at ninety degrees, staring down towards the metal bedstead, and she kicked off her evening shoes, curled her toes and sighed and rubbed her black-stockinged feet against each other, and he tapped them with his great muddy boots, once, twice.

'Hey!' she said. 'You were meant to take your boots off!'

And then they were kissing and though it would be hard to say exactly who started it, there was no doubt of the mutual enthusiasm. She had never kissed a man with a beard before, had imagined it would be like rubbing your face on a coconut, but it was soft as was his mouth, which was still sticky and sweet with the sloe berries, with a lingering trace of whisky and the pub curry, something slightly numbing anyway, or perhaps that was the taste of her own mouth, but either way it was delicious and she felt and remembered it: desire. *There it is again. Hello, desire! God, I missed you!*

Another squall of springs as they shuffled down the bed so

that they could lie flat, facing each other, her hand on his neck, his on her waist, and she had a momentary worry that she might have food between her teeth, a grain of rice or the trace of a nut that might become dislodged and get kicked around. She wondered, too, if she should do something about the radio, which had settled on Radio 3, an arts programme and a review of a new production of *The Crucible*, which, thankfully, all of the critics had admired very much, finding it 'powerful', 'timely' and 'compelling', but his hand was on her ribs now, his finger and thumb along the underwiring of her bra, and she wondered how to reciprocate, unzip his trousers at the knee perhaps. Perhaps she could make a joke about it, but that would mean breaking away from the kiss, which she didn't want to do, finding it powerful, timely and compelling. Now she wanted to laugh, not mockingly but with a kind of glee, a rollercoaster laugh as they shifted again, the bedsprings like an accordion, his leg between hers, pushing her dress up and now his hand was on her thigh at the top of her hold-up stockings, which she was suddenly embarrassed about, my God, hold-up stockings, as if this were a touring production of *The Rocky Horror Show*, aware too of his erection or perhaps his GPS device brushing against her hip and now she was tugging at his shirt, the famous shirt, and he whispered something like *Hey, careful with that, it's delicate* so that they were both laughing again until she heard another noise from elsewhere, a tap on the door. He must have heard it too, because he broke away and they lay facing each other, very still.

'What was that?' he said.

And then a rustling sound from the landing, as if someone were eavesdropping. 'Hold on,' and she disentangled herself, swung her legs to the floor, pulled down her dress and stepped lightly across the room.

A postcard, a glossy picture of the perfect valley they'd seen that afternoon, the words 'Greetings from Viaduct Country!' italicised across the bottom. She turned it over and saw, written neatly in fat black pen – 'No Guests After 10, Please!'

'Oh, God, no.'

'What is it?' said Michael.

'She's throwing you out.'

He laughed. 'Really?'

'No gentleman callers.' She showed him the postcard and he scrubbed at his hair with both hands, winced and sat at the edge of the bed. 'I suppose there's no arguing with that,' she said, 'house rules.' He found her hand and held it.

'You could come back to mine. It's a single bed, but—'

'No, I think not.'

Some time passed, sat looking at the biscuit barrel, the small kettle, holding hands. She thought she could feel the blood pulsing in his palm, or perhaps it was hers or perhaps both. He sighed. 'Tomorrow then?'

'I'll see you tomorrow.'

'I feel pretty drunk,' he said, then quickly, 'though that's not the reason.'

'Me too,' she said, 'by which I mean me neither,' and they kissed again, more hesitantly, gently and for some time, until Marnie broke away. 'I feel like she's writing another postcard.'

'I'll go,' he said, 'make a run for it.'

'If she tries to stop you, just push past her, she's elderly and small.'

'I will do that,' he said, hand on the door, 'I will push her down the stairs,' and she thought how handsome he looked and how much she wanted him. 'That was fun,' he said, and those might have been his parting words had she not bolted him in. There was some confusion, tugging and rattling the handle until he managed to pull back the bolt and smile and leave. She heard his boots on the stairs, then the front door closing softly in the hall below.

And then she lay there, staying very still so as not to sound the springs, the room moving very slightly, its dimensions changing, smiling to herself, confused and excited and yet not so excited that she didn't fall into a profound sleep, on top of the bedclothes, in her second-best dress with one stocking rolled below her knee, at a little after ten past ten.

Night Messages

And then he woke at three, head pounding, his tongue a rolled-up bar towel, stumbling on blistered feet to the tiny bathroom basin where he bent to drink, cracking his forehead on the hot tap, pissing noisily and stumbling back to bed. He touched the screen of his phone to check the time and saw a message, from Marnie, he guessed, he hoped.

Sure. I'd like that. Let's make a plan.

It was from Natasha. Confused, he tapped the message and saw that he had completed and sent the draft earlier that night.

All IS well. In fact I'll be near you Friday night if you want to meet.

Possibly a mistake. He wondered if it might keep him awake but he too fell into sleep, deep but full of wild and brilliant dreams.

Day Six:

KIRKBY STEPHEN TO IVELET

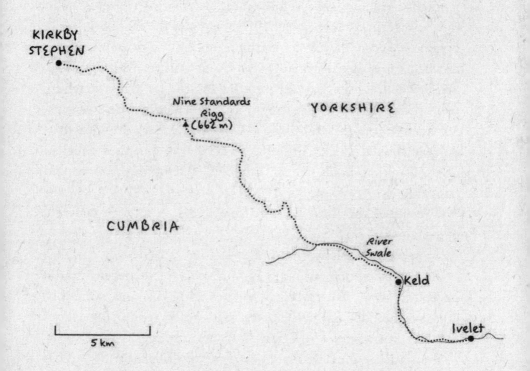

The Watershed

She packed the postcard. *No Guests After 10, Please!* It was a funny souvenir but she also had a secret, sentimental notion that it might someday have significance, become a future relic. In the short term, she would have to face down the landlady. In the breakfast room there was no mention of the scandal, just a pinched smile as she asked for no fry-up, just toast and coffee, and before long she was out into the day, the landlady watching from the doorstep, Marnie with an insolent swing in her hips, Michael waiting a safe distance from the house, the local bad lad. He looked pale, a little bashful. No kiss but they touched their shoulders against each other as if chinking glasses and laughed.

'I feel like the local floozy. I feel like I should be chewing gum.'

'Hop on my Harley,' he said.

'And what about my marriage prospects? No decent man'll have me now.' They settled their backpacks and were off, crossing the Eden River, the pretty side-streets turning into lanes that began to ascend towards the Pennine ridge.

She had the illusion that they were walking not just across the country but through the seasons. The sky made her think of the phrase 'robin's egg blue', though she'd never seen a robin's egg. The hazy blue of an airmail letter then, and soon there were hawthorn blossoms as white as A4 and gorse flowers in Post-it note yellow, and everywhere a bright highlighter green so vivid that it seemed to fizz. They passed a shallow black pool, bubbling like a cauldron, which, on closer inspection, was dense with writhing tadpoles and she didn't find this gross. Even with her sore eyes and a hot, aching head, she felt that time was passing quickly and lightly and that a real summer, the first for many years, lay ahead. In the years of the great seclusion, she'd found herself wishing for the darkness so that she could justify going to bed. Now she wanted to prolong the days, to wish them brighter and to occupy them fully. It would be a mistake to name it, but what was this sensation of optimism and receptiveness?

Eventually they left the clear track and began to clamber towards the horizon and nine spikes of stone, each a different size, like teeth set far apart. 'That's Nine Standards Rigg,' he said in his teacher's voice, though she didn't mind, 'marking the ancient border between Cumbria and Yorkshire.'

'And do you have some interesting facts about it?'

'I do! It's significant because— Are you listening?'

'Yes! Tell me more.'

'When we get there. That's your incentive. Local interest.'

Despite the dry days the ground remained boggy, the path badly eroded, so she endeavoured to tread lightly, as if walking on a mopped floor. Soon breathless again, her sweat carrying a sour, hoppy taint, they climbed, not looking back until they were on the ridge itself, the jagged teeth revealed as cairns, intricate and sturdy but sinister even in the sunlight and stillness. The air was as clear as the vacuum of space, the view to infinity and only the eastern high moors prevented them from seeing the North Sea and then on to . . . Holland? Norway? They were quiet for a moment, taking in how far they'd travelled, where they were heading, looking everywhere but at each other until she said, 'So. Tell me.'

'Well, this is a watershed, which in geographical terms means that if it rains over there,' he pointed west, a little downhill, 'it will end up in the Irish Sea, and if a raindrop lands where we're standing, it will end up in the North Sea.'

'And where do you stand to end up in London?'

He pointed to her feet. 'There, I suppose.' A moment passed, and then they were embracing, his chin on the top of her head just as when they'd danced last night, and in return she patted the sides of his rucksack, a little drum riff. A close embrace, sober and in daylight. Another landmark, she supposed. 'Let's keep going, shall we?' he said, and they broke apart.

They turned to follow the ridge and began the descent towards Swaledale, striding along on flagstones set in the mud, the land-scape a series of embankments and swampy hollows. On the next ridge, they saw a group of four walkers, heads down, standing a little apart as if waiting for a bus, and she braced herself for the banalities. *Nice day for it. Where are you heading? Maybe we'll see you there!*

But as they got nearer, she saw something on the ground, a fifth figure reclining beneath a silver sheet, the light foil blanket that athletes wear at the end of a marathon. It seemed almost comical here, like a joint resting after the oven. Perhaps one of the group had overreached themselves. Even so, it was unusual for the face to be covered like that.

But as they got nearer she recognised them: Barbara standing stunned and expressionless, her family too, faces fixed, their eyes red-rimmed, shifting from foot to foot as if they'd been caught out in something. She was close enough now to see Brian's pale hand protruding from the silver sheet, palm upwards. 'Oh, no,' she said, and looked to Michael, but he was already running over to them, and while they spoke in low voices, she stood alone in the glare of the sun.

Walking Away

They had to walk some distance before either of them could speak and even then, 'I don't know what to say,' said Marnie.

'No.'

'Should we have stayed with them, do you think?'

'I asked that and they said no, and look . . .'

They turned back and saw other figures arriving, an ambulance on the road below, a Land Rover too, pitching unsteadily on the low slopes as it climbed over rough ground. They watched for a moment, then turned and walked on. 'What was it like?'

They all seemed in a state of shock. No one was crying. That would come, and for the moment they were too dazed, too numb to do anything but stand there and wait. He was ashamed to realise that he couldn't remember their names, but Brian's daughter-in-law, the only one who seemed able to speak, had told him that it had happened very quickly, that Brian had sat down and then lain down and they'd all laughed at him at first, at his hangover. *Come on, Dad, keep up!* But then they realised he was already gone. They did what they could but . . . 'I'm very sorry,' Michael had said. 'He seemed like a very nice man.' And his daughter-in-law had said thank you, and yes, he really was, and please don't wait, people are coming to help, we're fine, you're kind, it was nice to meet you both, nothing you can do.

For a moment, running towards them, he had thought he might save the day. He was trained for these things, he had strategies and procedures, but like Marnie, he'd seen the pale hand, its palm upwards, fingers slightly curled and, shamefully, he realised that the instinct to comfort and assist was no match for a compulsion to get very far away and to demote these people, whom he had spent time with, whom last night he might have called friends, back to strangers. Perhaps the daughter-in-law had sensed this: 'Really, there's nothing to do here.' Brian's two sons stood immobile a few feet apart, eyes set on the ground, as if they didn't want to be disturbed. He'd looked to Barbara, but she had turned her back and was staring towards the east, to the horizon, calm for now, though you could sense the rumble of terrible grief rolling towards her. 'Really, thank you, but you can go,' said the older son, so he'd nodded, turned and now here they were, walking away.

They didn't speak much for the rest of the morning. The day had become vicious and bleached out, the promise of the morning discarded, the beauty of the scenery dishonest. To remark on the view as if it were some consolation would have been trite and so they descended through boggy ground to a lane then a river, the Swale.

'I realise,' she said, 'that I've never seen that before,' she said. 'Have you?'

'No. No, both parents still alive. Dad's frailer now, a cancer scare, but he's all right.'

'How's your mother?'

'Healthy. She has her piano, her church. I don't see them as often as I should.'

'Who does?'

'Yours?'

'They don't move much but they're alive. I phone them, but

when I'm doing something else. I've got to clean the fridge, best phone Mum.'

'That's what I do.'

'Even so, I can't imagine . . .' She tilted her head back to the hill. 'I dread that. Just dread it. Are you close?'

'To my dad? No, but I don't think he minds. He's . . . traditional. We don't really talk like that.'

'Like what?'

He looked for the word. 'Normally.'

'Do *you* mind?'

'A little. I tried once or twice, to talk about, I don't know, love or emotions, almost like a dare and you could see the panic in his eyes. *Don't ever do that again.* Dad's closer to Natasha if anything, adores her. I mean it was embarrassing, how moony he used to get, all tongue-tied. The only time I've seen him cry was on our wedding day. He hated her moving out, they both did, but we don't talk about it. And my mum's quite religious, conservative, so she didn't understand and, I don't know, it's a mess.' They were at the valley floor now, a wide, lush plain, the Swale a broad black ribbon draped along its length. He asked suddenly, 'Do you worry about being alone?'

'In life? In general or when I die?'

'Both.'

'I am alone. 'S all right. A lot of the time I quite like it. No one to please but myself. I work, I read. And I've dreaded someone coming home, so compared to *that*, it's bliss.'

'Did you dread it?'

'By the end I did.' She shrugged. 'I realise that this sounds like I'm putting on a brave face, but we make too big a deal about being alone. People aren't meant to spend their whole adult lives with one other person. In fact, very few do. Well, not very few, but your parents, mine, they're not the majority.

And lots of people live without a life partner. I don't know why this perfectly common thing's thought of as odd or sad.'

'No, I know. But living alone for the rest of your life, being alone when you die, d'you think about that?'

'No, course not.' They walked on. 'Every now and then.'

Prizes

At some point, Marnie thought, *we'll have to stop talking about death*. This was not how the day was supposed to go and she didn't mind, not really, but she had also hoped to have some kind of conversation about . . . not love, not that, but what had happened last night, and not just last night, the last few days, some acknowledgement and discussion, kind and honest, about what might happen next. In the Lavender Suite she had felt like a teenager but also exactly her own age, and that combination was thrilling and rare, lust and experience, together at last. What might have happened in a different room, without boots on a quieter bed? She felt sure that he'd wanted more too but now there seemed no easy segue from the scene they'd witnessed to whether they might kiss again. Something about seizing the day? *Life's short and painful, so let's make the most of it and with that in mind . . .*

But it was a tough transition, harder now that he'd asked her if she expected to die alone. Heigh-ho. She didn't mind, or not too much, and perhaps this was the kind of conversation students had, late at night in a room lit by tealights. Will I die alone? Well, maybe, but don't we all? 'For company when I die' was a terrible reason to want a relationship, an even worse reason to have kids – good luck with that. Besides, look at where we are right now. We're not alone, so can't we talk about the present instead?

The walk stretched long into the afternoon past ancient stone barns with tiny high windows, the river always in sight. The path was easy, broken only by the dry-stone walls that spanned the valley, like the frets on a guitar, and every hundred metres or so they'd squeeze through a new stile into another meadow populated by new-born lambs, a week or perhaps even a few days old, their fleeces graffitied with numbers so that they seemed like a kids' football team. Tactless in their brightness and youth, they were delightful but also a bit much, the frisking, the baby-talk bleating, as if they were trying too hard. Was that how she'd been with Conrad?

But not with Michael. Instead they spoke about their childhoods and their parents' marriages, which were similar in their constancy and restraint. Michael spoke the most and she thought, not for the first time, that if you wanted to get a man to talk with real emotion, you should ask him about his father.

But it was rarely a fast track to a good time. He had clearly been shaken by the scene on the hill and in this shaking something had come loose. For her own part, she had two consoling thoughts about what they'd seen, and both were such clichés that she had resolved not to say them out loud. The first, 'At least he died doing what he loved', had always seemed a poor consolation. She enjoyed going to the cinema in the afternoon but liked leaving too. Still, to be with people who care for you, and somewhere beautiful, for it all to be, she hoped, relatively quick, well, there were worse ways.

The second thought was connected to the first and it was this: in the brief time she'd spent with Brian and Barbara, they had seemed very happy. The phrase 'love of her life' occurred to her, a phrase that had always made her wince a little. It was melodramatic, the notion that this accolade might be handed out on your deathbed, a trophy to the one person who had made it all worthwhile. Marnie certainly didn't have a love-of-her-life and neither did she expect to fulfil that role for anyone else, and that was fine too. Many people live full and happy lives without making that much of an impression, and even if someone were to say it of her, she would probably frown and ask, *Really*? Are you *sure*? Have another think.

Perhaps the idea would be less queasy and oppressive if the honour could be shared out equally so that everyone got a prize, like a children's birthday party. But the mathematics was hopelessly off. A select few beautiful souls might pile up the trophies but many people would never be the love of anyone's life and it was silly and pointless to worry about this. What could you do about it? What she hoped for was to be liked very much by someone for a certain period of time. That seemed achievable.

But the couple they'd sat with for a few hours had seemed very much in love and it seemed natural to envy that a little. What she didn't envy was the look that Michael had spoken of on the hillside, the widow's shock at the sudden absence, and perhaps solitude is more frightening when something is snatched away.

Yurt

'The reservation was for a single person,' said the landlady, standing in the doorway.

'Yes, it's a last-minute thing.'

She puffed her cheeks. 'There are two single beds, if you don't mind sharing the same yurt.' The woman was tired, greasy hair pulled back into a functional knot, and somewhere inside the house a baby was crying. 'I'll leave you to think about it,' she said, and disappeared inside. It was a whitewashed farmhouse that had long since ceased to be a farm, the remaining few acres now occupied by four drum-shaped structures swaddled in red fabric, like miniature circus tents pitched high on the dale's northern flank.

'We could try the next village along—' he said.

The sky was reddening, the river path far beneath them. 'No, I don't mind.'

'—because I know your feelings about tents.'

'It's not a tent, it's a yurt. And, anyway, it's good to rough it. It'll be like one of your field trips. I'll get drunk on Cinzano, give a Frenchie to a local lad.'

The remark hung in the air for some time.

'So I'll say yes?' he said.

'Let's run away to the circus,' she said, and he went inside to find the landlady, confused and unsure about what was happening and how he might explain things: *Marnie, can we wait, it's just what happened today, and I'm seeing Natasha, and I need to think, and the timing, give me a day, thirty-six, no, forty-eight hours, but I do want to kiss you again at some point.* Yes, that was what he'd say, without the phrase 'at some point', which lacked passion.

Inside the farmhouse, he found the landlady feeding banana to a sticky-faced child in a high-chair, and she explained how the food and showers worked, how they could order drinks and breakfast. The signal was poor and he made conventional noises about this being a good thing, going off-grid, et cetera, though in truth he'd need Wi-Fi to make plans.

The tent, the yurt, was effectively a large circular room with rough wooden floorboards concealed beneath a ragged Oriental carpet. The reddish light gave it a vaguely boudoir air and they stood for a moment at the end of their two beds. 'Left or right?' she said.

'I'm easy,' he replied, and that hung in the air too, all these remarks, hanging in the air like scaffolding, cracking them on the forehead. She took the left-hand bed, where she usually slept, and he usually slept on the right, so that was fine, that worked, and off she went to the shower block.

For the first time since the incident on the hill he was alone and in her absence he felt the depression crawling back inside him, almost a physical thing, its symptoms as tangible as the beginning of flu: smarting eyes, a tightening in his neck and shoulders, a sense of helplessness and a sudden exhaustion that caused him to lie back on the bed. He draped his arm across his eyes, like a compress, and felt a sharp sense of shame, loathing really, for fleeing today, and though it was irrational, it was enough to make his breath come faster. At such times his doctor had instructed him to breathe in for five then slowly out for seven, but he was always troubled by the imbalance, because if you're breathing out more than in, surely you're suffocating . . .

'Are you all right?'

He sat upright, pressing his palms into his eye sockets as an alibi. 'Sorry, I was just falling asleep,' and he blinked and yawned and turned to smile.

Marnie stood in the entrance, her old clothes bundled up in her arms, her hair wet and slicked back in a way that was unfamiliar, her face shining, and she looked so bright, warm and new and so patently a great thing, that he wanted nothing more than for her to cross the room and hold him. Or perhaps he could go to her, perhaps, he wasn't sure, and in the time it took to consider this, she said, 'So what do you do, on these famous field trips, to pass the time?'

Firepit

They sat outside in the smoky air and played Gin Rummy. They played Whist and Double Solitaire and silly games like Shithead and Spit. Like talking to waiters, the manner in which someone plays cards was a litmus test for Marnie. In both scenarios, Neil had turned into Caligula, capricious and spiteful, and his grin as he laid down his winning cards made her want to pin his hand to the table with a dagger. Michael did not bray or preen when he won, there was no whining or questioning the shuffle when he lost, and he was just competitive enough for it to be fun. Still, she should remember, 'better than Neil' was the very lowest of bars to set.

The field in which the tents were pitched was a kind of mantelpiece – not the proper term – over the valley and in between games they watched the sun set, lights coming on in the scattered cottages below. Dogs barking, wood smoke. With darkness came the cold, and Marnie was obliged to put on the last of her clean clothes and some dirty clothes too. Michael set and lit the fire and they sat in folding chairs, muffled up against the night air, drinking the cheap jammy wine they'd bought from the landlady, along with baked potatoes, pulpy and buttery and delicious. The fire was warm on her face and while the sadness of the day was still present it did not feel inappropriate, this contentment. Someone outside a neighbouring tent was picking at an acoustic guitar. 'Do you mind?' he shouted across the darkness and Marnie, who had a horror of anything folky, said that she did not.

Eventually it became too hard to see the cards and, with their devices charging in the kitchen, she had the new experience of being outside at night away from the city. Was she supposed to look at the stars? They were bright and lovely, she supposed, but she wished they would dance or shoot or something. At least the firelight was flattering – she could tell by glancing at Michael, who had, she thought, a Gabriel Oak thing going on and might at any moment put his finger to his ear and sing of bonnie banks and loved ones 'cross the sea. As if he'd heard the thought, he turned to her. *Quick, say something.*

'I think,' she said, 'I'd be a lousy cavewoman. Apart from the cold and brutality, once you've got the nuts and berries, what d'you do of an evening?'

'Tell stories by the campfire.'

'I'd edit other people's. "You mentioned five mammoths but earlier it was three." You, on the other hand, you'd fit right in.'

'Thank you. Is it this?' he said, scratching at the beard.

'Maybe. How long have you had it?'

'Only a couple of years. I got this scar,' and he traced his finger along his jaw. 'You've probably noticed.'

'I have. But scars are cool.'

'It didn't feel cool at the time.'

'What happened?' she said. 'Unless you don't want to talk about it.'

He frowned. 'I don't come out of it well, I should say.'

'I'm sure that's not the case.'

'Well. You'll see. So . . .'

The Pen Lid

He was silent for a moment, then.

'It's all quite ordinary, in the sense that it happens a lot, but I always struggle with the word, because if I say "accident", it suggests it wasn't deliberate, which it really was, and if I say "fight" it suggests there was some back and forth, combat, which there wasn't, and if you say, "Oh, I got my head kicked in", it's a bit pathetic.'

'I don't think so.'

'Well, anyway. We were coming back from town, Friday night, Nat and me, and there were some kids on the bus, seventeen, eighteen years old, and they were hassling people, you know, throwing chips, trying to get a reaction. Daft kids' stuff but vicious too, sexual, to these girls, not just banter, upsetting. So, ever the teacher, I went up and said something and they stopped for a bit.'

'Well, that was the right thing to do.'

'In theory. And there was this murmur of approval from the passengers and I sat down, all pleased with myself, and Nat squeezed my hand and my heart was racing but, you know, community hero. I could see them watching me, watching us, and I thought, Well, even if we ride all the way to the depot, we're getting off this thing eventually. And I could see them, hear them, laughing, whispering, five of them. We left it to the last minute, ran for the doors, and I thought we'd got away with it but sure enough they'd got off too and started following us, walking just a bit behind, waiting for it to get quiet. That was the worst bit, walking with Nat and she's brave, you know, she doesn't take any shit, but she was really frightened. She'd heard what they'd been saying to the girls and she was gripping my arm and I was saying, "Listen, don't worry, it's me not you. We'll wait till we see someone or you run to someone's door and knock, call the police, let them know you've called the police." It seemed to go on for ages, this conversation, should we both run, could she run in her shoes, should we call the police now, look for a shop or a pub to go in? I could see how frightened they'd made her and I was so . . . angry, full of this rage, frightened of it, of what I might be capable of, thinking, should I bunch my keys, what if I take an eye out, will I go to prison? What about a pen, have I got a pen, can I stab someone with a pen, have I got that in me? A pen, fuck's sake. Anyway, we decided we'd knock on someone's door and just as we turned the corner there was this rush, feet slapping on the pavement.

'I let go of Nat. I was holding her hand and then I wasn't. She ran up someone's front drive, they left her alone, thank God. I suppose I thought, *I'll draw them away*, that's the generous interpretation. Anyway, they're young and I'm not and they tripped me up and I went down, bang, on my knees, elbows, face, and all that fury I'd been saving, all that anger . . . Didn't even get the lid off my pen. By the time it was over I had a broken collar bone, lost these teeth – these are implants – broken fingers, deep cuts here and here and inside my mouth, scar on the top of my head, you can see me worry at it sometimes, very charming. And this big cut here on my jaw, from this kid's shoe.'

'Oh, God, Michael . . .'

'And it went on for a long time, that was the strangest thing,

I mean ages, so long that I actually had time to think, Well, this is interesting, an experience, I'm getting beaten up. I can feel my collar bone, there it goes.'

'Shall we talk about something else?'

'No. Anyway. Nat was knocking on doors and eventually there were enough people for it to get embarrassing, watching and filming and so they ran off.'

'And were they ever caught?'

'No. In that sense, it was the perfect crime.'

'And you went to hospital.'

'For a couple of weeks, then home again on sick leave and that became lockdown, which, you can imagine, made for a very relaxed atmosphere. Then when I went back to work there was this whole exciting new adventure, panic attacks, breathlessness, crying jags in the car park, anxiety with noise and crowds, and at school, well, it's all noise and crowds. I loved teaching the kids, always had, and they give you a hard time sometimes but I always thought there was something fundamentally decent and good in them. But I'd be in class, especially with the older lads and there'd be a flash of something, a sneer from some little . . . and I'd . . . fall apart. So I was off sick again. Depression. Spent a lot of time in bed. For a while I couldn't even ride a bike, didn't believe the physics any more, kept imagining catastrophes, feeling guilty about everything, and with the pandemic happening, I thought – see?'

'Can I just reassure you,' said Marnie, 'that the pandemic was almost certainly not your fault.'

'Well, you *say* that.'

'You were traumatised.'

'I wonder if people use that word too much.'

'It's the right word for something traumatic.'

'But it wasn't war. People get beaten up every Friday night.'

'And are traumatised by it.'

'Maybe.'

'And do you think . . . ?'

'What?'

'D'you think it had anything to do with your break-up?'

'With Nat? I don't know. I don't think she thought, *What a wimp, it's over*. And if I'm honest, it wasn't great before, what with all the stress and tests and working out what to do, IUI, IVF. When something like that happens, you're very aware of your dignity being taken away, quite methodically, with every minute you're down there, and it was definitely – daft word – emasculating, which it's meant to be, and you do feel ashamed and even if the person you love says, "Don't be ridiculous, I don't think less of you," you still carry it with you. So I did push her away for a while and eventually she pushed back.

'And it hurt to be touched, physically I mean, and even when it stopped hurting . . . I was in the spare bedroom because of insomnia and nightmares, and even if you don't know a lot about infertility, you know it's a good idea to be in the same room.

'And suddenly there were kids, babies everywhere, all the teachers off on parental leave. It was in the air, not in the air, in our faces. And the house felt so sad. We were either snapping at each other or not talking at all or talking in that weird, formal voice, the flatmate voice, *I wonder if it might rain, we need more milk*. That's no way to live, is it? So we talked about it. She went to her parents'. It's fine now.'

Sleepover

The valley was dark now, the campers long since retired, the fire burning down.

'I think it's a shame.'

He shrugged. 'Not as much as staying together. I used to watch my parents and they weren't . . . affectionate as such, Dad anyway, but every now and then you'd catch something, a little touch or look, and you'd feel reassured. For me as a kid, it was enough, and I remember thinking, I want that.'

'I didn't think that with mine. I looked at my parents and thought, *I want something bigger.* Passion, something . . . volcanic. So *that* worked out.'

'Maybe that's what Nat wanted too. Maybe it wasn't enough, but I liked being a husband, same as being a teacher. Four things I wanted to be: good son, good husband, good teacher, good father. And I'm a good teacher.'

'I'm sure you're more than that.' She hesitated, wondering if it was dark enough to say such a thing out loud, then; 'D'you think she was the love of your life?'

He thought for a moment. 'So far. But come and see me on my deathbed.'

'"Michael, can you hear me? We've got a visitor for you."'

'"She says she's got a question, she's very insistent."'

'"Hiya! You won't remember me but . . ."'

'I'm sure I will remember you,' he said.

'Ah, that's nice.' She placed her hand on his, patted it and then took it away, now needing somewhere to get rid of her silly hand, as if it were an empty crisp packet.

He reached for it and took it and, after a moment, said, 'The thing that happened last night.'

'You mean . . . Curry Club?'

'Yes, Curry Club, but after too.'

'Ah. Okay, the *snog*.'

He laughed. 'Is that what we're calling it?'

'Well, that's what it was, wasn't it? Two friends, too much to drink.'

'I don't know. Maybe. But can we?'

'What?'

'Put it on hold, for tonight. I feel a little, I don't know, a bit blue.'

'Well, that'll be all this sexy deathbed chat.'

'Yes. Maybe tomorrow we should talk less about dying alone.'

'As a last-day treat. Is it far?'

'Fifteen miles, a couple of hills, you'll be on the London train by seven.'

They sat in silence for a while. 'I'm exhausted,' she said. 'What's the time?'

'Nine forty-five!'

'Our usual bedtime.'

The glow inside the tent had been replaced by the stark light of rechargeable LEDs, breath visible in the frigid air. There was a demure and overly chivalrous process whereby Michael spent a long time brushing his teeth so that she could get undressed and under the covers, cocooned in thermals, swaddled under heavy blankets, a nun on a sleepover with a monk.

'Hey, you didn't wear your sackcloth shirt.'

'It's too cold for revealing clothes,' he said. 'Also, I've got three more days in that thing. I didn't want to get it smoky.'

She sniffed at her own shoulder. 'I smell like a Christmas ham.'

'I like it,' he said, 'it's a nice smell,' and she accepted that this, being told she smelt like ham, would be as close as they got to intimacy tonight. If she hadn't slept through her alarm, if the landlady had been more liberal, if today had turned out differently, if they'd talked of something else, if the tent wasn't so cold, the precise circumstances required to get together were so specific that it seemed as unlikely as seeing a shooting star. And yet they sometimes appeared, and tomorrow perhaps, or in London or York in the near future . . .

All the great changes in her life lay in the future except this one, meeting Michael. It seemed like a great and marvellous stroke of luck and enough for now. 'Shall I turn the light out?' she asked.

'Sure.'

But she had not slept so near to someone for years, not heard the sound of their breathing or felt the changes that the presence of another body brings to a room. She ought to acknowledge it somehow so pulled her arm out from under the blanket, and he reached out too and for a moment their hands touched, her fingers moving a little, as if under the chin of a cat.

Then her arm got tired and her hand got cold, and she thought, *Fuck's sake*, and pulled it back, turned over and went to sleep.

Omissions

He did not fall asleep straight away, instead lying there and thinking of the things he hadn't said.

He'd not mentioned his complete absence of courage. When he'd realised that violence was inevitable, he'd wondered if perhaps he might summon up some innate fighting ability, unleashed by righteous fury. That's what happened in films, he thought, to ordinary men forced to defend the thing they loved. But no such power manifested itself, and while there was no shame in being beaten up by five fit young men, he undoubtedly felt shame. In the version he'd told Marnie, he'd made it sound as if he'd simply curled up and taken it, so that it was a story of resilience, with no mention of the pleading that Nat had witnessed.

He'd made it sound as if he was forgiving about his attackers when in truth he thought quite often about killing them, the grinning boy in particular, a kid no older than the lads he taught, bringing his foot down with all his might. The grin, the glee, it seemed to Michael a terrible thing, the boy's face the figure-head for all his intrusive thoughts and an image he'd never escape, no matter how far he walked. He'd never had a use for the word 'cunt' before then and now, in his moments of panic, jolting awake in the night, he pictured that little cunt's face, and the rage he felt, the violence, would set his heart racing again. Michael would never stop hating that boy for the time, the peace of mind he'd stolen, and he'd never stop being frightened of him either.

This hatred was shameful in another way. A central tenet of his teaching had always been that all of his pupils were of equal worth, all possessed a quality or talent that might be drawn out and nurtured. But his attackers, he thought they were worthless and felt compelled to tell them this, whisper it, make it their last thought each night, that he wished them nothing but unhappiness, sickness and failure. Such hatred was a cumbersome thing to carry, yet there was undoubtedly excitement in hatred too, in his own fantasies of revenge, and this was also shaming.

Something else unspoken. Did he still love Natasha? He did, though it had been so long since they'd been in the same room. He didn't expect a reunion, though he thought about it. He was no longer quite the wreck that she'd abandoned, and perhaps if they talked, really talked, who knows? As to whether she was the love of his life, it was certainly looking that way, and while this was not ideal, there seemed little he could do about it. With the exception of the woman sleeping a few feet away, he'd not felt anything for anyone in years, had presumed all that was behind him.

With the exception. She was exceptional, and there was no doubt that he was happier with Marnie around and to be happier in someone's presence rather than alone felt like a breakthrough. Perhaps he should say it now. *I don't love you yet but I'll see if I can.* Not that, but something like it. In the darkness, her face was not much more than a few smudges, her hair across her eyes, breath clouding the cold air.

'Marnie,' he whispered, 'are you still awake?'

And, as if in reply, she turned her back.

Finally, he should have told her that he was meeting up with Natasha the following night. She had texted that afternoon, saying, yes, let's meet at five thirty. Marnie would be on the train to London by then, and since nothing was likely to happen, there'd be nothing she needed to know.

Day Seven:

IVELET TO RICHMOND

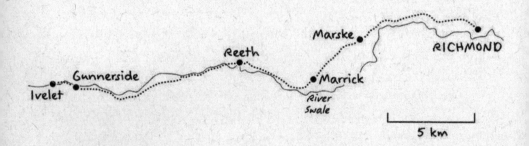

'You Are Here'

She'd have been hard-pushed to find it on the map but there must have been a point where she thought she was falling in love, somewhere between Marrick and Marske perhaps, in an area of woodland, shady, damp and pungent with wild garlic, where the path had started to rise once more above the river. No majestic vista, just a steep, muddy incline, dim and chilly on an overcast day.

The whole morning had been like this, teetering uncomfortably in single file along the verges of busy B-roads, then picking their way through scrappy, litter-strewn birch woods, past signs that warned against fly-tipping. The solemnity of the previous day had dissipated but gloom seemed to linger in their surroundings, the grey sky sagging above them, like an old plaster ceiling that would surely collapse soon.

'I'm sorry it's not prettier,' he said, 'on your last day.'

'I don't mind,' she said, meaning it, happy in his company. Before long they left the river and roads behind, clambering up through Steps Wood, so-called because—

'Is it because of the band Steps? Was the band Steps formed in these woods?'

'If you don't want to know—'

'Okay, is it because of all the steps?'

'Because of these flagstones, so the nuns could get from the abbey to Richmond. These are called Nuns' Steps.'

'Which was also the original name of the band Steps,' she said, and he smiled and she thought, *Look at us, sparking off each other.* 'Can we stop for a second?'

They stood for a while, her hand on his shoulder, his on hers. It was exactly the kind of place where they might kiss and she looked up and waited. 'How are you feeling?' he asked.

'Like a sweaty nun.'

'It's all downhill from here.'

'Yes, you keep saying that and it never is.'

'One or two small climbs, but I promise we'll be in town by tea-time and you can be on your way.'

'Sounds like you're trying to get rid of me!' she said, a blatant feed line but they moved on. She was becoming increasingly aware of the clock, of it counting down with the miles, of what needed to be said. Instead they descended into a valley, lapsing again into companionable silence. Note: 'companion' sounds like a golden retriever. 'Comfortable silence' better? In the long, dead hours with Neil, at the breakfast table, in front of the TV or in restaurants, she'd sometimes tried to persuade herself their silence was to be expected, because what was there to talk about? It was not even silence, more of a drone, the humming of a pylon or the buzz of a fridge as she wondered, How do I break this? What can I say? But in these last few days with Michael the silences were no more alarming to her than the gaps between songs, easy and ordinary because soon another song would start.

Halfway across a meadow he stopped, finger in the air. 'Hear that?' It was a bird's call, a little upwards scale and then a wheeze. 'What's that?'

'Chaffinch?'

'No.'

'Blue tit? Starling? Is it a kestrel?'

'You're just listing birds.'

'Okay, tell me, nature boy.'

'That is the song of the yellowhammer. It's very distinctive, it's meant to sound like words, a phrase. Listen. What's the phrase?'

She listened. 'Is it "I like you but just as a friend"?'

'It's "a little bit of bread with no cheese".'

She laughed. 'Yeah, right.'

'I know.'

'The bird's not talking about *cheese*. It doesn't understand the concept of cheese.'

'I realise that. It's, you know, country lore.'

'Ah, country lore!'

Of course conversation wasn't everything and passion would have to be part of it too, and it was true, that if forced to describe 'a type', she would not automatically have gone for 'middle-aged geography teacher'. This was not love at first or even fourth sight and when she tried recalling his face on the train, it had a blurred quality, like something seen through a steamy window. Now she could see it when she closed her eyes – she'd tried – and perhaps a face was like one of those magic eye pictures that everyone had been crazy about as kids, made of abstract shapes and patterns, perhaps the trick was simultaneously to concentrate and relax until it becomes clear and you think, *There it is*. Concentrate and relax. Certainly she loved looking at him now, his mouth, his eyes, his body too, which she could piece together from glimpses, not one of those silly, sleek, lightly muscled things, but appropriate: the body of a once-gifted amateur footballer who now plays a little badminton. Again she thought of the Lavender Suite, his leg between hers, his hand beneath her dress. Was she meant to be looking at this tree? Look at the tree, Marnie. The tree. Concentrate and relax.

Or perhaps she'd simply fallen for this landscape, rolled him into the fells and the forests. She'd never met someone on holiday but knew that such relationships did not always survive a change of background. She tried to picture him away from the moors and mountains, dropping him into her world like a figure in an architect's model. Here was Michael outside Brixton tube station; here he was outside the Ritzy Cinema. Brockwell Park seemed a little restricting but perhaps she could take him to Kensington Gardens, let him run around. In her local Italian, she imagined him alarmed by the prices but saying nothing. Now here he was climbing the stairs to her flat behind her. He seemed larger in a small room, but now he was at her table laughing, and now in her bedroom, kissing her, lifting her dress over her head, yes, that all worked, that all made sense.

Of course there might be a tweak or two. She felt ambivalent about beards but the grey was fetching and perhaps with a trim, a dab of oil . . . My God, was she really contemplating grooming him? She was, in the same way that she wanted to smooth down his hair, which had no style at all, just a permanent exasperated air. It would be a blow to discover that *all* his trousers unzipped at the knee and she expected there to be two or three more shirts, but all of these things were fixable.

Fixable. A mistake to think of an adult as an old chest of drawers to be stripped and oiled and almost certainly he would have his own notes, but she'd caught the looks too, even on the train when they were strangers. No one could have called her vain but there was something very attractive about being found attractive, and perhaps attraction was like sound, the slightest whisper bouncing back and forth, amplifying itself in a feedback loop until it became almost unbearable, until someone surely had to say something about all that noise.

On the approach to Richmond, they passed a sign, a large board with a map of the path they were following, the scrawled red line from west coast to east, an arrow two-thirds of the way across labelled 'You Are Here'.

'Look at what we did together,' she said.

'I know,' he said. 'It's quite something.'

'And this . . .' She measured out the remainder of the journey, a hand-span. 'This is *nothing*,' she said, and wondered, What if he asked me to stay on and finish the walk? Is that what he wants? If he asks me, *if* he asks me, I will. I will stay with him and walk into the sea.

Slide to Answer

Marnie would be gone by four thirty, which would give him an hour to get ready. That morning, while she was showering, he had walked a little further up the hill to find the internet, searching for *best restaurant richmond yorkshire*, peering at tiny photographs of leaking steaks and gargantuan roasts and glossy curries, wondering, What would go best with regret, with analysis and reflection? He settled on an Italian place that seemed intimate without being needy and checked the menu to ensure it served something other than pizza – all that sawing and folding, all that hot cheese unspooling. Nat would order the Caprese salad and the bream, but beyond that, he really had no idea what to expect.

He was making the reservation when the phone rang in his hand. Natasha's number. He'd not heard her voice for four months and for a moment he was unsure how a phone worked. Slide to answer apparently. 'Hey,' he said, turning his back on the valley as if the valley might listen in.

'Hiya! How are you?' Her voice, the light north-east accent.

'I'm good, I'm good. I was about to text you.'

'Okay. Where are you now?'

'Swaledale, just looking at the valley. Lovely.'

'And the weather?'

'Okay. Bit overcast.' They were talking about the weather. 'So.'

'And how is it, the walk?'

'Lovely.' Why was everything lovely? 'Tiring.'

'Still okay for tonight?'

'Yes, yes, of course.'

'Cleo said you were walking with a friend, and I didn't want to—'

'Oh, what? No, Marnie, she left days ago, two days ago.'

'So . . . it's not a problem? Tonight?'

'No. I'm looking forward to it.'

They made plans. He would text her the hotel address. Nothing could happen because she was seeing a guy (early days), was still proceeding with the divorce (also early days) and pressing on with the sale of the house (no takers yet, easy enough to pull out). Yes, she'd been the one to instigate this meeting, but it was probably just a sense of obligation, like a hospital visit. Even so, he upgraded to a better hotel, a double room, because nothing was going to happen.

Through Reeth and Grinton, Marrick and Marske, these thoughts preoccupied him and the day saw long stretches of awkward silence, though Marnie didn't seem to mind. 'Look at what we did together,' she said, measuring the distance travelled on the map with the span of her hand, but the coast was still some way off, four days at least. Soon they were walking through municipal woods, past joggers and walkers and benches dedicated to the deceased who had loved it here, and soon Richmond was in view, housing estates and churches, the Swale making its return in the valley below. What looked like a cathedral tower was in fact a castle keep high above the town. 'Richmond, from riche-mont,' he said, 'meaning "strong hill",' and she pushed him from the path. 'I think you'll miss it.'

'I won't miss *anything*,' she said, and he felt a small panic at the prospect of her absence.

Richmond left them wide-eyed. Traffic lights! Shops and timbered pubs and fine Georgian houses, and soon the market-place, a grand egg-shaped arena, picturesque even when crammed with cars. They walked around its edge to the hotel and now it was time to say goodbye.

'So,' she said.

'So. Here we are! The end of the road!'

The Day After Boxing Day

'Nice hotel you've picked for yourself. Very swanky.' It was a Georgian townhouse, imposing and elegant. 'I get the Black Dog, you get this four-star coaching inn.'

'Budget room, last minute.' Silence. 'They can get you a taxi if you . . .'

'Train's not for ninety minutes. I thought I'd have a look around. There's a wool shop that looked exciting.'

'Okay. Okay, I'll come with you.'

'No, no, you fire up your jacuzzi—'

'Or we can get tea or—'

Hesitancy. 'No, let's say goodbye. Though I might leave my bag here for a bit.'

The lobby was low-lit and wood-panelled, with a cigar-box smell. She didn't belong in this place, and Michael, now stiff and shifty, clearly thought so too. Was this shyness? No one said goodbye at airports any more because no love was worth the journey there, but surely there'd be some acknowledgement of what had happened, even if it was 'Let's be just friends.'

Instead she asked the receptionist if she might leave her bag for an hour, ordered the taxi, stood around while Michael checked in, both of them self-conscious and tongue-tied. The room key was in his hand.

'What's the theme here?'

'Grape varieties, weirdly.'

'There's posh. What are you?'

'I'm in . . .' He showed her the fob. 'How would you say this?'

'Gewürztraminer?'

'Gewürztraminer.'

Rooms named after grape varieties. Instinctively she began to scroll through the jokes she might make about this but, honestly, what was the point? She felt very tired, the soles of her feet bruised, so that standing hurt more than walking. Time to go home. She didn't want to go home, but there was nowhere else to go.

'You're sure you don't want me to come out into town with you?' he said, looking to the staircase.

'No, no, you go up to Gewürz-is-name, I'm going to hit the streets. I hear talk of a strong hill!'

'Okay.'

'I'll leave you in peace.'

'Finally!' He took a step forward and they embraced, stiff and somewhat formal, the kind of embrace you see at a funeral. The fireplace lean was back. 'We had fun, didn't we?' he said.

'I don't remember *that*,' she said.

'I wasn't expecting any fun at all.'

'I'm sorry to disrupt your plans.'

'I'll see you next time you're up in York.'

'Or you're down in London. I know it's frightening, with the big red buses.'

'If I get the nerve.'

'I'll see you there.'

'Bye.'

'Bye.'

'See you.'

'Bye.'

And then she was out, a grey afternoon in a strange town. She wandered around but even the celebrated indoor market, even the cheese vendors and fudge shops, couldn't shift her sense of disappointment. She bought a sausage roll and ate it out of the bag, scalding the roof of her mouth with the hot pink paste, then scalding it again with hot tea, then worrying at the scald with her tongue, waiting for the time to tick away before her taxi arrived, feeling like she did as a child after Christmas, not just sad it was over but disappointed at how it had been, a sense of something unachieved, the difference being, she supposed, that Christmas would come again.

No, it couldn't end like this. If it was over, if it was all a mistake, if she'd imagined it, then she would hear him say it. The taxi was due in fifteen minutes. She tossed the greasy parcel into the bin, then strode back to the hotel, walked past Reception and crossed directly to the staircase. There was a system, French grape varieties on the first floor, Italian on the second, Spanish and Portuguese on three and German on four, and she felt a moment's indignation on behalf of Riesling wines, and began to climb the stairs. A corridor took her past Cabernet Franc, Merlot and Shiraz, then up to Chianti and Valpolicella then Rioja and Tempranillo, Garnacha and Albariño and finally in a corridor in the eaves of the hotel, Gewürztraminer. Next to the lift she'd missed, a hallway mirror, where she took a moment to catch her breath, swipe the perspiration from her forehead and the grease from her lips. The sausage roll had been a mistake. Her breath would smell of pork and tea. Would it even matter? She crossed the corridor and knocked.

Someone entirely new opened the door.

'Oh, I'm sorry, is your dad in?'

'Marnie—'

271

'I was looking for Mr Bradshaw but . . . What have you done?'

Smooth-faced and handsome, straight from the shower, he'd already changed into the famous shirt and even this looked new and pressed.

'I thought I'd . . . freshen up.'

'I hope you shaved it off in stages. Sideburns, mutton-chop, little toothbrush moustache . . .' He'd seemed delighted when opening the door, but now stood unamused, almost irritated, and she glanced into the room, saw a bottle of champagne in an ice bucket, and wondered, How did he know I'd be back?

Later, on the train to London, she would struggle to recall the exact words she'd used, but within moments she was walking away, jabbing at the button and stepping into the lift that seemed to be waiting to escort her from the premises, down, down, down, through the vineyards of Spain and Italy and France.

In Reception, she retrieved her rucksack from behind the desk just as the taxi-driver arrived, followed by a woman of about her own age, neat, carefully dressed and visibly pregnant. The woman smiled and somehow Marnie smiled back. Then she followed the driver out to the minicab and on, in dazed silence, to the station and the train that would carry her home.

The Romantic Weekender

The champagne was a mistake. He'd thought it might be charming but now it seemed corny, even a little sleazy. Never mind, too late now. He emptied the contents of the bag on to the bed, some small scissors, a razor, shaving cream. To avoid bumping into Marnie, he'd had to sneak out to the chemist, a spy behind enemy lines, and that had felt sleazy too. Now he showered then snipped off as much of the beard as he could, rinsing the sink with the tips of his fingers, then shaved the rest carefully, twice up, twice down, trying not to imbue the act with too much symbolism. Bare-faced, that was the phrase, and there was something exposed and unmasked about it, a younger face from before everything had gone wrong. Somewhat nervously, he pulled the skin tight and examined the raised line of the scar, pale with no pores or follicles. While he could never think of it as raffish or cool, it had lost its repulsiveness. Perhaps it was fading. He buttoned up his freshly pressed shirt, the first time he'd ever used an iron in a hotel room, the first time he'd used an iron for some months, and there was something nostalgic, domestic about the warm cotton smell, though he hoped Nat wouldn't notice that he'd gone to any trouble.

It would be harder to pass off the champagne as something casual. He had bought it on impulse, a special offer on the hotel website, the Romantic Weekender, and now here it stood in a bucket on its little stand, two flutes upended in the melted water, presumptuous and intrusive, as if a small, silent child were standing sentry by the bed. Could he hide it behind a curtain, or would that be more sinister? He made it stand in the corner.

He felt both exhausted and adrenalised. Was this what it was like to have an affair, an assignation – was that the word? Champagne warming, waiting for Reception to call up. It can't be an affair if you're meeting your wife, but even so, he wondered whom he was betraying.

A knock. Perhaps she'd slipped past Reception. He pulled his hands down over mouth and chin and opened the door.

'Oh, I'm sorry, is your dad in?'

'Marnie—'

'I was looking for Mr Bradshaw but . . . What have you done?'

'I thought I'd . . . freshen up.'

'I hope you shaved it off in stages . . .'

She was off again, making jokes though he couldn't quite take them in. 'No, no, just in one go.' There was a silence. 'I thought you'd left.'

'I'm sorry, I know,' said Marnie, 'I know, we've said goodbye and I am going . . .' Her eyes darted around the room. 'Are you busy?'

'No, not at all, but your taxi—'

'It's coming, but I wanted to say, before I go . . . this is weird, isn't it? Leaving like this? Because I thought we had something. I mean I really, really liked you and I haven't had that for – I was going to say decades, and I thought, *That's not right*, but it is more than one decade, and I don't just mean friendship, not just nice chats but attraction. Fancying. I mean I really want to kiss you, *all* the time. It's the weirdest thing . . .'

'And I did too.'

'Did?'

'Do, do very much want that too, I do,' he said, and yet he didn't move.

'So why don't we walk to the sea! Sixty miles is nothing – it's that much.' She held up her hand and showed its span. 'It's a stroll, and I feel like something is happening and it seems crazy to go home. I'd miss you and I had an idea you might miss me. So why don't we . . . ?'

'Keep going? Yes, okay.'

She laughed. 'What – that's it?'

'No, I think let's keep walking and talking and . . . see what happens.'

'Okay. Okay.' She looked confused. 'So, what, I should cancel the taxi?'

'Yes, yes, do it. Cancel. Good.'

'Okay. Okay.' She looked confused and he found himself glancing down the corridor, over her shoulder. She saw this. 'I'm sorry, it's none of my business but is there a call-girl coming?'

He smiled tightly. 'No. No, I'm meeting Natasha.'

'Oh. Okay. What, now?'

'Any minute.'

'Okay. Okay, I didn't know that.'

'No.'

'It feels like something you'd mention.'

'It's not a good time to talk about this, Marnie.'

She jerked her head back. 'Oh, is that your teacher's voice?'

'No, it's just—'

'Fuck off, sorry, I mean you've got every right, it's just why didn't you . . . ?'

'Because probably nothing's going to come of it and you're meant to be gone. So.'

'I see. I see.' She was chewing her lip, getting ready to go. 'But you still think we should carry on walking to the sea?'

'I think it's a great idea!'

'Okay. But can I ask, do you still love her?'

He had not always been honest with Marnie and it seemed important that he should be entirely honest now.

'I do love her,' he said, 'at this time and place.'

And here she smiled, not pleasantly. 'But, Michael,' she said, 'that's where we are.'

Part Four

THE MOORS

—

THE FOOL   *This cold night will turn us all to fools and madmen.*

Shakespeare, *King Lear*

Daffodils

Stupid, stupid, stupid to care, stupid to hope, stupid to change the way things are.

The Friday-night train from Northallerton was packed before she even stepped on board, hen parties, stag parties, football fans and tourists, raucous and boozy, the seats overflowing into the aisles and between the carriages. She found a spot on the floor, rucksack on, her view the knees of passengers as they opened the toilet door and recoiled.

She would need a distraction but *Wuthering Heights* was no use to her here. Impossible to work and impossible not to worry about work. If she'd kept walking, she might have begged an extension but there was no excuse now: the edit was due on Monday. Perhaps if she worked all weekend – what else was there to do? – but all this could have been avoided if she'd simply gone home last Tuesday as planned. She'd have been reacclimatised, back in her rhythm, deadline met, serene – well, not serene but at least not furious, raging at her own foolishness. Stupid, stupid, stupid to have been suckered by hope, scammed by human interaction. At York, Michael's station, she stood to stop herself tumbling backwards out of the automatic door then slid back to the floor, and returned to her phone, scrolling through the emails she'd ignored, new phone bills available to view, an update to our privacy policy. The Ullswater hotel wanted her to rate her stay, but where was the tick-box for 'misleading' or 'delusional'? She was hungry again and ate a sticky, wadded energy bar that she'd found in a side pocket, a pellet so sweet and dense that she immediately got the shakes. Jaw clenched, jittery and nauseous, she wondered, Is this what a speedball feels like? How can it possibly be legal? They were speeding through the East Midlands at 120 miles per hour and she was coming up on fifty grams of pure glucose and still it wasn't fast enough, with the karaoke party in Carriage H reaching its wild height, the train manager joining in on the speakers, congratulating Pete and Claire in carriage E on their marriage this weekend. Cheers, applause, Marnie off her face with exhaustion and energy. Should she track down Claire and tell her, 'Don't do it, get out, you're making a terrible mistake'?

The last week had changed her and now she must change back. For the most part she'd been offline, so she set about restoring her own default settings, scrolling through her old websites and social media. Deep-sea divers returning to the surface have to acclimatise to their old environment, and this is how the internet felt, absorbing the fights and feuds she'd missed, the rage and the predictions of the world's end until she got the old feeling back, tension tightening her shoulders, all sense of pastoral well-being gone. Once she'd imagined that she might post a photograph or two online, a view or a selfie with a self-deprecating comment. If she'd made it to the North Sea, she might have posted a wholesome snap of her boots in the surf, *went for a walk, got carried away.* Just this morning, she'd been learning bird songs! Well, screw you, yellowhammer and your bread-and-no-cheese. At Finsbury Park she scrambled upright, rolling past the spaceship lights of the football stadium and on into King's Cross.

The crowd pressed against the doors then tumbled out,

tourists and lovers rushing to restaurants and hotel rooms in Shoreditch and Soho. Hoisting her rucksack, she felt as if she was arriving in some foreign city, dazed and disoriented but with none of the tourist's anticipation. Sky like a blackout blind, the smell of diesel and fried food, she crossed the forecourt and descended, standing with the partygoers to the end of the Victoria Line, absurd now in her boots and waterproofs. Outside Brixton station they were still preaching the good news about Jesus but she'd no time for good news, running for the number 3, a Londoner again. In the late-night supermarket, she bought bread *and* cheese, milk, eggs, juice, a banana as hard as a cosh, green leaves in a chlorinated balloon, enough food to allow her to remain indoors, as well as wine and chocolate and gin in a can, the return of the treats. Cheap daffodils were in season and recklessly she bought some to cheer the place up. *And then my heart with pleasure fills/And dances with the supermarket daffodils.*

Her keys were buried at the bottom of her rucksack and on the steps of her flat she was obliged to unzip the pack, searching through the tangle of old underwear and charging cables. On the shelf in the communal hall, bills and flyers from takeaways and estate agents, nothing friendly or hand-written. Legs aching, knees complaining, she climbed six flights, past the sound of the TV in 2B, an argument in 3A, someone gaming in 4B, and opened the door to 5A.

It felt like opening a sealed tomb, the air frigid and stale. She shrugged off her rucksack – deal with that tomorrow – and unlaced her boots so as not to provoke the downstairs neighbours. The soles of her feet felt flayed as she padded through the flat, turning on lights until it was too bright, reacquainting herself with the sounds of her world, the click of the thermostat, the whoosh of the boiler igniting, the tick of the radiators, the lip-smack of the fridge door. She put away the groceries and placed the daffodils in a small jug, but the buds were not yet open, and it looked like a display of five spring onions. *And then my heart with pleasure fills . . .*

In the bedroom, the smell of her sheets, the laundry basket, the dust warming on the radiators. Grimy and sticky, bruised and exhausted, she longed to be warm and clean in fresh linen, the weighted blanket a hand pressing gently down.

But it would take an hour for the water to be hot enough to bath, and changing the sheets seemed far beyond her. Instead she lay back on the bed with her feet on the floor and looked up at the ceiling, its familiar topography of stains and bubbles and cracks. She felt suddenly overwhelmingly alone, and this was absolutely fine and might only be a problem if you'd been anticipating something else.

Day Eight, Part One:

RICHMOND TO OSMOTHERLEY

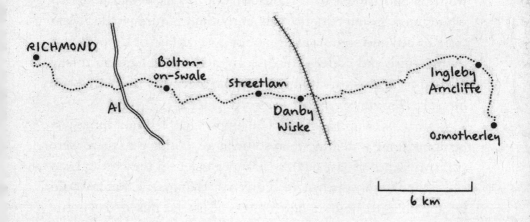

Kippers

Remember, the solitude is the point.

In the wood-panelled breakfast room, he was greeted by the waitress and shown to a table for one by the window. Crisp white linen, heavy cutlery. This early on a Saturday, the lovers were in bed and so he was alone for a breakfast of kippers and orange juice and coffee, a little king with no obligation to say a word to anyone or do anything but check his route and tell himself, *Do not fall apart, keep it together.*

Time to pack up his room. The kippers had left him thirsty, so he drank some water and then some more, noting that there were still two inches of last night's champagne left in the bottle. Even chilled and freshly opened, he didn't love champagne, but it would be appalling to pour it down the sink so he raised the bottle experimentally, sipped and grimaced and dropped it back into the bucket. He half made the bed – he liked a hotel room to be tidy when he left – headed down, handed in his key and stepped out into the marketplace, still quiet at this hour on a Saturday. A cloudy day, not unpleasant, good walking weather as he strolled down the hill, past the castle and along the river. Today was the longest walk, twenty-six miles on flat ground with a final ascent into the Hambleton Hills. A day of fields and country lanes and light showers, the biggest challenge boredom, boredom and perhaps despair, *This is fine it will pass just keep going*

And so he walked around the perimeter of housing estates, through recreation grounds and past sewage works, the messy edges of every-town. It would get better once he'd crossed the motorway and put some miles between him and last night, *Oh, God, last night stupid stupid stupid*. For now, he walked muddy paths churned by trail riders and dull minor roads towards the brown noise of the A1. On the approach to the crossing point he took a wrong turn and found himself in a deserted farmyard, wandering between sheds and barns and outhouses, the ammonia of silage stinging his nostrils, still alone but feeling observed, as if through the sight of a rifle. He walked the circumference of a silo and came upon a muddied yellow digger, the corpse of a calf lolling in its bucket, legs stiff, stomach taut, yellow eye rolled back, and he laughed out loud, and thought, *Oh, come on, you've made your point.*

Stay calm. Look at your map, retrace your steps. He walked the motorway's margins until he found the river, a path, a tunnel. Things would get better soon, he was sure of it. In the meantime, he thought, I'm glad that Marnie isn't here for this and wished that Marnie were there.

Day Eight, Part Two:

BEDROOM TO KITCHEN TO RECEPTION

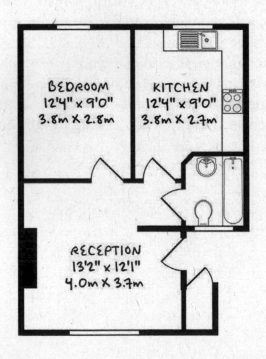

BEDROOM
12'4" x 9'0"
3.8m x 2.8m

KITCHEN
12'4" x 9'0"
3.8m x 2.7m

RECEPTION
13'2" x 12'1"
4.0m x 3.7m

Work

And wasn't it a pleasure to return to work? To put the chain on the door and fill the kettle, make things cosy and secure? There were aches in her thighs and knees and feet but she would not add to them today, her mission solely to keep her step count in double figures. The aches would fade, like the suntan after a normal holiday. She showered and ate her usual breakfast, made a pot of coffee, wiped the crumbs from the table and began.

She was barely a quarter through *Twisted Night* and the deadline was Monday, but now she found her flow, racing through the chapters, sex scene, murder scene, sex scene, murder, guessing the killer (the agent did it), finding a kind of comfort in the rhythm of it, entering a pure and heightened state of copy-editing, like a kid at an arcade game, shooting down 'lied' for 'lay', 'brought' for 'bought', the blue eyes that were previously grey. Eroticism couldn't touch her now and the hours flew by with barely a thought of Michael, of where he was and what he was doing, what had happened last night and what had gone wrong between them, whether he was thinking of her and whether he might text or call, how angry she was with him and how sad and stupid she felt and whether she might ever see him again and what the weather was like in Yorkshire and the landscape and how his feet felt and how far there was to go. Blissfully, she was free of all those thoughts.

Marching

Only the cows saw him eat his lunch. This was by no means the most remote part of the walk yet he'd seen no one on foot since he'd left Richmond. He knew that a landscape is not altered by one person's absence, but the woods and lanes did seem dull, the patchworked fields just that, patched together. If Marnie were still here, she'd be looking up bus routes by now, but she wasn't here, so . . .

On he walked, though he might as well have been on a treadmill. The simplicity of the route allowed him time to think, which was the last thing he wanted, and he found himself wrenching his mind away from last night as you might wrench a steering wheel to avoid a collision. Instead he tried to focus on the physical act of walking, marching, one-two, one-two, towards the high scarp of the Hambleton Hills and beyond that, the Cleveland Hills curving north. On the plateau at their summit, unseen, were the North York Moors, so that he felt like a child who can't see the top of a table. On the maps, they looked formidably bare and unmarked, like reading a book where the pages become suddenly blank and even the word 'moor' seemed to carry an atmosphere of gloom. Of course it needn't be like that, and it must be possible to have a fun time on the Moors, but even so, he felt apprehension at what lay ahead.

For now, he marched on through Danby Wiske and Oaktree Hill, Harlsey and Ingleby and finally along the edge of the plain, the path now rising abruptly into woodland that provided some shelter from the steady rain. *Typical spring*, he'd said. He climbed, descended again into a pretty town, the houses neat and sturdy, built from blocks, the village green unnervingly silent. In the pub, he spoke to a human being though only to collect his key. The room was Hawthorn, the Wi-Fi code wainwrightc2c.

A single bed, military-style. *The Haywain* in a clip frame. Biscuits, long-life milk, a small kettle. It was 5 p.m. and he had no idea how to fill the hours before sleep. He checked his phone but with no expectations. Any further communication with Marnie would have to come from him and he'd no idea what to tell her. Instead, he read three messages from Nat.

Hope you're okay
Please reply
All okay?

He remembered last night in Richmond. *My God*, he thought, *I bought champagne.*

Feta

She worked hard all morning, barely looking up. For lunch, she found that open pack of feta cheese, softening at its edges and with a mauvish-tint, which she ate from a saucer with a teaspoon as if it were a slab of ice-cream. It fizzed on her tongue but did not make her sick, and while that was the least you should expect of a meal it meant she didn't have to stop working.

By mid-afternoon, in need of something to punch, she thought of her ex-husband. Quickly she opened an email and wrote:

Dear Neil,

How are you? I hope that the family are well, and that parenthood suits you.

I'm well too. In fact, I've just returned from a holiday where I did some thinking and also took some advice.

I'm writing to say that the time has come for you to return the money you owe me. Ideally you would pay in one lump sum, but I understand your financial obligations so, if that's not possible, a monthly payment would be acceptable. Please make a proposal. I am willing to forgo interest but you do have to pay me what is mine. I have financial obligations too.

I sincerely wish you well for the future and hope that we can settle this amicably. I think we will both feel better

when this is all brought to a close and we can get on with
our lives.

Best wishes, Marnie.

She read it back, changing the phrase 'took some advice' to 'got some legal advice', pressed send, then rose from her chair and paced as much as the kitchen allowed. She'd hoped for some elation, the kind of satisfaction that traditionally comes from confronting a bully, but it was hard to imagine the Neil she'd known accepting her demands. All she'd done was restart hostilities.

Sure enough, the sound of a text arriving made her jump. Retaliation, she thought, or perhaps it was Michael. She'd resolved yesterday to delete his messages unread. She picked up the phone.

Hi! Are you back? Shall I alert mountain rescue? Have been thinking about you. If you are here, how about that drink? I promise – no walking. Let me know, Conrad x

She read the message twice then once again, alternating between feeling annoyed and flattered by his persistence. Perhaps it might be fun or a chance for revenge. Were 'fun' and 'vengeance' compatible? She didn't see why not.

The orthodoxy in the books she'd edited seemed to demand that she wait a couple of days before replying, but who had time for that? She read the text again then replied in two words, **Yes** and **Tomorrow?**

Last Night in Richmond

'Mike,' said Natasha, 'you bought champagne!'

'Yes, but we don't have to,' he said, indicating the armchair by the window. Why wouldn't she take her coat off?

'Nice hotel. Swankier than usual.'

'Well, you know. Do you want to . . . ?'

'Okay. I will.'

And there it was, the soft swelling below the waistband of her skirt, the one he'd longed to see, year after year, and he felt the air squeezed out of him in a great sigh. *Hold it together, try to smile.*

'Obviously this is why I can't drink the champagne.'

He breathed in. 'I understand.'

'But if you want to . . .'

'I'm all right. Maybe later. Maybe I'll . . . Anyway, congratulations, Nat.'

'Thank you.'

'How long?' That was something people said, wasn't it? His brain wasn't functioning as it should.

'Seventeen weeks now.'

'Wow,' he said, a meaningless response to meaningless words. Then, 'So I guess it's not mine!'

She looked shocked but only for a moment, then smiled. 'No,'

292

she said, her coat draped across her arm as if she might leave. 'It's not.'

'Please, sit. Take the weight off.' She laid her coat on the bed and sat, and he sat in the other armchair, both set at forty-five degrees to face the bed as if something might happen there, as if it were a stage. Clearly this was intolerable.

'Shall we get out of here?' he said.

'Let's,' she said, standing, one hand on her belly.

'I booked us a table at a restaurant. Are you hungry?'

'I will be.'

'I booked it for eight o'clock.' He looked at his watch. It was five forty. 'But maybe we could go for a walk, get there early.'

'Sure. Sure, let's do that.'

In the lift, they caught each other's eye, smiled, and then he looked to the floor, hands linked in front of him, like a priest. He wondered if Marnie might still be in the lobby. Perhaps she might throw a vase, but Marnie was long gone now.

They stepped out into the marketplace and he had a very vivid memory of their first date, not lunch in the staffroom but a formal date, the city centre on a Saturday night, how nervous he'd been and how she'd taken his hand as they walked towards the restaurant and, before they'd entered, turned and kissed him. She had always been the forthright one. *There. Now we can concentrate*, she'd said, and he remembered how hard it had been to do so, sitting across the table from her, a nice Thai place, nothing special, talking happily but thinking all the time, *It's here, I've found it, it's sitting right in front of me.* It was silly, but he remembered, too, how the news had been received at school, the cheers at the next disco when they'd danced together, all the cheeky questions from children who might now have children of their own. Kids loved it when teachers got together, as if they were responsible, were less sure how to react when teachers broke up. Now in the quiet of the back-streets, he felt self-conscious about the clomp of his boots, the rustle of his clothes. There were so many things to say but he didn't yet trust his voice, so Natasha took over, as she always had.

'How are your legs?'

'Oh, fine. It's not hard, it's just long. It's for tourists, really.'

'But ten days. You look well on it.'

'Do I?'

'Got some colour.'

'Tanned from the rain.'

'But it hasn't rained every day.'

'No, it's been mixed, you know, spring, typical spring.'

It was absurd to be talking about the weather again, yet he was incapable of anything beyond bland chat about where he'd stayed, the route he'd taken, how many miles. They walked the lanes and back-streets, shops shutting up now, people heading home. The restaurant was not yet open so they walked another circuit, Michael answering her questions in a strained, sing-song voice. A light rain began to fall so they circled back and tapped on the restaurant window, a waiter letting them in warily. The place was brighter, more modern and less intimate than he'd hoped, more like a works canteen, the table still wet, a sharp citrus smell in the air. The chef had not arrived, would they mind waiting with a drink? He ordered a beer, Nat asked for sparkling water, ice and lime. Time passed, and he was suddenly aware of his shirt cuffs, the frayed edges, a loose thread holding the button.

'Cleo said you were walking with someone.'

'I was, with her friend. She stayed on, just for an extra day or so.' If he pulled the thread he'd lose the button.

'And how has that been? Having company?'

'It was . . . fine. You've met her before. Marnie.'

'Have I?'

'At the christening.'

'Oh, right. Cleo's friend from London.'

'Yes.'

'Married to that terrible man. Cleo *hated* him.'

'Divorced now.'

'Well. Good. Did you get on well or . . . ?'

He knew what she was doing. She was probing, hoping there was something more than friendship. What a relief that would be, like offloading a subsiding house, and he felt a little spur of irritation, no, anger. How would it feel to flip the table over? It was futile, of course, the rage of a man at the bottom of a pit. Instead, he asked, 'How is it going with Frank?'

She pulled her head back. 'Okay. Things have got a little more serious,' she said, glancing down. 'Obviously.'

'Of course.'

'I've moved out of Mum and Dad's. I'm at his now.'

'That makes sense.'

'And he's excited about – the baby.'

'Well, that's all good news.'

She sighed and looked to the door. 'Michael, don't be—'

'What?'

'We're getting along. We both wanted it, it felt like the right thing. It's good.' She looked to the door again as if contemplating fleeing. Perhaps he ought to let her. There was nothing that could remedy this situation and she must have felt so too, her cheeks red, her eyes a little wet. Unfair to torment her with this great hulking, incoherent sadness, and yet it occurred to him that if she left now, he would probably never see her again. Was that melodramatic, an exaggeration? What would be achieved by meeting in person? The bureaucracy of the separation could be carried out remotely, her dwindling mail forwarded; she could get her things when he was away; perhaps she should just go. Yet if she left he knew his heart would crack, he was sure of it.

'If I'm honest about him, about Frank,' she was saying, taking his hand, 'we don't have what you and I had.'

'Please, don't do that.'

'I just mean—'

'I can think of one thing we didn't have.'

'Yeah. I know.'

'And I'm pleased for you, I mean I will be pleased at some point in the future, for you, for both of you. I – I know how much you wanted it.'

'I did want it,' she said, then stopped herself. *With you*: was that what she was about to say? Every consolation was another blow, and for a terrible moment, he thought, *My God, what if she asks me to be godfather?*

The door opened and a man hurried in, swiping the rain from his hair with the flat of his hand, the chef, he supposed. They'd not eat for some time yet and it seemed intolerable to sit and make small-talk when he had thought they might get back together. He had tried to suppress the notion but that was what he'd thought, that she might say, Let's try again, get to grips with the situation, do what we can and talk, honestly and openly, find what we'd once had. He'd thought she might stay the night. Why else had he bought the room, the ridiculous champagne? Now he felt sulky and self-righteous. 'I wish you'd warned me in advance.'

'I thought I should tell you in person.'

'But you could have let me know this morning.'

'Then it wouldn't have been in person, would it?'

He opened his mouth, then closed it again. She was moving things on briskly, talking about selling their house.

'We might need to speed things up a little.'

'Of course.'

'Maybe register it with more than one estate agent.'

'Fine. I'll do that.'

'How is the house? How does it feel?'

'You mean . . . is it tidy?'

'I'm sure it's tidy.'

'Am I washing out the bath, making the bed?'

'I mean is it . . . appealing?'

'Does it smell of freshly baked bread?'

She pressed the heels of her hands into her eyes. 'Yes, Michael, that's what I mean.'

'It feels sad. It's a sad house. I can't bear the place, actually. I cannot bear to be there.'

'I can imagine.'

'That's why I'm wandering around on the fucking heath like a lunatic all the time, because I can't stand being in *our* home.'

'Then perhaps you should move out, rent, you'll have to eventually.'

'I can't afford it.'

'Then we should speed things up a little. Like I said.'

He remembered this, too, the cadence of their arguments, his petulant outbursts, her forced attempt at reason, the performance of patience, the sudden silence. He put his hand to his mouth and was startled by the feel of the bare skin, unpleasant and clammy. 'I will look for somewhere. I'll look. I haven't got round to it.'

She said nothing, her hand bracing her forehead and he realised that she was crying. 'Hey, I don't want to make you upset.'

'You're not *making* me, I just am.'

'I'm pleased for you, that it's happening, I am. I will be, eventually.'

'Thank you.'

'But it's not what I'd hoped for or what I wanted. It's not what I thought our marriage would be.'

'No.'

'And I thought about kids a lot.'

'I know, me too.'

'How stupid, to just presume, but I took it for granted we'd be parents, Mum and Dad, we'd be good at it.'

'And we would have.'

'And I know it would be easier for me to . . . If I could just, you know, give you my blessing, say I'm happy for you both, new chapter, he's a lovely fella, but . . . I'm just so fucking sad, Nat, nearly all the time.'

'And what can I do about that?'

'I don't know. Stay away?'

She looked up, her mouth open. 'I don't want to do that.' And now she took his hand across the table, holding it still. 'I want you to be happy.'

He laughed for a moment. 'Fucking hell, so do I.'

They were both crying now and the waiter was approaching. 'Oh, *now* we get served,' said Natasha, urgently dabbing her eyes with a napkin and they were both laughing too, hiding their heads in the menus, shoulders shaking.

'Would you like to order?'

'Actually,' he said, without looking up. 'Something's come up.' He glanced at Natasha, who gave a small nod and perhaps the waiter was relieved because within a few minutes the bill was settled and they were on the street. The rain had eased and it was a relief not to face each other as they walked slowly to her car, the conversation turning to easier stuff: village life, the health of her parents (they send their love), the management of the new school, the kids. The countryside there was wild but lovely. Lots of nice walks.

And then they were at the car and it seemed that everything was happening too quickly, like a conversation through the window of a departing train. There was no reason why they couldn't continue but she should get back. 'It's a quarter to seven.'

'Wild nights,' he said, and thought how strange that she was returning to a home he'd never seen, would never see. *How did it go?* Frank would ask from their sofa. *How did he take it?*

'I hope you enjoy the rest of the walk.'

'I'm sure I will,' he said, far from sure.

'Good luck. Be careful on the Moors. I'll see you with Cleo and Sam. Send Anthony my love.' He promised he would but she must have pressed the button in her coat pocket because the car door was unlocking and now they were embracing, her body subtly arched away from him so that only their shoulders touched and then she was reaching up and holding his face, pressing her cheek to his.

Then, just as quickly, she had turned, holding her coat across her belly protectively and climbing into the car. He stepped back and saw her face once more, managing a smile, eyes glinting. She raised one hand, then turned the wheel sharply and was gone.

Back at the hotel, he asked if it was possible to return the champagne but it was tricky because it was part of the Romantic Weekender package. Perhaps he could take it with him. That, too, would be tricky so instead he ordered a sandwich and went to his room.

In his efforts to hide the ice bucket, he had pushed it too

close to the radiator so the bottle was now warm and, when he opened it, foaming and unpleasantly flat, but he forced it down, taking care not to drink the whole thing, leaving a couple of inches in the bottle for the morning.

Day Nine, Part One:

HERNE HILL TO BATTERSEA

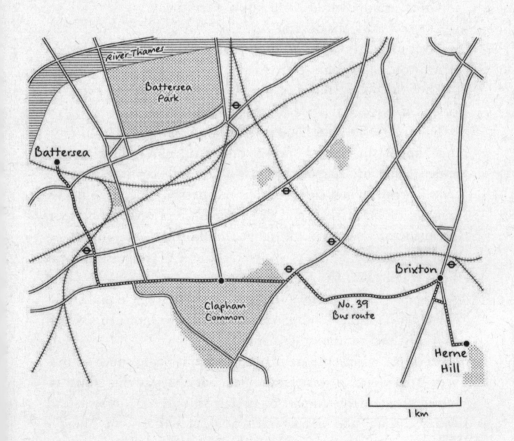

Brains and Hearts

'So how's it going at the chemist's? I mean, the *pharmacist's*.'

'Great!' said Conrad. 'You know, very tiring.'

'Do you work six days or . . . ?'

'Five. I have an assistant manager, so.'

'Are you a late-night pharmacist?'

'Only in my private life,' he said, with a raised eyebrow, though it was six thirty p.m. on Sunday.

'Flah-nah,' she said. The private language was back. Forty-eight hours since she'd spoken out loud. How quickly she'd settled back into her old ways, working all day, hoping for a cancellation. When none came, she dressed in her old city uniform of black skirt and coat, her blisters now rubbing on the inside of opaque black tights and flat black strappy shoes. They sat on high stools at the zinc counter of a tapas bar near Battersea Bridge, Conrad in a leather jacket, open shirt and blue jeans, like a Premier League footballer on a night out. There wasn't a nightclub in the world that would turn Conrad away. Michael on the other hand . . .

He began with some standard digs about being south-of-the-river, how weird it was, how quiet, but she put this down to nerves, resisting the temptation to slag off Barons Court, instead leafing through the menu, which came in a sticky vinyl binder and was the length of a novella. 'Ah, tapas,' she said, 'the original small plates!' And she considered how close the Embankment was, how easy it would be to run from here, hurdle the railings and leap into the fast-flowing river.

They ordered a bottle of 'red Vino tinto', which Marnie noted was a tautology, the capitalisation all over the place, then debated what to order, the ratio of meat to fish to vegetables, the number of plates, the etiquette of sharing, Conrad noting the candidates on a red napkin ('*Boquerones*?'), the process so complex and political that it could easily have taken the whole night. 'We can always order more but we can't order less,' said Marnie, and Conrad liked this philosophy so much that he repeated it, more than once, as they sipped their red wine, which was as sticky as the menus and tasted like the headache it would bring about.

A silence. Then. 'Cheers!' said Conrad. 'To cities!'

'To normal shoes!'

'And flat ground. To being warm and dry.'

'Foxes and pigeons!'

'Foxes and pigeons.' They drank. 'I'm amazed you lasted so long.'

'Oh,' said Marnie, 'why?'

'Well, seven days! What did you talk about?'

'You know – love, life, death,' she said, and Conrad laughed, though in fact this had been true. 'There's something about walking, things slip out. It's like taking a truth serum or something. Also it was very beautiful. Look.'

Though she'd resolved not to do it, she found herself reaching for her phone. Here was the photo of a view down to Grasmere, where they'd been surrounded by all the dogs, here was Angle Tarn where they'd almost swum, here was Kidsty Pike, the highest point, and eerie Nine Standards Rigg, the watershed, and after this they'd found, well, best not tell him about that.

On that wretched New Year's Day she'd promised to change the nature of her photographs and she'd done it, but even with the brightness turned up, the pictures lacked any hint of the sublime, and perhaps landscapes were like photos of the full moon, always underwhelming. 'They don't look like much, I know.'

'Let me see,' he said, and took the phone, swiping back to the one she'd skipped. 'There he is!'

It was the photo they'd taken by the dam, by no means flattering, Marnie smiling goofily, Michael's arm heavy and unnatural across her shoulders, the one new face she'd managed to add.

'How did you get on?'

'Oh, okay.'

Shortly afterwards she'd asked for his number and he'd asked her to stay.

'Did he make any moves? Late night in the lounge bar, boots all muddy—'

'Don't be ridiculous.'

'I think he had a thing for you.'

She laughed. 'Oh. Why?'

'I saw it a couple of times, that night in the bar, little looks, leaning in. Where is he now? I wonder.'

She wondered too. She felt the need to confide in someone, tell them about the scene in the Lavender Suite, what a thrill it had been to kiss again, to want and to be wanted. The cliché was 'like a teenager' but she had a right to those feelings too, to the dizziness and elation of it all.

But none of this seemed appropriate on a date and she realised that the only person she could talk to about her confusion was the person who had caused it. For the moment, she should concentrate on Conrad, who was exactly as handsome as he'd been a week ago, as confident and free of guile and pores and humour. The food came quickly, and he talked about his work, the famous university experience, places he'd live abroad, and he was nicer, she thought, less gauche, and even though there was no romantic feeling, she was doing what she'd vowed to do, to be out in the world, listening.

And yet it no longer seemed so important merely to fill the photo frame. The question she needed to ask: Is this someone I'd turn to in a crisis, someone whose memory or image I might summon up when they're not around? Someone I need? If they came to visit me on my deathbed, would I be pleased, or would I think, *What are you doing here?* It was a ghoulish criterion to apply on a casual date but this perfectly nice man didn't qualify, any more than she'd pass the deathbed test for him. One or two more people, that was all she really needed, one or two that she could love.

They drank the first bottle quickly, ordered another, and he began to confide about his ex-fiancée, telling her the story he'd been too self-conscious to share a week ago, and she sucked the sweet garlicky brains from the heads of the prawns, benevolence fading. She had read somewhere that prawns' hearts were in their heads, which sounded like a metaphor for something, though perhaps it wasn't really a 'head' as such, more of a thorax. Meanwhile Conrad was saying that it had all happened so quickly, the engagement, and maybe he'd panicked but maybe she'd been right, they weren't young any more, didn't have time to waste and blah-blah-blah. He was playing the sadness card. Men, she thought, overestimated the appeal of sadness. Marnie slipped an empty prawn head on to the tip of her index finger, made a little puppet, sniffing the air, nodding, yes, yes, tell me more, and so pleasing was the effect that she slipped on three more. 'I swear,' she said, 'my manicurist . . .'

'Sorry?'

'Nothing. You sound like you still love her,' she said abruptly.

There was a pause. 'Yeah,' he said eventually, 'I think you might be right,' and she wondered if this was how she was doomed to spend her evenings, listening to men who were heavy and dull with love for somebody else. Perhaps she'd snapped, because Conrad was silent now, staring mournfully at his greasy wine glass, and out of respect she removed the prawn heads from her fingertips. 'Why don't you have this conversation with her instead?'

'D'you think?'

'I think it would be a good idea, yes.'

'Okay. Maybe I will.' He sat up straight, resolved. 'Do you want pudding or . . . ?'

'No, I'm fine. Let's go.' They surveyed the table, spines and shells and pools of red oil.

'We didn't over-order after all.'

'No,' said Marnie, 'we did very well.'

They walked along the Thames towards Battersea Bridge between circles of orange light. 'I should have said this earlier but I feel bad about when we were away.'

'You were fine! You were great!'

'Just boring on about Formula One. You're not interested in racing cars.'

'I was just as bad! Is it "chemist" or "pharmacist"?'

'And then running off.'

'Yes, that was strange.'

'I know! And I didn't want you to think it was because I didn't like you. It was just everyone watching, the pressure.'

'I understand that.'

'And, I hope I can say this, I fancied you, I did, but it wasn't the right place. I mean, I fucking *hate* the countryside.'

She laughed. 'Well, then, it definitely wasn't the right place.'

'Still. I wish you'd stayed over in my room.' They were at Battersea Bridge, buses heading north above them, and they stopped and turned. 'I was thinking I'd like to kiss you now but that's probably a bad idea.'

'Almost certainly.' She pointed to her mouth. 'Prawn brains.'

'I don't mind.'

As a girl, she'd once tried kissing the cast of *Friends* on the television screen, one by one, to see what it was like and perhaps this would be the same. 'Go on then,' she said. 'Just the once.' They kissed for some time. Yes, it was the same. 'Thank you very much,' she said, as if she'd been given a book voucher.

'But . . . just the once?'

'I think so. It's nice to see you again. I just don't know if we have the pharmacy. We lack pharmacy.'

There was a moment before he smiled, and then looked to the bridge. 'I'd better . . .'

'Yes, before they close the border. The nineteen, the forty-nine, the three four five . . .'

'You really know your buses, Marnie,' he said, and she bobbed her head modestly. 'What'll you do now?'

It was cold but crisp, still early, and she felt the need to clear her head. The blisters weren't too bad. 'D'you know?' she said. 'I think I'm going to walk.'

Day Nine, Part Two:

OSMOTHERLEY TO BLAKEY RIDGE

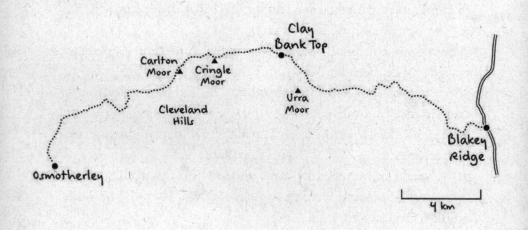

Fun on the Moors

On Sunday he fell apart then, without realising it, he began to put himself back together.

A 100 per cent chance of rain, said the weather app, but rain can be a mist or a monsoon and perhaps it wouldn't be too bad, the peaks and troughs of the Cleveland Way in the morning, then a level march across the moors. He would treat it like a physical challenge, a marathon or an assault course. There'd be nobody to urge him on but there might still be some fun in that, on the moors, alone, an assault course in the rain.

But he was exhausted before the first ascent. He'd gone to bed early but it was pub quiz night and the old wooden floors had meant he was able to take part from his bed, doing well on movie themes and rivers of the world, increasingly frustrated during the picture rounds. Should he give up on sleep, go and offer his services to the Four Quizeteers? Or lie there and strain his eyes looking at the room's tiny TV, placed too far away on the chest of drawers? There were two working channels, both showing quiz shows, so he spent the evening under intense interrogation, distant voices demanding to know who had had a number-one hit with 'Smalltown Boy'.

Still exhausted, he climbed through woods straight out of a horror film, the mist dense as cigar smoke so that he had the illusion of walking in a small, portable grey cell, open only to the rain. His thoughts felt similarly confined. He would have to tell his parents Natasha's news. His colleagues at work, their mutual friends, would need to know, perhaps knew already. He would have to get serious about finding a place to rent – renting at his age, my God. Would he have flatmates? He was too old for flatmates. The path opened in front, closed behind, and now the rain was seeping down his back and into his boots, and he could definitely feel the skin starting to rub. Only one idea brought relief and it was too late for that.

Finally he left the tree line, emerging at the top of the scarp, a great expanse of the north-east unrolling before him, green and yellow fields spiked with pylons and turbines and, just visible through the grey wash, Middlesbrough, Stockton and Redcar. It was a view he might once have taken in, but now he merely glanced at it, as if it was a postcard intended for someone else. He'd be heading south-west of here, but first there'd be a hill to climb, then another and another, five in all. This took up the grim, wet morning, the walk along the plateaux too brief so that the sudden descent and steep climbs seemed spiteful, enraging, and he began to doubt the wisdom of the whole project. Landscape no longer worked. There was no walking cure, and it was impossible to put the past behind you because it would always find a way to sneak ahead and obstruct your path. Round Hill and Carlton Moor, Cringle Moor and Clay Bank Top, he trudged across and up and down, the cold, steady rain seeping into every seam, into his clothes, through his skin, and into his joints so that he felt as if he was rusting. If Marnie had been here, they might have found comedy in it. Was there a way back, an apology or explanation by text or call? He did not have a gift for emotional eloquence as Marnie had discovered, but perhaps if he was honest and straightforward . . .

But it was a myth that talking made things better. Just keep on, get it over with. One last climb and he was on Urra Moor, exposed and bare and seemingly infinite, and he remembered Marnie's description of looking at the world atlas as a child, that fluttering fear of great distance and empty space. He had never felt such solitude in all his life and he found himself imagining terrible things, falling overboard and watching the ship sail away – Christ, don't think about that – his childhood nightmare of drifting through infinite space or being buried alive, spiralling fantasies of terrifying loneliness, the thoughts so relentless that he had to stand, hands on knees, struggling to breathe. Fun on the Moors! No wonder people went mad here. There was beauty in its severity, but couldn't he find beauty in something bright and noisy and alive, somewhere populated even by just one person?

Too late for that. Keep on. Hours passed and he entered a fugue state of exhaustion, the light fading before he saw a sign of human life, a small cluster of modern houses on the lonely road that bisected the moor, their location so remote that they must have been built there by mistake. A burst of rain urged him on to a drab, pebble-dashed house, four windows and a door, like a child's drawing, a mud-spattered minicab on its gravel forecourt. Was this really somewhere that took paying guests?

'Good God, look at the state of you. Let's get you indoors.' His host was a white-haired man in his late fifties, short and stocky and blunt, like an old-fashioned football manager, ushering him into the hallway, helping him with his wet clothes.

'You on your own?'

'I am tonight.'

'All this way on your own?'

'I was with a friend, but she had to go back.'

He followed the man up the narrow stairs. His son, he said, had just joined the Royal Navy so, rather than let the room go to waste, they were trying out the B-and-B game. It was 'early days, so please bear with us'. His wife, he said, was finding it hard and had gone to stay with her sister in Scarborough. 'She doesn't like people in his room.'

'Won't that make it a bit difficult? For a B&B, I mean?'

'Yes, well, like I said. Early days!'

And it was true, the tiny spare bedroom still carried the son's presence – a pull-up bar above the door and a set of weights in the corner, Blu-Tack marks on the wall where the posters had once been, football stickers on the mirror and, on the chest of drawers, a huddle of trophies in black and gold plastic. The duvet was emblazoned with red and white lions, the colours of Middlesbrough FC, and the landlord, Graham, hoped he wouldn't mind. 'Not a Magpies' fan, I hope!' and Michael assured him that he was not.

'Do you have kids yourself?' asked Graham.

'No, no, I don't.'

'You miss them when they go.'

'I can imagine.'

There was a pause as if Graham wanted to say more. Instead it would be lads together for dinner, if that was okay, or he could run him to the pub if he preferred. 'Well, I'll leave you to it,' said Graham, and gave a last forlorn look around the room as if to check, absolutely once and for all, that his son was no longer there.

And then Michael was alone again, sitting on the edge of the narrow single bed. It seemed inconceivable that he would spend the night here and inconceivable that he might leave, for where would he go? With one finger, he pulled the curtain aside and looked eastwards. Daylight had gone, the wind now spattering the window with rain. This – now *this* was wuthering. It was a view of such featureless desolation that he had no choice but to laugh. Leaning his phone flat against the glass, he took a photograph as a kind of joke: fat dark bands, like the view through a blindfold.

What to do with the photograph? What are photos for? He heard footsteps on the stairs, a light tap on the door, and here was Graham again, excitement in his eyes.

'Just to say I'm about to microwave a chicken.'

'Thank you very much, Graham,' said Michael. 'That sounds terrific.' He heard Marnie's voice, *Oh, 'terrific', is it?* and went downstairs to help.

Mark Rothko

She returned home and found her rucksack waiting in ambush by the door just as she'd left it, but she didn't have the energy for that now. Neither could she sleep. At her kitchen table, she scanned the last few pages of her copy-editing to check that she'd not rushed things, then wrote the covering email for the editor. Yes, it was a spicy read as promised and she'd enjoyed it and hoped this would help. Was there anything else she could look at? She was available. Invoice attached.

She would send this in the morning but now here was a new email, 'From Neil' the subject. She held her breath and opened it. In its entirety, it read –

Fair enough. Sorry it's late. Will this be okay?

– and below this a screengrab of a standing order for five hundred pounds, monthly for the next two and a half years. It was the first time that a message from her ex-husband had brought any kind of satisfaction and she replied with a simple 'Thank you' and closed the laptop, just as she heard the sound of a text arriving.

She lifted the lid once again.

It was from Michael, the first she'd ever received, an abstract vertical image, horizontal bands of industrial grey and black.

She clicked on it so that it filled the screen and stared at the monolith, waiting for some further explanation. Time passed. Nothing seemed to come. She ought to go to bed now.

Marnie waited.

The Boy's Duvet

He should have sent the text first before the photograph because now he wasn't sure what to write. The buttons seemed too small, his thumbs too fat, he should really have drafted it first, and now it was as if he'd knocked on her door then run away.

What did he want to say? There wouldn't be space in a text but at some point he wanted to tell her about his evening, eating dinner in front of Graham's TV, their plates on matching trays with cushioned bottoms, par-boiled potatoes, marrowfat peas like gallstones, the chicken an anatomy lesson, an impression underlined by the surgical glare of the big light overhead. Microwaving, it seemed, was the process whereby a real chicken was rubberised, the skin pale and bobbled, the flesh grey and weeping some sort of white sap. 'My wife does most of the cooking as you can probably tell,' Graham had said, and Michael had done his best, really he had, his stomach engaged in a battle between hunger and nausea. On a low brown leather sofa, they'd drunk beer from cans poured into Middlesbrough FC-themed tankards and watched *Antiques Roadshow*, Graham assessing each item as either old tat or worth a few bob, and while he was a decent man and warm company, it was a meal that would haunt Michael until his dying day. For pudding they'd eaten strawberry yoghurts out of the pots, then stood at the sink by the kitchen window, Graham washing, Michael drying, looking out into the darkness as he was quizzed about his life. The game was to answer truthfully but with the bare minimum of detail.

'Married?'

'We're getting divorced.'

'No kids?'

'No.'

'Well, that makes it easier.'

'So they say.'

'Got to move on, haven't you? Are you courting?' said Graham, nudging him and Michael had smiled. 'What?'

'I've not heard it called that for a while,' said Michael. 'I was, I think, in a way.'

'Surely you'd know.'

He laughed. 'You'd think so, wouldn't you?'

'And where's she now?'

'Oh, back in London.'

'Well, you should go down, get on with it. Good-looking fella like you.'

Michael frowned and changed the subject, talking instead about Graham's family, the minicab game, his wife, his son's travels with the Navy, how he missed them both when they weren't around, eyes fixed on the window throughout as if he hoped to see them stepping out of the rain. Had his own parents felt his absence this intently when he'd left home? It had never crossed his mind and he resolved to visit them as soon as he got back, tell them in person, talk honestly. He'd said no to a bedtime milky coffee and *Match of the Day*, went upstairs and lay on the bed, phone in hand.

Finally, he wrote: This is the view from my window on the Moors. It is raining! Hope you got back safe. Needless to say I feel bad about our goodbye. Not sure why I didn't tell you I was meeting Nat. It was rude and I apologise. She is well but I am going to try and move on. Two more days to go then I head home Tuesday night. It has been an 'experience' but all the best bits were with you. I am sorry you left but understand. I am fool. Hope you are well and that I might see you again some time, indoors or out.

He took a deep breath, pressed send, at the same time noticing the error. 'I am fool', as if he was the essence of Fool. She would notice too, that was her job, but would think he had a point. Still the message felt unfinished, as if he was loitering in a doorway. Say what you mean. He wrote:

I miss you now

Thought and wrote again:

PS Never microwave a chicken.

He washed his face, brushed his teeth, checked his phone. He climbed under the Middlesbrough FC duvet, which was clean but still had a young man's muskiness; he imagined it would never quite leave. Outside, rain rattled against the window like handfuls of gravel. Two more long days. He should sleep but his phone kept him awake past twelve and one and two a.m. despite, because of, not making any noise at all.

THE LAST DAY

Unpacking

There really was no reason to get up the next morning yet she couldn't stay in bed. Still in pyjamas, she sat at the kitchen table, opened the laptop and sent the copy-edit so it would be waiting when the editor arrived.

And there was Michael's message from last night, which she read again. *I am fool* sounded about right but what about *I miss you now*. Did it mean *I miss you now that something has happened* or *I miss you at this precise moment*? What did *try to move on* mean? It was neither here nor there, of course, but she wondered where he'd written it. Feeling furtive, she dragged the photo on to her desktop. Command-I opened what she thought might be called metadata and, yes, sure enough, there were the co-ordinates. Pasting these into the map gave a precise location, a cluster of four buildings so remote that she worried for him. In Street-view, she peered at the plain modern house from the roadside, puddles on the forecourt, pebble-dash, the red and white of a football flag. He was behind one of those windows at this very moment, either sleeping or eating breakfast with his hands. She clicked to step closer. Was that a human shape? The image was months, even years, old but for a moment she felt as if she were about to order a SWAT team raid to pull off the duvet, swipe the socks from the radiator, truss him up in cable-ties. Or perhaps this was just stalking. Either way, it was not appropriate or useful. On Street-view, she turned away and scanned the landscape he'd be crossing. It had a certain bleak beauty. Certainly it was bleak.

Her rucksack stood in the hall where she'd left it more than two days ago and now she hauled it to her bedroom, unclipped and unzipped, wrinkling her nose as if she'd found it on the street. The compass, the water bladder, *The Central Fells*, the mashed-up protein bars, who was this stranger? She consigned the paraphernalia to the drawer where she kept her dead batteries. This stranger's clothes smelt of peat and old sweat and she tossed them into the washing-machine, shedding grass and dried mud as she went. Here were her three good dresses, the optimistic evening wear. She sniffed her second-best dress: deodorant and the tang of her sweat, the hoppy smell of the pub. She remembered its hem rising up to her hip. It would need dry-cleaning. She tossed it into the wardrobe and when the rucksack was finally empty she took it to the bathroom, held it by the base and shook it vigorously over the bath to remove the last of the debris.

A skittering noise, as something fell into the tub and rolled around its base like a marble. It was a pale red stone, the size, shape and colour of a supermarket raspberry. Red sandstone from the beach at St Bees, it had indeed dried out, and was disappointing in a way she could not have anticipated, but she placed it on the glass shelf with her toothbrush for the moment, rinsed away the grit from the tub and shoved the rucksack to the very back of the wardrobe.

She found the postcard too, Greetings from Viaduct Country, *No Guests After 10, Please!* This she tore smartly into four and put into the recycling bin.

The Path

On waking, he immediately looked for Marnie's reply and, in its absence, finished packing. Opening the curtains made no difference to the light in the room and through the rain's veil the Moors looked dank and saturated. He would not get lost, he was sure of that, but it would be a long, wet march to Egton Bridge, in clothes that were still damp from yesterday, with nothing to see but the inside of his hood.

'I can run you into Scarborough if you fancy,' offered Graham at breakfast. Microwaving bacon had not been a success either and Michael brushed his teeth to shift the taste, then left the money for the accommodation on the chest of drawers, plus twenty pounds extra, and went downstairs to say goodbye. The stay had been top-notch and he would be sure to give it five stars, and now the front door was open. He hesitated on the threshold as if it were a parachute jump, and Graham laughed. 'I leave for Scarborough in an hour.'

'No, it's got to be done.'

'Well, here's my card if you change your mind.' Michael slipped it into his pocket. 'Just get to the nearest road. I'll find you.'

'Can I ask something?' said Graham.

'Go on.'

'Why on *earth* would you do something like this?'

No one would know if he gave up now. No one would care

if he dipped his toes in the North Sea or dropped his pebble on the beach. No weight would be lifted from his shoulders. There'd be no sense of closure, of liberation or change. The only mild motivation was a sense of completion, the ability to say that he'd done it, though Cleo aside he was not sure whom he could tell. Back in the Honister Pass, that first day alone with Marnie, he'd refused a lift on the bus because he would only be cheating himself. He remembered her face in the back window, writing in the steam as it drove away.

'Because I don't want to go home,' said Michael.

'We all have to go home sometime.'

Michael smiled, raised his hand and stepped out into the rain. 'Silly bugger,' said Graham, and at the front gate, Michael stopped, then turned and walked back to the house. Graham had not even closed the door.

'Actually,' he said, 'I think I will take that lift, if you don't mind.'

Part Five

AUTUMN

–

Summer was ending, and the evening brought her odours of decay, the more pathetic because they were reminiscent of spring.

E. M. Forster, *A Room with a View*

The Post-Romantic Era

The seasons came around in their tiring way, Marnie noting the events in Nature's almanac: fox-scream night, the changing of the duvets, the rodents moving outdoors, the start of moth season. In May she retrieved the winter clothes she'd put away prematurely in April, exchanging them in June for her summer wardrobe, more accurately her summer bin-bag, a wad of ancient T-shirts that she kept on a high shelf with the Christmas decorations. In the park, the first burnt-black patches from disposable barbecues were springing up. Pomegranates gave way to mangoes in the Turkish grocers' and strawberries were on special. Soon it would be spider season.

In the meantime, she worked steadily, taking on every assignment she was offered, thrillers, romantic comedies, Napoleonic adventures, YA weepies, locked-room mysteries, a high-concept thriller that took place over twenty minutes, a sci-fi saga spread over twenty thousand years, all from her kitchen table. Love came up a lot, sex too, but she tried not to editorialise. 'Yeah, right,' was not a useful note. When not reading for work, she read for pleasure, and one bright, vacant afternoon in June, she put her book down, hauled her terrible window-boxes indoors and emptied out the lunar soil. At a stall in Brixton Market, she asked, 'What's the hardest plant to kill?' and now here they were, two rows of invulnerable red geraniums that she could see from the sofa. The beginning of her gardening years.

There were other changes too. An old friend got in touch, saying she was 'out the other side' now that the kids were older, and they met for a drink and laughed, and this led to other reunions with re-emerging friends, a few dinner parties, nothing wild. Whenever talk turned to school catchment areas or exam results, she simply disassociated, made shopping lists, hummed in her head until it passed. At some of these events she was conspicuously paired with recent divorcés – that word, the suave little accent like a tip of the hat – and this in turn led to an agreeable solo dinner with a very nice older man, which led nowhere. She tried not to fret about this. It was, she thought, like picking up a book, reading a paragraph and knowing with absolute conviction that it isn't for you. The analogy didn't quite hold – books aren't upset when you put them down – but in this instance they both walked away unscathed, grateful for the other's indifference.

But life seemed fuller, more populated than it had a year ago. She went to exhibitions and films, sometimes alone, sometimes with a friend, and when she'd saved enough of Neil's money, which was her money, she went on a solo trip to Italy, role-playing a character in a Forster novel. In Florence, she read performatively in cafés and sat in the cool of exquisite churches, straining for some kind of spiritual feeling. In Rome, she visited the Non-Catholic Cemetery and sought out the graves of Keats and Shelley and found herself moved and mortified by being moved.

She thought of Michael often, though had no reason to say his name out loud. Cleo had told her about Natasha's new life, and while she was pleased for her, it felt like hearing that a friend had been hit by a car. She recalled his face in the hotel corridor, clean-shaven, shiny and hopeful, and while she'd not forgotten her own hurt and anger, she felt for him too, her old friend, and hoped that he was managing to move on. More often when she thought of his face, nights usually, sometimes first thing, it was the one she'd seen on the beach, old-fashioned, handsome without knowing it, the face she'd watched for days as they'd walked and talked.

Still, she resisted mentioning him to anyone. In the summer holidays, Anthony came to stay but he was unlikely to raise the subject and instead she focused on keeping him entertained, taking him to places he'd loved, the South Kensington museums and Forbidden Planet, though they seemed to have lost their appeal. Instead they went to fashion stores in Soho – stores not shops – where customers queued as if it were a nightclub. She'd not queued to enter a shop since the pandemic but she loved seeing his excitement, and once inside she'd find a chair and read her book, nodding to the music, godmotherly but never grandmotherly. In the evenings they'd get take-out – take-out not takeaway – lie on the sofa and watch old nineties action movies, and it was here, between explosions, that she asked, in her most casual voice, 'How's Mr Bradshaw getting on?'

'He's all right.'

It was unclear what else she'd expected, and if she wanted a fuller report, she could always ask Cleo. But raising that subject would have opened up all kinds of speculation, so she tried again.

'He seems okay? At school?'

'Yeah. He's a teacher. I don't know much about it.'

On screen, a mansion exploded, the hero scorning to watch.

'Is the beard back?'

'No, his girlfriend didn't like it.'

'Oh. Oh. He's got a girlfriend.'

'He did have,' said Anthony, 'not any more,' and she felt two emotions in quick succession, as if bouncing over a pothole.

Summer ended and Nature's cavalcade continued. Flying Ant Day came and went, sweetcorn took the place of mangoes. Schools returned and the buses became busy, the rodents moved back indoors and suddenly it was spider season once again, Marnie catching the webs full on when she took out the bins, swiping madly at her own face.

Boot-camp

Cleo had been appalled. 'I just think it's terrible, to get so far then give up!'

'Why?' said Michael. 'You thought the whole thing was ridiculous.'

'But you were so keen!'

'The weather was really horrible.'

'No such thing as bad weather!'

'And also, it just seemed a bit . . . futile.'

'I can't believe it's *you* saying this. Why didn't you just *lie* to me?'

'What if you'd asked for a photo?'

'I wasn't going to *ask for a photo*. Just tell me you did it. Lie!'

'But then I'd be cheating myself.'

'I'd rather you cheated yourself than left me hanging like this. I was going to talk about it in assembly. What lesson will that teach them now? "Here's Mr Bradshaw, with a wonderful story about chickening out."'

He laughed. 'I didn't *chicken out*!'

'Obviously. You've got to go back and finish it.'

'Let's forget about it, shall we?'

But the subject came up again in May, at a party where he was introduced to Tessa, or 'the famous Tessa', as Cleo called her. The portrait he'd imagined was not nearly flattering enough. 'I'm sorry I couldn't make it to the walk,' she said.

'The walk that he *abandoned*,' said Cleo, leaving.

'Well, it's nice to meet you now,' he replied, summoning up the gambits he'd prepared in the spring. 'I hear you're a triathlete.'

This was the first time he'd allowed himself to be out in company since his return and he still felt shaky and self-conscious, capable only of the most basic conversation, asking questions at regular intervals, like a machine that launches tennis balls. But as he left the party he heard footsteps on the path behind him and Tessa was there, asking for his phone number. He grinned – a grin rather than a smile – and when she asked why, he said it was because no one had ever asked for his phone number before, though this was not quite true. 'And this is my landline,' he said, and smiled again.

The relationship with Tessa began a week later, continued for two months and ended without regret or anger. It was, while it lasted, extremely outdoorsy, kayaking, sea swimming, long bike rides, though she was less keen on walking, preferring to run. Cleo called these dates 'boot-camp', and he did sometimes feel as if he was in training for something undetermined, life in general, perhaps. If he'd been asked to sum up the relationship in one word, it would have been 'rigorous', but he felt better, happier, certainly fitter, and a large part of this was down to sex, which was rigorous too, with a good mix of cardio and strength work.

When they weren't out of breath, they talked. He began to feel a little more eloquent, as if conversation was another skill he was training for, though every now and then he'd find himself telling a story or making a joke he recognised from his week with Marnie and he'd feel guilty. The jokes and stories rarely landed anyway. They did not make each other laugh, but perhaps too much emphasis was placed on that sort of thing.

Or perhaps not. The fact was that he thought of Marnie often, nights usually, sometimes first thing, and missed her very much. He missed her jokes, of course, and her conversation, the way she'd take a remark and play with it, examine it, hold it up to the light. He missed her face, which he would sometimes look at in his one terrible photograph, using his thumbs to crop out his own gormlessness, placing her at the centre of the frame. Surprisingly, he missed the feel of her, moments of physical sensation, arms touching along their length, his hand on her lower back or under the swell of her breast, all as potent as the sensations you have in a dream, with the same lingering disappointment, too, at waking too soon. Teenage really, the stuff of his pupils' lives yet apparently now his own, the thoughts and feelings so persistent and surprising to him that he was forced to ask the question, not 'Am I in love with her?' but 'Could I be in love with her?' The answer to the second question, he decided, was unquestionably yes, and he felt it with such conviction that it became the answer to the first question too.

Clearly, he would have to stop seeing Tessa, a rare instance of someone ending a relationship because they were not seeing someone else. He found the prospect of the conversation mortifying, like telling someone you loved the gift then asking for the receipt. While he summoned up the words, they continued to go for dinner, watch films and even discussed going somewhere in August, but nothing really changed or developed, so that you could shuffle the order of their meetings and it would make no difference. It was less a relationship, more a protracted pep-talk, and while he was grateful, it was intolerable to spend time with someone while wishing they were someone else. At the end of an exhausting, mud-spattered weekend, he saw his chance but Tessa, the superior athlete, saw it first. 'Michael,' she said, 'you're a lovely guy but I'm not sure this is going anywhere.' Dropped from the squad, he conceded and said goodbye, and went home to shower and rest.

Home. An offer was made on the house by a nice young family, and accepted, and Michael was obliged to try to conjure up a life without Natasha's influence. A home divided into two makes something less than half a home and he would have to think about new furniture, new plates and pictures on the wall, new holidays and habits. He would need a new watch, though he would put the old one away with care. For the moment, he discussed the practicalities with Natasha, first by text and then, in September, over the phone and he found that he was able to do this perfectly well, without anger or recrimination. 'How are you feeling?'

'About to burst,' said Natasha. 'Huge, nauseous. But I'm fine. You?'

He was fine too. In the past, this had been another way of saying *Leave me alone*, but he was surprised to find that it was true, and while he could still recall his grief at the end of their relationship, it was an emotion that belonged to someone else. For now, he was not happy but not unhappy, content in all but one respect. Even so, he did not want to be there when Natasha came to take her stuff away. Thankfully, they found a time that corresponded with the autumn geography trip, which this year, at Michael's suggestion – at his insistence – would be a little different.

Day Ten:

HYDE PARK CIRCULAR

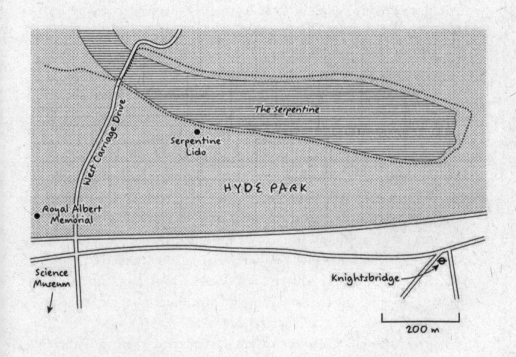

Serpentine

'So — a super-volcano is defined as a volcano that produces a massive amount of what we call ejecta. Why is that funny, Ryan? Would you like to explain to everyone? Okay, where was I? So this magma builds under the crust, the pressure increasing until you get this super-eruption, sometimes more than one thousand cubic kilometres of ejecta . . . Will someone pat his back, please, before he chokes? Ryan, do you want to wait outside until you've calmed down? No? Right then, I give up, I'm not going to tell you any more, you can find out in the exhibition.

'Now, that should take an hour and then you'll have some spare time to do whatever it is you do. Please, I beg you, don't just run to the shops. Hyde Park is to the north of us, so come out of the Museum and turn left and left. You know what to do. You can read maps. We are heading for the Royal. Albert. Memorial. Who knows who Albert was? . . . Yes, exactly, thank you, Amit. The Royal Albert Memorial at four p.m., no later. Careful crossing the roads. Ryan, can you breathe again? Good lad. Mrs Fraser and I will see you at four.'

They scattered. Cleo and Michael watched them go, then walked the aisles, half reading the labels, pressing buttons, their minds elsewhere. The London trip had been Michael's initiative, surprising in its passion, this shift to urban geography. They'd see the Thames Barrier, explore the city's hidden rivers, discuss transport policy, spending two nights in a Soviet-style budget hotel near Hanger Lane gyratory.

'Missing the mountains, Mrs Fraser?'

'I like the mountains,' said Cleo, 'but the shops are better. In fact, I'm off.'

'But you have to see the exhibition!'

'A million billion cubic metres, sixty trillion years. Is that the gist?'

'I don't know why you're here if you're going to be cynical.'

'If I'm cynical about anything, it's our reason for being here.'

'Geography's not just lakes and mountains, it's cities too.'

'And people.' A giant cross-section of the earth, animated orange magma simmering beneath the mantle like an angry boil. 'The movements of people.' Pressing buttons forced the lava up through the earth's core towards the danger zones. 'I like this,' said Cleo, jabbing buttons. 'God-like power.'

'You're sure you don't want to come? Say hi?'

She laughed. 'Oh, no. You're on your own for this one. There goes Yellowstone. Shouldn't you be going?'

'I've got a while yet. We're meeting at two.'

'Go now. In case you get lost. You look nice. It's fancy dress and Michael's come as autumn.'

'Sounds depressing.'

'Not at all.' She checked quickly that no kids were watching, then embraced him. 'Don't fuck it up, Michael. See you at four.'

He set off, pausing in the gentlemen's toilets to check his appearance. A jacket, corduroy but fitted, even a tie, knitted, bulky, practically a scarf. He'd shaved that morning in the tiny bathroom cubicle, brushed his teeth, clipped his nails and flossed and brushed his teeth again. Was this grooming? It was not how Marnie would remember him, but perhaps that was a good thing. New start, clean slate, all among the phrases he'd rehearsed.

337

He brushed his fingers along the mark on his jaw — scar was such a melodramatic word — then headed out on to Exhibition Road.

He'd first made contact in early September, with a text.

Dear Marnie, It has been a while I know, and feel free to ignore this but it turns out I have to come to London with school in early October. Do you want to go for a walk? It is fine if not, but I would love to see you. Michael

It was a functional message that seemed to have gone through many drafts, retaining a slightly formal air — no contractions, proper punctuation, that 'dear' — so that it was like a request to call in an Edith Wharton novel. Why no 'yours sincerely'? No 'x' either and 'love' was there only to express enthusiasm, as in 'I'd love a biscuit.' Still wary, still bruised, Marnie spent some time drafting an appropriately insouciant response, something she might toss over her shoulder while walking away, indifferent. After some thought, she came up with *le mot juste* —

Sure.

— her masterpiece. Several more coded exchanges followed, days, even weeks apart, each as contained and considered as a haiku.

Let us meet at two
On the south side of the bridge
Look forward to it

She'd had her hair cut a week before so that it could settle a little and considerable thought had gone into her outfit too. A long black coat, long black pleated A-line skirt, black tights, black jumper in budget cashmere, the look was 'wronged woman in modern-dress Chekhov production'. Ideally she'd have come without a bag but there was now a package to give to Michael, or to take away again, depending on how things went.

338

For a change, Nature had decided to play along and it was the most exquisite autumn day, honey-coloured and cool, one last flourish before the evenings closed in. Maybe they could talk about it a little, what the leaves were up to and all that. They had two hours and she was not yet sure if this would be too much time or not nearly enough.

She saw him coming some way off, striding alongside the traffic on West Carriage Drive, raising one hand. She hadn't wanted him to jump out on her but these slow approaches were always awkward – he must have been a quarter of a mile away – and was she meant to look at him, look at the trees? Go and get a coffee and come back? She had adopted a wry smile, but unless he'd brought his binoculars the wryness would not register and so she looked at her phone, up and down again, until he arrived.

'Hello.'

'Hello, there.'

He put his hands on her upper arms and they touched cheeks. *Why is she in mourning?* he wondered. It didn't bode well.

'It's so strange to see you without your . . .'

'Beard?'

'Rucksack.'

'Thank you.' Don't say *thank you*, it's not a compliment. 'And you.' Don't say *and you*.

'Beard or rucksack?'

'No, I meant, you look very nice.'

'And you look very different.'

'Oh. Well. Thank you.' Again, not a compliment.

'How is London?'

'You were right. It's so big!'

'But you found this all right?'

'Well. I'm here.'

'You are. You are.' It was not going well, and they both felt

339

that this was their own fault. 'Shall we get off this main road? Go and see the lake?' she said, as if the lake might provide the answer. 'We can walk around it and it won't take nine days. You're meeting at . . . ?'

'Four, by the Albert Memorial.'

'I'll get you there in good time.' Now she was the guide as they crossed the road and followed the southern edge – shore was not the right word – alongside the joggers and tourists.

'Maybe we could both go for a swim!'

She knew what he was doing. He was being nostalgic, but it was too early for that. 'You can swim here, actually. That's the Lido coming up. I'm talking about it like it's something I've done, swim in the Serpentine. I've always meant to do it. I know that's not the same thing.' At one point, when she'd first thought she was in love, she had imagined him in this exact place, walking arm in arm, exchanging fond looks and laughter as if in a flashback, everything settled and understood. In the present tense, it was all so much harder.

For his part, he was appalled at his unnatural demeanour, galumphing and tongue-tied, a teenager without the alibi of youth. Doggedly, they worked through questions and answers – where are you staying? How far away is your flat? How is the hotel? Are the kids wild? What are you editing? – and it was fine and fond enough but it felt like clearing the furniture from a room to make space, either for a dance or a fight, and half an hour passed before he found a chance to say, 'Obviously, I wanted to apologise.'

'Why "obviously"?'

'What?'

'Why "obviously"? What do you think you did wrong?'

'What did I . . . ? Well, clearly I should have told you I was meeting Nat.'

'She's your wife. You don't have to tell me everything.'

'I was a bit abrupt, saying goodbye.'

'You had a lot on your mind, you were nervous—'

'And maybe I wasn't very open or clear with you about what I was thinking.'

'You told me, the night before, she was probably the love of your life. If anything, it was a little *too* clear.'

'So, you're fine?'

She shrugged. 'I'm just not sure it's that big a deal.'

They walked a little further, and after a while, he said, 'You see, you say that, Marnie, but ever since I arrived you're just giving off this tremendous sense of rage.'

And here she laughed. 'I thought we had something, Michael!'

'And so did I!'

'I thought something was happening!'

'I thought so too!'

'Yes, but something different. You thought you were going to have, I don't know, a little holiday fling or something—'

'That's *not* what I thought—'

'—and I thought I was falling in love with you.'

'Did you?'

'"Holiday fling"! It wasn't even a proper holiday.'

'But is that what you thought? That you were—'

'Yes! Yes, and it was extremely rare and extremely new to me and quite alarming actually, because that hasn't gone well in the past, and what's worse is you knew all that, I'd told you, for hours and hours, why I was wary and it was, well, it was humiliating, frankly.'

'So you *do* think I should apologise.'

'Oh, I should think so, yes.'

'And that's why I'm here!'

'Now, you're here because of . . . super-volcanoes or what-ever.'

'That was just a ruse.'

'Oh, a *ruse*, an ingenious *ruse* . . .'

'I'm here to see you. I wanted to see you because I felt the same.'

'I'm sorry, I don't think you did.'

'But I was getting there. I was thinking the same things, asking the same questions. I was just a little bit . . . scared, I suppose.'

'Scared! Men always say that, like it's a reason, but you're not using the word properly. What are you scared of? You're a grown-up! I mean, if I had a taste for human flesh or something, that'd be a cause for fear but even then—'

'You said yourself, it's a big deal at our age—'

'Hey! Four years younger—'

'—even at *your* age, to fall for someone—'

'—especially if they're in love with someone else.'

'I am not in love with anyone, Marnie, except you.'

She went to speak, hesitated, held her breath and then exhaled.

'Why don't you believe me?' he said.

'Why would I? You don't stop loving someone because you can't have them. People have written books about it.'

'I did love her. Very much, some years ago, and it didn't work out, and I won't forget that. But I think I can . . . I think I'm ready to start something new. And I do feel happier with you, happier than I've been for ages, years, more than I thought I could be. Even arguing with you like this I'm happier. I can talk, I can say things I couldn't say before, and coming here today, I was so . . . excited. You're like, I don't know . . . a view. I just want to look and look. I'm not making sense but the point is I want to be with you, Marnie, more often and as more than friends. I don't know how it's going to work but I want to be with you as much as possible from now on.'

They stood silent for a moment. She was not unmoved by this and for a while she didn't know what to say. 'I think . . . I think we need some time.'

He held up a finger. 'And with that in mind . . .' He reached into his pocket, and then another pocket, then a third until finally he produced an object which he held out in his hand as if it were a ring box rather than a dull grey stone with a white stripe.

'My god,' she said, 'You're *obsessed*.'

'D'you remember?'

'I'm sure I've seen it somewhere.'

'I was meant to take it all the way across, but I didn't make it. Did Cleo tell you?'

'She did. She said you'd chickened out. We laughed about it.'

'I thought you might. But I had this idea that I might go back, autumn half-term, walk the last two days, and I thought you might come with me.'

'I think I'm walked out, Michael.'

'No, but listen, you come up early Friday, I meet you in Scarborough in a cab, we go to the Moors where I left off, then walk the last two days to Robin Hood's Bay. It's all downhill, not all but most of it, it has to be, sea-level, the last of the Moors, then cliff-tops, beautiful in autumn, and we stay in a nice hotel, spend the day by the sea, and then head back to York.' He felt silly about the stone now, something he'd hoped might be charming. Should he throw it into the lake? 'It feels wrong not to finish it together. I mean you won't have done *all* of it, obviously, only seventy per cent.' Here she gave him a dangerous look. 'You caught a bus!'

'Only for half a mile!'

'But the principle of it . . .'

'Two hundred yards. It was an emergency!'

He smiled. 'Fine, we'll say you've done it all. And it's not far.'

'I've heard that before . . .'

'Really, it's not, and it'll be fun, and we can talk about everything, where we are now, where we want to be—'

'And the hotels—'

'Yes.'

'—the same room?'

'That's what I want. I mean I really do, if you want it too. Do you?'

She paused and thought for a moment. 'Well, it would save money.'

'Very much a cost-cutting exercise,' he said, and here she laughed and kissed him, standing at the south-east corner of the Serpentine, pausing only to step politely to the side to let the tourists pass, then continuing until she suddenly pulled away as if remembering something.

'Go on,' she said.

'Go on?'

'And then what? What happens the day after that?'

'Well. We'll take it one step at a time, I suppose.'

'Sounds a bit vague.'

He opened his eyes wide. 'I know!' he said, and they kissed again. 'So will you come?'

'I will give it serious thought. I will think about it. Okay?'

He'd hoped for something more definite but this, he felt, was enough for now and so they talked of other things and walked the north side of the Serpentine, which, as Michael pointed out, doesn't really deserve its name, given that it barely bends. Marnie smiled.

'What?' he said.

'I was just thinking. Look who's back.'

They sat and watched and rated the roller skaters on Serpentine Road, then headed west into Kensington Gardens, wary of getting too close to the Memorial for fear of bumping into the class, and in a quiet spot under the trees, they held on to each other, storing up the sensation, committing it to memory before saying goodbye.

'Oh, by the way,' said Marnie, reaching into her bag, 'this is for you. Don't open it until I've gone.'

It was a parcel wrapped in brown paper, tied with her green gardening string, the size of a hardback book but soft.

'Thank you. I should have got you something from the Museum gift shop . . .'

'Plastic dinosaur. No, I'm all right. The Memorial's over there, the Victorian space rocket.' One last kiss and then she was walking away across the park and once again there was the problem of distance. She knew he would be watching so she put her hands deep into her pockets, swishing the coat just a little, as if it were propelling her, seeking out piles of dry leaves for the full effect.

He watched her for some time, then found a bench, sat with the parcel on his lap and tugged the string. There was no note, just a new shirt, white, large-collared and French-cuffed, in some heavy material, soft and expensive. It was, he thought, the most beautiful item of clothing he'd ever seen.

He rewrapped the parcel carefully, tied the string again, waited until he'd pulled himself together, then went off to meet the kids.

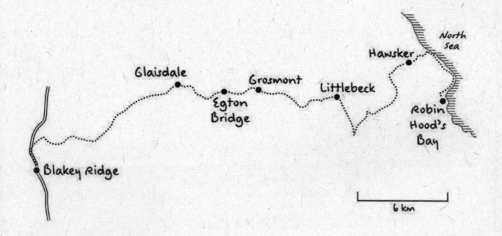

Glaisdale

Grosmont

Hawsker

North
Sea

Egton
Bridge

Littlebeck

Robin
Hood's
Bay

Blakey Ridge

6 km

A Note on the Journey

While I've tried to describe the landscape as accurately as possible, the pubs, hotels and restaurants along the way are all entirely fictional. Angle Tarn and Urra Moor are real, the Black Dog and Sunnyview Lodge are not and walkers will search in vain for a pub on the shores of Ennerdale Water. I've also taken a few small liberties with the route; for example, the path around Nine Standards Rigg is heavily eroded and best avoided in winter or after rain and even Michael would take the low road here.

During research, I was assisted by *The Coast to Coast Walk* by Terry Marsh (Cicerone) and of course Alfred Wainwright's fine *Pictorial Guide*, in the walkers' edition revised by Chris Jesty (Frances Lincoln), both of which were invaluable.

Acknowledgements

I'm indebted to my early readers, Damian Barr, Hannah MacDonald and Michael McCoy for their insights and suggestions, and to Jonny Geller – my agent for twenty years – and all the team at Curtis Brown, especially Viola Hayden and Ciara Finan, Kate Cooper, Nadia Farah Mokdad, Emma Jamison, Sam Loader and Atlanta Hatch.

At Hodder and Sceptre, thanks to Holly Knox, Emma Knight, Vicky Palmer, Saffron Stocker, Catherine Worsley, Alice Morley, Melissa Grierson, Eleanor Wood, Katy Aries, Sarah Clay, Richard Peters, Kerri Logan and all their teams, as well as Katie Espiner, Oli Malcolm, Charlotte Webb and Hazel Orme, who copy-edited with Marnie-like attention and care. I've always wanted to write a book with maps, and so am grateful to the cartographers at Barking Dog Art, and Dolly Alderton for conversation and advice. A line in the chapter 'In Shelley' was suggested by the song 'I Do This All The Time' by Rebecca Lucy Taylor.

I'd like to give a special thank you to Nick Sayers, my brilliant editor for many years, for his wisdom, encouragement and enthusiasm. And I'm immensely grateful to Federico Andornino, my editor this time, for his invaluable suggestions and for keeping me on the right path.

Finally, thank you to Romy and Max and dear Hannah for their endless patience and support.

About the Author

DAVID NICHOLLS is the bestselling author of *Starter for Ten*; *The Understudy*; *One Day*; *Us*, which was long-listed for the Booker Prize for Fiction; *Sweet Sorrow*; and *You Are Here*. He is also a screenwriter and has written adaptations of *Far from the Madding Crowd*, *When Did You Last See Your Father?*, and *Great Expectations*, as well as his own novels, *Starter for 10*, *One Day*, and *Us*. His adaptation of Edward St Aubyn's *Patrick Melrose*, starring Benedict Cumberbatch, was nominated for an Emmy and won him a BAFTA for best writer. Nicholls is also the executive producer and a contributing screenwriter on a new Netflix adaptation of *One Day*.